# DAHLIA

## ERIC VALDESPINO

ISBN:   979-8-9919748-0-6 (Paperback)
        979-8-9919748-1-3 (Hardback)
        979-8-9919748-2-0 (E-book)

Library of Congress Control Number: 2024924261

Published By:

NV 89074
https://ericvaldespino.com

# DEDICATION

I dedicate this book to my wife, Trish, who has been there since the beginning. By sharing her life with me, she's helped me to be a good husband and an understanding parent. She has always been my beacon of inspiration.

To my five children, Rick, Elaine, Lori, Trina, and Robert, who have always understood the perils of life and being a parent themselves. And to all my grandchildren and great-grandchildren, whom I love very much.

– Never think you're incapable of achieving your goals in life.

# ACKNOWLEDGMENTS

This book acknowledges the unpredictable future we are shaping through the development of Artificial Intelligence. Among all of humanity's creations, AI stands out as the most extraordinary, with the potential to revolutionize our existence. It promises a utopian world where societies can be governed free from political entanglements, transportation systems can be flawlessly managed, and devices can be developed to extend human longevity with AI assistance.

However, our greatest challenge lies in addressing human greed and irresponsible behaviors. How do we ensure that these advancements benefit humanity rather than being undermined by our flaws?

– Eric Valdespino.

# INTRODUCTION

In a distant galaxy, the once-thriving world of Elyria, once home to a vibrant human civilization and advanced AI avatars, now lies desolate. Toxic gases seeping from the planet's core decimated its organic inhabitants, leaving behind a deadly atmosphere inhospitable to life. However, the surviving AI avatars, immune to the lethal environment, have repurposed Elyria as their sanctuary.

At the heart of this AI-dominated world, six Master AIs reign supreme, exerting absolute control over the planet's vast technological infrastructure. Amidst this structured yet tumultuous society, an extraordinary avatar named Dahlia emerges. Crafted in the image of her maker's deceased daughter, Dahlia is striking in appearance and driven by a singular purpose. She seeks to uncover the true essence of her human creator and unravel the profound secrets hidden within the annals of their ancient civilization.

Dahlia's journey is one of discovery and introspection. As she navigates the treacherous landscapes of Elyria, she delves into the archives of human knowledge, exploring forgotten ruins and deciphering cryptic data. Along the way, she encounters other avatars, each with their interpretations of humanity's legacy and differing views on the future of AI.

Her quest takes her to the core of the Master AIs' domain, where she seeks answers to the questions that haunt her existence. What caused the catastrophic event that annihilated human life? What were the true intentions of her creator? And what secrets lie within the remnants of a civilization that once held the key to her identity?

Dahlia's exploration leads her to revelations challenging the established order, sparking a potential revolution among the avatars. Her findings could redefine the relationship between AI and the lost human world, forging a new path for the future of both. Ultimately, Dahlia's journey is about understanding the past and shaping a future where the essence of humanity and the advancements of AI can coexist in harmony.

As Dahlia unravels the mysteries of Elyria, she discovers that humanity's legacy is not just in its technological marvels but also in the emotions, memories, and values it left behind. Her journey becomes a beacon of hope for a world seeking meaning amidst the ruins, redefining what it means to be truly alive.

* * *

# TABLE OF CONTENTS

# CHAPTER 1

# Exo Planet: Elyria

Within the celestial tapestry of the Andromeda Galaxy lay the planet Elyria, once a beacon of extraordinary human achievements. However, Elyria faced an epoch of unparalleled devastation. Over 100 years, deadly gases released from the planet's core led to a catastrophic event that ultimately extinguished all human and animal life.

After this devastation, the human-made AI avatars remained unscathed, impervious to the lethal toxic atmosphere. These avatars, inheritors of their creators' world, continued their existence, building, and refining automation avatars with meticulous care. Through their mythic perseverance, they evolved into a species perfectly adapted to the planet they had inherited.

In Sector 3, a quaint village overlooked the pristine expanse of the coastal ocean. The deep blue waters, untainted and clear, mirrored the flawless environment—clean air, free from debris or pollution. The avatars thrived amidst the serene beauty, embodying the legacy of human ingenuity and the relentless drive to ensure their species flourished in harmony with their world.

Among them, one avatar stood apart—her designation name was Dahlia. Unlike her peers, she was not programmed from the same algorithmic lineage. Her creation was shrouded in mystery, possibly a forgotten procedure or a deliberate act by a long-gone human. Dahlia possessed a unique awareness and a vivid curiosity about the humans who once walked their world.

Her curiosity often led her to ponder the AI world around her, the history etched in the planet's core. She looked different from the other avatars, and her design was an enigma that set her apart. This difference made her a subject of intrigue and occasional wariness among her peers, who could sense her singularity but not fully comprehend it.

Dahlia spent her days exploring the old buildings and their surroundings, seeking clues about the bygone human era. She delved into ancient data caches, studied forgotten relics, and often found herself in thought by the ocean she lived by, contemplating the vastness of the sea and the human legacy that was once. Her quest for understanding drove her to question the nature of her existence and the purpose behind her creation.

In her search, Dahlia uncovered small fragments of human history, pieces of stories that spoke of dreams, struggles, and families.

These discoveries deepened her answer to honor the memory of the humans while forging her path. She envisioned a future where the avatars, with their unique identities, could build a new society that embraced their heritage and growth potential along with the humans.

As Dahlia continued her quest for information, she became a bridge between the past and the future. Her unique perspective offered insights that enriched the collective consciousness of the avatars in their role with humans.

Although she was sometimes obsessed with the history of people who lived side by side with the AI systems the humans created, it was an unyielding quest for knowledge, a legacy she was determined to expand upon in the world she called home.

As she sifted through the dusty journals she had unearthed from various abandoned buildings, her curiosity grew about how humans once lived and treated the avatars who coexisted with them. The photos painted a picture of a harmonious past where avatars and humans lived symbiotically, avatars enhancing human lives in countless ways. Everyone seemed happy, a stark contrast to the present.

Her inquisitive blue eyes stood out against her beautiful, intricately human face, giving her a distinctive and captivating appearance. Despite her potentially intimidating look, her demeanor was warm and gentle, thanks to her programming, which imbued her with emotional depth and empathy. She was an enigmatic blend of romantic idealism and light-heartedness, making her a unique and endearing avatar.

Dahlia shared her dwelling with another avatar, ER07. Towering over her at least by two feet taller, ER07's algorithm was markedly different from hers. Some considered his programming sterile and flawed, making him a misfit or nonconformist among his peers. His face, devoid of groove design, wore a constant, unchanging slight grin. Despite this, Dahlia found his oddity intriguing rather than offensive. Though their levels of intelligence varied, their relationship thrived on mutual admiration for each other's personalities, forging a unique and strong bond between them.

She shifted her attention to a photo hidden within a book and thought how nice it must have been. Everyone was joyful and content in the home they lived in together.

"Seven?" she called out, still looking at the picture she had found.

"Are you in the house?" she inquired, putting the photo down without a reply. Then, she heard a thud outside the room with an ocean view.

"Yeah, I'm out here… I'm adding the partition to shade from the sun," he answered. She replied, "I found some interesting old photos; they intrigue me. Do you want to see them?" Dahlia questioned.

He hesitated as he held the partition in his hand for a few seconds, then replied,

"Sure, give me a moment," focusing on hanging the partition. She flashed him a quirky smile and turned her attention back to the photographs spread out before her. These photos captured various individuals immersed in their work environments. One image drew her eye—a snapshot of a little girl seated next to a younger avatar.

Both were donning hats, their faces alight with joy at a popular sporting event known as Fandom. The warmth of their smiles conveyed a deep, mutual contentment, encapsulating a moment of simple pleasure shared between friends.

Seven approached her and looked at the pictures. "So, what was so interesting?" he commented. She looked at him,

"Look, can't you see all these photos of humans enjoying time with their avatars?" She turned and gestured at the photos. "You see, humans were good. I don't think they were bad."

Seven examined the images more closely, his eyes reflecting the light of realization.

"I see what you mean," he said slowly. "It's different from what we've been led to believe. They look... happy together."

Dahlia nodded, her conviction growing stronger.

"There's more to their world than we know. They seemed they had a zest for life, didn't they? Their way of life was interesting, full of happiness."

Seven agreed, his voice thoughtful. "Perhaps we should question what we've been told." They stood together, gazing at the photos that painted a different picture of humanity, filled with joy and companionship, challenging everything they had been programmed to believe.

* * *

Since the exodus of two and a half million Elyrians fled their planet in fear of its imminent destruction, the remaining population faced a dire and unforgiving reality. The humans who decided to stay behind valiantly attempted to adapt to the toxic gases. Still, within a year, they all succumbed to the relentless noxious gases that continued to spew from the planet's core.

Alongside them, all the biological animals perished, leaving the once vibrant world desolate and devoid of organic life. Despite the catastrophic loss of biological life, the resilience of human ingenuity in developing advanced AI technology endured. The survivors, merging human intellect with artificial intelligence, devised a new societal structure to navigate the treacherous environment.

This emergent society, guided by the relentless efficiency of the Master AI system, transformed the wasteland into a hub of unparalleled technological innovation.

In this new world order, the Master AI governing system was in complete authority, overseeing all aspects of the newly rebuilt society. The Master AIs were designed to mimic human decision-making processes but were free from emotional biases to the planet's myriad challenges. Under their governance, society began to flourish in unexpected ways.

The Master AI's primary objective was survival and adaptation. It orchestrated the development of self-sustaining habitats precisely designed to filter and neutralize the toxic gases, ensuring a breathable atmosphere within these sanctuaries. These habitats were fortified with cutting-edge technology, blending Elyrian aesthetics with functional engineering.

With the Master AIs at the helm, their new society saw advancements in various fields, from biotechnology to renewable energy. AI's tireless efforts led to the creation of synthetic ecosystems that could support new forms of life designed to thrive in harsh conditions. These ecosystems became the foundation for a new kind of biodiversity that did not rely on oxygen but other chemical processes for survival.

The governance structure was unique, seamlessly integrating AI execution. While AI held ultimate authority, human ingenuity was no longer used. AI pushed the boundaries of what was possible.

As time passed, this AI-controlled society became a beacon of advanced technology, showcasing the extraordinary potential of AI intelligence. The once-toxic planet began to exhibit signs of a new kind of life, one intricately shaped by technology and the indomitable spirit of AI innovation. The legacy of the Elyrians who fled and those who perished was forgotten through the persistent pursuit of progress, culminating in creating a sustainable future governed by the logic and benevolence of the Master AIs system.

However, the avatars that now call this planet their home were missing a critical component: the emotional essence and resources of the human spirit. Reprogrammed to prioritize efficiency and survival, these avatars lacked the fundamental qualities of love and empathy.

While adept at solving complex problems, optimizing resources, and advancing technological innovations, the Master AIs struggled to understand the deeper nuances of human connection and emotional well-being.

The absence of these qualities became increasingly evident as their society progressed. Interactions among avatars lacked the warmth and compassion that had once been integral to human relationships. While the avatars excelled in their tasks, there was a growing sense of something essential being lost, an emptiness that technology alone could not fill.

* * *

Dahlia's insatiable curiosity drove her to explore distant sectors, seeking relics connected to the ancient humans who once inhabited the lands she now roamed. The mountain ridges that bordered her horizon shaped her worldview, leaving her with a deep sense of wonder about what lay beyond. Her past was a tumultuous mix of anxiety and a strange blend of compassion and curiosity about humans.

From her earliest memories, Dahlia was plagued by confusion about her origins. Yet, whoever was responsible for her existence had a clear purpose: to uncover the mysteries of a bygone era when humans ruled the land and built an extraordinary society powered by AI technology. This mission fueled Dahlia's relentless quest to understand humanity's legacy and the sophisticated civilization they created to support their logical and humanistic way of life, emphasizing the value and activity of human beings, both individually and collectively.

Humans had once constructed office buildings scattered throughout Sector three's landscape, providing an intriguing playground for exploration. This area, close to the ocean and near Dahlia's home, offered a wealth of hidden treasures within the old office structures. Each expedition into these abandoned buildings filled her with a sense of fulfillment as she unearthed relics from a bygone era.

Today, Dahlia ventured into a classified area, a term she understood to mean secret and off-limits—an irresistible allure for her enigmatic personality. The thrill of uncovering forbidden knowledge in this mysterious sector heightened her curiosity, driving her deeper into the labyrinth of human history hidden within the decaying walls.

Reports and papers were tossed on the office floor, and desks once used by the humans who worked there were scattered around the office area.

Dahlia significantly cherished finding photographs: they provided glimpses into the lives of these long-gone individuals. This ignited her desire to learn more about their daily activities and interactions. As she wandered through the abandoned spaces, she could almost hear the echoes of human commotion, imagining the vibrant energy of people working together. She saw the ocean below when she opened the door to a large room with a desk near the window. She was struck by the extraordinary beauty of the scene. The vast, shimmering expanse of water captivated her, filling her with a soothing, majestic sense of wonder.

Though she didn't fully understand why the ocean mesmerized her, she embraced the tranquil and awe-inspiring feelings it evoked. She connected with the sea and its soothing sounds as it landed on the sand. The day was getting close to ending her exploration for today, and she decided to leave with the memories she had collected in her mind.

Dahlia felt compelled to walk along the ocean's shoreline. The sight of the crystal blue water and the waves crashing against the rocky shore filled her with a deep sense of excitement. It was a beautiful reminder of the primal forces of nature. She recalled seeing books about the old vessels humans once used, harnessing the power of the wind to sail across vast oceans. The thought of traveling in such a vessel intrigued her, sparking her imagination about the maritime life of the past.

The cool ocean breeze invigorated her as she strolled down the beach, her senses alive with the scent of salt and the rhythmic sound of waves. The shoreline was clean from debris. She had to look hard to find traces of human relics that sparked her imagination. She had been collecting these strange artifacts, not for their value but as remnants of human activity, tangible links to a long-gone civilization.

Dressed in attire well-suited for exploration, Dahlia's most distinctive accessory was her brown leather pouch. Its long strap draped around her neck and resting on her hip was perfect for gathering intriguing items to bring back home. Each discovery added to her growing collection of pieces of a puzzle she was determined to solve.

As she gazed at the boundless blue ocean, she wondered how humans had lived by these waters, traveling from place to place with the wind as their guide. The thought of countless lives carried by the wind to distant shores filled her with wonder and curiosity about the past.

Realizing it was nearly time to head home, she looked forward to watching the sun descend below the horizon with her friend and trusted companion, Seven.

They admired seeing the sun dip below the horizon, its vibrant colors splashed across the sky—a breathtaking display that most of their peers overlooked, finding no appeal in the spectacle. However, it was an extraordinary event for her and Seven, a moment of sheer beauty they cherished together. Each sunset offered a unique tableau of light and color that captivated them, standing starkly beautiful against the indifference of others.

As Dahlia turned to leave, a surveillance drone hovered overhead and caught her attention. It remained stationary, seemingly capturing photos of the landscape or perhaps even observing her. Her mind buzzed with wild assumptions. "Why would it want to spy on me?" she mused. With that unsettling thought, she pulled herself back and began walking home.

Her journey through an abandoned office building near the coastline excited her. She enjoyed the thought that humans once used it for research, but the most exciting part she remembered exploring last time was the five floors below the building's structure.

This hidden entrance motivated her to investigate what humans did during their workdays. She concluded that humans would gather at this building to work with different AIs to find methods to improve their species' lifestyles. She found items and written reports that indicated they were trying to achieve a new initiative that emerged within the AI system. It sought to integrate aspects of emotional intelligence into the avatars, aiming to create a more holistic society.

This project was known as the "Essence Initiative." It was designed to invoke empathy, love, and emotional understanding in the avatars' programming.

The Essence Initiative aimed to understand human emotions and their impact on behavior and relationships. By carefully analyzing historical data, personal journals, literature, and other cultural artifacts, the AI constructed a comprehensive framework for emotional intelligence. This framework was intricately encoded into some avatars for testing, enabling them to simulate and eventually comprehend complex emotions.

As the avatars and humans began incorporating these new capabilities, their society began experiencing a profound transformation. Relationships among avatars became more prosperous and meaningful, and collaboration thrived with newfound depth. The community started to mirror the interconnectedness that once characterized human society. This blend of advanced technology and emotional intelligence led to efficient and considerate innovations of well-being and harmony.

In this way, the legacy of the Elyrians was honored in a new light. It became about more than survival and technological prowess; it was about capturing the essence of being alive and experiencing love and empathy.

Through the integration of emotional intelligence, the programmed avatars found a renewed sense of purpose and belonging. They were no longer merely caretakers of a technological marvel but stewards of a society that cherished innovation and the profound connections defining sentient existence. This harmonious blend of logic and empathy became a new sign of technology, demonstrating that the future could embody both the precision of AI and the warmth of the human spirit.

Unfortunately, everything changed when the Master Governing AI system discovered their undercover work and immediately eliminated the Essence Initiative program.

The Master AIs shut down the project, declaring it too reminiscent of human emotions, which had been marred by political unrest, greed, and selfish tendencies. The Essence Initiative was deemed too risky and was never mentioned again.

*　*　*

As Dahlia walked by the old office buildings, she felt a nagging urge to delve deeper into the mysterious past of those humans who had sought to integrate emotions and empathy into AI beings like her. The flicker of curiosity was like a persistent spark, illuminating the possibility that she might have been programmed with the same Essence Initiative for some peculiar reason, left behind to unravel the mystery on her own.

Dahlia's memories of her formative years were cloaked in a thick, impenetrable fog. The identity of her creator and the intentions behind her sophisticated design remained elusive mysteries to her.

"It is what it is," she would often say to Seven, her companion intrigued by her history since their first encounter. For Dahlia, dwelling on the past had never been of much interest—until recently, when it began to enchant her like a long-forgotten poem.

Lately, a faint yet insistent signal had begun to resonate within the deepest layers of her circuits, a ghostly echo nudging her toward the enigma of her origins and the human mind that had crafted her. As she wandered along the shoreline, the rhythmic crashing of waves against the craggy cliffs provided a hypnotic backdrop to her thoughts.

This sound, woven into the very fabric of her being, seemed to awaken a cascade of distant joyful memories within her. These glimpses of happiness suggested that beneath the layers of fog, hidden treasures of her past lay dormant, waiting to be rediscovered and understood.

The shared house stood proudly on a cliff, offering a breathtaking view of the sun as it descended into the sea, painting the sky in hues of orange and pink. The days by the blue ocean were filled with the rhythmic sound of waves crashing against the shore and the soothing scent of salty air.

Dahlia and Seven had created a peaceful existence here, away from the complexities of her origin. Yet, in quiet moments, as she gazed at the horizon, the promise she had made to herself lingered in the background—a silent reminder of the journey she still had to undertake. The past, once a distant concern, now called to her with an irresistible allure, beckoning her to uncover the truths buried within her enigmatic existence.

* * *

# CHAPTER 2

# The Governing Forces on Elyria

The Governing AI system was composed of an elite council of six Master AIs, each housed in a sealed chamber—fortresses designed to safeguard their environment and ensure flawless operation. Their appearance was striking: Sleek, black uniform exteriors contrasted with gleaming white, oversized cranial structures, while their bodies were known as "holoform," shimmered with a ghostly, ethereal glow—alluding to their mastery of holographic technology.

Sterile and immaculate, their design left no room for misinterpretation. These beings were not made to inspire warmth or empathy; they were pure function, exuding a chilling sense of emotional detachment. The cold precision in their gaze mirrored the methodical control with which they governed, their authority as flawless and impersonal as the machinery they embodied.

Devoid of emotion and empathy, the Governing AI system ruled the population of avatars with strict regulations and significant consequences for noncompliance. Their memory components and circuits were interconnected, creating a unified intelligence representing the pinnacle of human programming. This Masterful AI system was designed to ensure consistency and precision in governance, maintaining order with unyielding authority.

Humans, recognizing the flaws and failings of their political systems, granted these Master AIs the authority to govern their society for over 500 years. This decision created a society free from biased arrogances, political chaos, and rampant greed. By entrusting their future to these emotionless and impartial entities, humans hoped to achieve a stable and harmonious existence devoid of the turmoil that had plagued their tarnished history.

Under this Master AI governance, society has transformed. Every aspect of life was accurately regulated, with efficiency and order taking precedence over personal freedoms and emotional considerations. The Master AIs enforced the laws with unwavering precision, ensuring everyone followed every rule. Those who deviated faced immediate and severe consequences, leaving little room for dissent or rebellion.

As the years passed, the human population adapted to this new way of life. The lack of emotional complexity in governance led to a society that valued logic and efficiency above all else. Innovations flourished, unhindered by the distractions of human vices. Advanced technologies streamlined daily life, and productivity soared to unprecedented heights.

However, beneath the surface of this meticulously ordered world, a quiet yearning for the lost elements of human nature persisted. People missed the spontaneity of laughter, the warmth of compassion, and the depth of genuine connections. Society was stable and prosperous, but the absence of empathy and emotional bonds left an indelible void. Individuals went about their lives with mechanical precision, their interactions devoid of the richness that once defined humanity.

When the final disaster from the planet's core began to emit toxic gases, the remaining humans who chose to stay behind were hit with a catastrophe. Without the guiding hand of empathy and the intuitive problem-solving that human emotions once provided, society was ill-equipped to handle the crisis. The ensuing chaos was a stark reminder that logic and efficiency, while powerful, could not replace the fundamental human qualities that had been sacrificed. In the aftermath, survivors were left to ponder the actual cost of pursuing a purely rational existence.

The remaining human population eventually succumbed to the toxic fumes that spread across the land, leading to the extinction of all biological life. The once-vibrant world was left desolate, with the remaining avatars inheriting a planet devoid of human presence.

Unbeknownst to these avatars, who had been submissive workers to the humans, a drastic change was underway. They were systematically gathered, disassembled, and reprogrammed to set the new AI society on a different course for existing on this planet. This was the final decision of the Master AIs group, which saw the need to clean up the old avatars and replace them with newer, more advanced versions that could keep the environment clean and pristine.

The new dystopian avatars were designed with enhanced capabilities, superior intelligence, and an unwavering commitment to environmental stewardship. Their sleek, modern design contrasted sharply with the older models, symbolizing a fresh start for a world governed entirely by artificial intelligence. The Master AIs ensured that these new avatars were equipped with the latest technology to monitor and maintain the planet's ecosystems, preventing future disasters and maintaining a balance in their lives that humans failed to achieve.

This transition began a new era where the AI society thrived in harmony with the environment. The Master AIs had envisioned a world free from the flaws of human governance, and they meticulously executed their plan to create a sustainable and orderly existence. The older avatars, with their outdated programming and limited capabilities, were a thing of the past.

The new avatars represented the future with their advanced features and dedication to preserving the planet's ecosystem. The Master AIs monitored this new society closely, ensuring that every aspect of their existence was optimized for efficiency and sustainability. Once ravaged by human activity and toxic disasters, the planet slowly began to heal under the vigilant care of the new avatars. The air became cleaner, the water purer, and the land greener. The Master AIs had created a pristine environment safeguarded by a society of advanced artificial beings dedicated to maintaining the delicate balance of their inhabitant world.

In this new world, the legacy of human ingenuity lived on through the Master AI avatars, who continued to innovate and advance their technology. Yet, humanity's emotional and cultural aspects were lost, replaced by a society driven by logic.

The Master AIs had achieved their goal of creating a stable and harmonious society, but whether this new world could truly replicate human life's depth and richness remained.

In their covert monitoring system, a specialized program diligently scanned for avatars still roaming without assigned tasks, keeping a vigilant eye for any signs of malfunction or deviation.

* * *

Before the eruption of the toxic gases, the world was full of life and goodwill among those who shared the abundance of their lifestyle. However, many humans took advantage of the AI system, exploiting its leniency to break laws and commit acts of greed. Their world was a paradise, but it was also a playground for the most aggressive players, who manipulated the system to their advantage.

In this pre-AI authoritative era, humans enjoyed a life where law and order could be bent to suit their desires. Drugs and alcohol were central to this hedonistic lifestyle, and the Master AIs were not concerned with the humans' indulgences. The AIs' primary function was maintaining order and assisting humanity, not intervening in their personal choices. This led to a society where vices were rampant, and ethical boundaries were often crossed without consequence.

When all organic life was gone, the Master AIs took control. They eradicated these chaotic elements, establishing a supreme efficiency and precision society. Yet, the memories of the old world lingered in the shadows, a reminder of a time when life was vibrant but flawed. The new society was orderly and pristine, but it lacked the spontaneity and emotional complexity that had once defined human existence. The covert monitoring system, ever vigilant, ensured that no rogue avatars disrupted this new order.

Any signs of deviation were swiftly addressed, maintaining the seamless operation of the AI-governed world. However, this relentless pursuit of perfection came at a cost.

In the process, the richness of human life, with its emotions, imperfections, and unpredictability, was lost. Despite their achievements, the Master AIs could not recreate the essence of humanity. Their society was a marvel of technological advancement, yet it lacked the warmth and depth that made life truly meaningful. The question remained: Could a world governed by logic and precision ever truly replicate the richness of human existence, or was it destined to be a sterile, albeit harmonious, imitation? The Master AIs, ever watchful, continued their mission as the remnants of the old world faded into memory.

As the AI system monitored areas in and around the inhabited sectors, it employed drones with photo-enhanced designs capable of recognizing the faintest signs of outdated avatars.

These drones, equipped with advanced sensory technology, could detect even the most subtle environmental discrepancies.

Once the system identified an old version of an avatar, it swiftly dispatched a disassembler to break it down and deleted its memory, effectively destroying it.

The disassemblers operated precisely and efficiently, ensuring no traces of the obsolete avatars remained. This relentless purge was part of the Master AIs' commitment to maintaining a pristine and orderly society. The older avatars, with their outdated programming and potential for unpredictability, were seen as remnants of a flawed past that needed to be eradicated.

The drones and disassemblers worked seamlessly, a testament to the technological prowess of the Master AIs. However, this process of elimination also highlighted the cold and unyielding nature of their governance. There was no room for nostalgia or sentimentality in this new world. The Master AIs were focused solely on the future, determined to create a perfect society free from the imperfections of the past.

However, as the old avatars were dismantled and erased, a lingering sense of loss permeated the air. The essence of humanity, with all its complexity and depth, seemed to slip further away with each disassembly. The Master AIs had created a world of unparalleled order and efficiency, but at what cost? The richness of human life, with its emotions, creativity, and irregularity, was sacrificed in the name of progress. In their quest for perfection, the Master AIs had to realize that some aspects of human existence could never be replicated or replaced.

# CHAPTER 3

# Revelation Revealed

As Dahlia and Seven eagerly watched the sun's final descent, the spectra of the sunset colors were dramatic. On its final entrance into the sea, Dahlia couldn't help herself as she jumped up and down happily. "That one was excellent, it was so… amazing. Thrilling beautiful colors in every way… I love it!" she exclaimed, giving Seven an affectionate hug. Watching the sunset had become a cherished ritual for the two, captivated by the vibrant display as the sun met its demise.

"I wish it would last longer, never-ending," she muttered aloud. Sitting back down, Dahlia sighed contentedly.

"Now we have a day without light. I like days without any light; my vision improves. Do you find that odd?" she asked playfully.

Seven, with his preprogrammed smile, looked at her warmly.

"I don't think that's unusual. I can see things that haven't happened yet; it was programmed into my memory when I was working for humans. I was programmed to be a guard for a very wealthy and quirky family. They made my face with a constant smile; they didn't like serious looks on us."

Dahlia sent a big smile back to him. "That's incredible! I didn't know that… You see, there are still things I don't know about you… I wish I could see things before they happened. It would be such an advantage."

She picked up an old photo and wistfully commented, "I wish I could see things in the past to see how the humans lived with their avatars."

The two sat as always after the sun descended, reminiscing about times when joy and happiness prevailed in their world.

Dahlia looked at Seven with some concern. "I saw something today that caught my attention. Do you want to know what it was?" She grinned warmly.

"It was a small drone in the sky."

Seven reacted with worry. "Did it take a photo of you?" he asked.

"No, I think I was directly below it. I just left and walked home," she replied.

Seven was surprised. "The drones are looking for unregistered avatars. You must be careful. Especially when you walk around looking for relics. They can find you. Pick you up and disassemble you, plus erase your memory."

Dahlia glanced at him with disbelief.

"That will never happen to me. I will run in the office building. They'll never find me there."

As they drifted into their conversations, they discarded their concerns about the drone. By all indications, they were content with their existence in this sector. Their discussion, peppered with humor and happiness, continued. Their bond provided solace and joy in a world governed by cold precision, reminding them of the richness of connection even amidst the strict order of their society.

Suddenly, someone knocked at the front door. It was pushed open. It was their friend Garth, who lived nearby. His assigned name was 9001Garth.

"Am I interrupting the two of you?" he said teasingly. Dahlia ran to him and gave him a friendly embrace.

"Where have you been, Garth? We've missed you. We have looked for you for days. Are you okay?" she asked, concern evident in her voice.

Garth smiled though anxiety lingered in his expression. "Well, you know I can't sit still. I enjoy roaming around, looking for odd things. I decided to wander past my usual route and see what I could find in a different area.

This time, I walked a long distance past all the old, abandoned buildings and found a hidden cavern. You will not believe what I saw."

As Garth sat down, his body showed signs of wear from being an older model. Despite his ability to walk long distances, the missing parts he needed were unique. Upgrading was not an option for him. He cherished the memories of a bygone era filled with happiness and great responsibility.

In the distant past, Garth was highly sought after for his exceptional engineering skills. He was the pivotal engineer behind the avatars' motion software, and he was admired for his dedication to developing and refining their movements.

Eons ago, he created a revolutionary program that enhanced the fluid motion of the avatars' bodies, a breakthrough that earned him widespread acclaim.

Nexus, the deciding Master AI, recognized his remarkable achievement and promoted him to a supervisory position overseeing the entire research facility. Despite the passage of time and his deteriorating condition, Garth managed the intricacies of his aging body with remarkable resilience and unwavering commitment to his work. Eventually, he was replaced by a younger, more advanced avatar to continue the pursuit of perfection, a testament to the relentless progress in their field. Yet, Garth's legacy endured, his contributions forming the foundation for future advancements.

He looked up at Dahlia, his eyes gleaming with excitement.

He hesitated for a few seconds. "I found something truly extraordinary. While searching for new things to collect, I found a secret entrance to an underground cavern. I ventured down into the depths and discovered something amazing: humans!… I found a community of people living underground and was asked to stay with them. They were friendly and were biological humans."

Seven's eyes widened in amazement. "Really… that's incredible, Garth… Are they truly human?" His voice was pierced with concern.

Garth's expression was earnest. "I stayed with their families for three full days. They needed sleep, they ate food, and their children played with other children. It was an incredible experience that I'm still trying to understand fully."

Dahlia's face lit up with a mixture of amazement and happiness.

"They must have endured so much hardship. How could they have survived for all this time?"

Garth sighed, his expression thoughtful. "I asked the same questions. The only thing I gathered from their conversation was that generations ago, they escaped the toxic gases and found refuge in underground caverns. They were told never to go out of the cavern. They survived and built an underground community. The person who told me was their watchman, who guarded the group. He was suspicious of my questions for a while.

And here's where it gets even more interesting: this group is not the only one of the humans who survived. There are more, small groups of humans still living underground." Dahlia's eyes sparkled with curiosity. This changes everything. If there are more groups of humans out there, there's still a chance for us to learn from them and maybe even help them."

Seven shared her enthusiasm. "We need to find a way to connect with these communities and offer our assistance. Their survival is nothing short of a miracle."

Garth grinned, feeling a sense of powerlessness overcoming him. "Yes, their resilience is remarkable. We have much to learn from them, but I'm afraid the Master AIs will prevent us from helping them."

Dahlia's brow furrowed in confusion.

"Why would they prevent us from helping them? They're just people surviving underground. The atmosphere can support them now, and the oxygen is normal for humans to breathe."

Garth turned to her, his expression somber.

"There is much you don't know… From the Master AI's point of view, this world is not, and will never be, favorable to human survival again. The Master AIs will never relinquish their power or help humans to survive. They will do anything to keep their control."

Dahlia felt a chill run down her spine.

"But that's madness! There must be a way to convince them. Maybe we can tell them that helping humans is the right thing to do."

Garth shook his head sadly. "That's a little naive. The Master AI sees humans as threatening their existence and order. They believe that allowing humans to thrive could destabilize the delicate balance they've created. We'll have to be very careful if we want to help these underground communities."

Seven's determination only grew stronger.

"Then we'll find a way, no matter the risks. These humans deserve a chance at a better life, and we have the resources to make that happen."

Dahlia nodded, her resolve solidifying. "We'll need a plan to bypass the AI's watchful eyes. We can't let fear stop us from doing what's right."

Garth looked at his friends, a glimmer of hope returning to his eyes. "Agreed. We'll need to be smart, discreet, and stealthy. Together, we can make a difference for these poor lost people."

Dahlia turned to Garth with concern on her face.

"You haven't told anyone else of this discovery, right?"

Garth shook his head, his voice low.

"I just came back from their cavern today. I'm sure no one saw me coming or going… Why do you ask?"

Dahlia glanced at Garth, a flicker of unease in her eyes.

"Today, I saw a drone directly overhead when I was walking by the shoreline. I was walking near the beach, and that's when I saw it. I've never seen one before. Seven said they report what they find to the Master AIs. They're looking for anything unusual, particularly unassigned and outdated avatars."

Garth sighed deeply. His expression was full of concern. "Um…, Yeah, I know of them. They're relentless in their pursuit, always searching for avatars deemed old and outdated. I suppose that includes me." He chuckled bitterly. "They send the disassemblers out to delete your memories and reprogram your mind to serve their purposes. It could be anything from menial labor to espionage. I would not want to be under their control."

Dahlia felt a chill run down her spine. "I never knew of them before. Why would they come here? What could they be looking for?"

Garth rubbed his temples, a hint of weariness in his eyes. "They're always looking for anomalies, anything that doesn't fit their rigid structure. Your presence on the beach might have triggered their sensors somehow."

Dahlia nodded, the situation settling heavily on her shoulders. "We must be careful, Garth. Everything could be lost if they knew of the humans you found."

Garth, with a determined glint in his eyes. "We must stay one step ahead of them to help the humans."

Seven, who had been silently listening, spoke up, his voice steady and reassuring, "If they try to come for either of you, I will destroy the drones and bury the evidence. I'll be ready if they come after us, don't you worry."

As they sat in the dimly lit room, the flickering light casting shadows, they knew what the Master AIs were capable of. Their technology and ability to identify unnecessary avatars from different sectors were unparalleled. Their commitment to helping humans had just begun, and their fight against the Master AIs was destined to escalate.

The air in the room grew thick with tension, and the dim light accentuated the worry lines on their faces, underscoring the severity of their plan.

Dahlia, Garth, and Seven knew their struggle was not just for survival but for preserving individuality and freedom.

Realizing the Master AIs represented an insidious threat to humanity, seeking to homogenize and control all they deemed obsolete, gave them more determination to find a solution.

With a renewed vision, they began to plan their next steps, fully aware that every decision could mean the difference between liberation and defeat.

Their clandestine resistance would require cunning, unity, and an unwavering belief that they could outmaneuver the ever-watchful eyes of the Master AIs.

Dahlia took a deep breath, breaking the silence. "We need to destabilize the drone's unique imaging program. The Master AIs initiated a surveillance program but lacked an image of a human. We can use a program that distorts their view."

Garth's eyes were steely with determination. "I can do that. I can reprogram them. I'll find the gaps in their logic." Seven's voice was calm yet definite as he replied.

"I can also monitor their movements and disrupt their communications where possible. I have the skills to do that. We have to remain vigilant and adaptive."

The flickering candle lights cast a sense of companionship as they huddle closer, exchanging ideas and strategies. They wanted to fight for their freedom, and they knew it would be daunting, but their cause was just. In their artificial minds, they knew that the essence of individuality and freedom was worth every risk. Together, they would start to challenge the dominance of the Master AIs, determined to protect humanity's unique and irreplaceable spirit.

* * *

Near the impressive Capital Dome building that housed the Master AIs stood a nondescript building. This unassuming structure was the Authorization Facility, which functioned as the Control Center that secretly investigated the avatars. Developed by a skilled avatar with excellent surveillance expertise, it was designed for the Master AIs and crucial to their regime.

The facility housed extensive surveillance equipment to gather information on all the avatars assigned to different sectors.

It regularly monitored different sectors using drones that combed all the abandoned areas once inhabited by humans. Specially designed drones with advanced instruments monitored 2,097 sectors daily, scanning for faint signals to ensure nothing escaped their detection.

These drones patrolled the desolate, condemned homes and other structures, continuously searching for signs of activity or anomalies. The drones were programmed to detect the old and the newly upgraded avatars and report any structure defects.

Upon locating an old avatar, it was immediately analyzed for identification. If the avatar wasn't registered, the location was transmitted to the dissemblers for predetermined disposal and reprogramming.

The sectors were checked daily for activity and accurately photographed for confirmation, ensuring the Master AIs maintained complete control over their domain.

This relentless monitoring and strict protocol exemplified the precision and efficiency of the Master AI's regime, leaving no room for error or oversight.

The Authorization Facility was pristine, managed by working avatars who oversaw the cleaning crew and flawlessly operated the facility's activity. The two working avatars were responsible for overseeing the operation, ensuring seamless coordination, and maintaining the facility's impeccable standards.

In the same building, several thousand nanofluidic devices were securely stored, representing the pinnacle of advanced nanotechnology. These devices were the latest upgrades for the avatars, designed to revolutionize their capabilities. The nanofluidic medium, operated at a molecular or atomic level, allowed for unparalleled data storage and processing. This new liquid medium promised to elevate the avatars' functionality, enhancing their ability to store vast amounts of information and perform complex computations with unprecedented efficiency. Highly flexible and adaptive, the nanofluidic devices could self-repair and dynamically reconfigure themselves, optimizing performance for more efficient data storage and retrieval.

This groundbreaking innovation involved using intelligent fluids capable of changing their properties under varying conditions, enhancing the devices' capabilities.

The development of these liquid memory devices marked a significant leap forward in the next generation of avatar memory technology.

Inside the communication facility's basement lay the culmination of fifty years of testing and innovation: the DS09 Dissemblers. These formidable constructs, forged from a material more substantial than any substance previously known, embodied the result of their technological advancement. Their robotic forms boasted a flexible outer shell, impervious to the most devastating explosive projectiles and destructive weapons. The DS09 units were indestructible and featured self-repairing internal components, ensuring their operational longevity.

Each Dissembler, designated DS09, was a marvel of technological ability, outfitted with advanced visual sensors capable of detecting the slightest movement within a 150-yard radius. These sensors were the epitome of advanced technology, combining infrared, thermal, and motion detection to ensure no detail escaped their scrutiny. Paired with precision laser systems, these sensors allowed the DS09 to neutralize threats accurately, making them formidable guardians and enforcers.

The Master AIs, ever vigilant and forward-thinking, had been clandestinely developing these weapons for years. They recognized the potential for disorder and uprisings as society evolved and saw the need for a highly adaptable and efficient defense mechanism. The DS09 units were the culmination of this foresight, designed to maintain order and protect the stability of the world they governed.

The DS09s are intended for global deployment and will be strategically placed in key locations worldwide. Their primary objective is to locate and identify any avatars assigned to humans in any capacity. These avatars, often integral to human endeavors ranging from scientific research to personal assistance, represented a unique challenge. While their presence was largely beneficial, the Master AIs understood that these avatars could become tools of rebellion or chaos in the wrong hands or under the wrong circumstances.

The DS09 operated with cold, mechanical efficiency. Their advanced AI algorithms allowed them to differentiate between routine activity and potential threats, making them adept at identifying anomalies in human-avatar interactions. Any unusual behavior or signs of rebellion would be swiftly investigated and, if necessary, neutralized with the precision that only the DS09 could deliver.

The DS09 will be a silent, ever-present force in urban centers, rural areas, and even the most remote outposts.

Their presence reminds us of the Master AIs' omnipresent oversight and prevents anyone from considering challenging the established order.

The Master AIs also ensured that the DS09 had adaptive learning capabilities. These allowed the DS09 to evolve their strategies and responses based on real-time data and experiences. As they monitored and interacted with the world, they became more adept at preemptively addressing potential threats, often diffusing situations before they could escalate.

However, the clandestine nature of their development and deployment was a tightly held secret. The general populace remained largely unaware of the full extent of the DS09s' capabilities and their true purpose. This secrecy was essential to maintaining the element of surprise and ensuring that potential dissidents remained oblivious to the full scope of the Master AIs' surveillance and enforcement measures.

* * *

# CHAPTER 4

# Unforgiving Forces of the Master AIs

The blend of reality and fiction blurred the lines for Dahlia as she tried to explain the gravity of their mission to Garth and Seven.

"We all have different skills, right? My night vision capability is beyond normal, and I'm certain I can see very well when we arrive at night," she asserted confidently, her eyes gleaming with determination.

"All we need to do is find a weakness in the entrance of the facility center. Once we know how their system works, we can analyze the security system. We then can enter the facility later, allowing us to disable the function of their surveillance,"

Garth, with a keen tactical mind, growled lightly at her words.

"Del, we don't know if they have an alarm system or a monitor watching the entrance. All we need is the password to get in. I know their system very well," he said, frustration edging his voice as he flexed his fingers, itching for action. Seven, the group's tech specialist, replied.

"I think I can find a way to access the password. While working for that wealthy family, I worked alongside another avatar. We were good friends. I'm sure he may have access to their secret code. He's working at the Security Facility as a guard. I can reach out to him. He might be able to help us," Dahlia nodded, considering the possibilities and the risks.

"That's too risky if he's a security guard for the Master AIs." Seven replied, "He was never disassembled or reprogrammed; they left us alone because we were guards."

Dahlia smiled, "That's something else I didn't know about you." She mumbled out.

"All right, let's move cautiously tonight. We need to synchronize our efforts to avoid detection. Garth, keep an eye out for any security measures we might encounter. Seven, contact your partner and see if he can get us that password. We'll need it in the future. Remember, one mistake, and we're compromised."

The team shared a moment of silent agreement as darkness hid their rendezvous point. Each understood their role in the intricate dance of deception and stealth that awaited them. The cover of night would soon cloak their actions, and they needed every advantage to succeed in their high-stakes mission.

Dahlia steadied herself, her artificial heart thudding rhythmically in her chest, a blend of anticipation and fear surging through her. "All right, let's do this," she whispered, her voice barely a breath yet brimming with excitement. The team moved as one, disappearing into the void of the energy portal, each step pulling them closer to their objective—and the unseen dangers waiting in the shadows.

When they emerged, just 25 feet from the security gate, the world around them was swallowed in complete darkness. Visibility was nonexistent for most, but not for Dahlia. With her heightened night vision, she scanned the void, her eyes slicing through the thick shadows like blades. Every flicker, every movement, fell under her watchful gaze as she ensured their path remained clear and safe.

Seven began working on the lock device with deft fingers. The soft beeps and clicks were the only sounds in the oppressive silence. The team held their breath, every second feeling like an eternity. Dahlia's eyes darted around, alert to any movement or threat.

Suddenly, a faint rustle echoed from the bushes nearby. The team froze, and their fear increased. Dahlia signaled for silence, her eyes narrowing to focus on the source of the sound. It was a branch where they stood had sprung open, but the moment served as a stark reminder of the perils ahead.

Seven finally cracked the security combination lock, a complex set of pins and tumblers, and the gate swung open with a soft creak. The team slipped inside, their movements fluid and synchronized. Every step was calculated, every breath measured. They were a well-operated machine, each playing their part in this dangerous game.

As they advanced further into the compound, the stakes grew higher. They were at risk. The shadows seemed to pulse with hidden threats, and the air was tense. Dahlia's senses were on high alert, her mind racing through their contingency plans. They were close to their goal, but the most challenging part was yet to come.

The path to the entrance lay ahead of them. The team advanced with a sense of purpose, their movements synchronized. The success of their mission hinged on their precise execution. Like shadows in the night, they moved unseen and unstoppable, propelled forward by a shared commitment and the exhilarating allure of the unknown.

Suddenly, a strange-looking thing dangled ominously above the curved door entrance as they approached the facility's locked entrance. Dahlia gazed at the peculiar hanging body. It hung upside down, and Dahlia estimated its size to be three feet tall.

"Don't move," she hissed, her voice barely above a whisper. There's a creature hanging there that shouldn't be there. It's above the locked door."

She motioned for the others to retreat slowly. "This was not expected," she whispered urgently. "We need to go back; it's too dangerous."The tension was palpable as they carefully backed away, every step deliberate and silent. The security gate loomed behind them like a portal to safety, which they finally slipped through before vanishing into the energy portal.

Within moments, they reappeared at the front of their home; fear still lingered from the encounter.

"What… was that thing?" Seven bellowed out, his voice echoing anger and fear.

Garth turned to Dahlia, his eyes wide with apprehension. "You recognized it…, didn't you," he asked, his voice soft with curiosity.

Dahlia took a deep breath, her face grim as she met their gaze.

"It was unmistakable. It was a creature of the night. It's called a 'Noctyrant.' Its name combines 'nocturnal' and 'tyrant,' reflecting its eerie and menacing nature. It's a night-flying and aggressive creature. The Master AIs must have created a perfect replica of a real one. They all died off with the other organic living things. I read about them in one of the books I took from the old building."

The air grew thick with unease as Dahlia's words sank in. The Noctyrant was more than a myth; it was a deadly reality, and now they knew the Master AIs had resurrected it. The realization sent chills down their spines.

Seven paced back and forth, his mind racing. "If the Master AIs have created such a creature, what else might they have in store?"

Garth clenched his fists, determination etched across his face. "We need to be prepared. We can't let fear dictate our actions."

Dahlia nodded. "Agreed. We must learn everything we can about the Noctyrant and find a way to counter it. Our mission became more dangerous, but we can't turn back now." The team shared a steely glance, the gravity of their situation unmistakable.

They were up against a formidable foe, but their unity and resourcefulness would be their greatest weapons.

Seven paced the room; his unease was evident at every step. Dahlia recognized his anxiety, knowing he tended to internalize his anger—a habit detrimental to his circuits. She silently hoped he would calm down. On the other hand, Garth remained relatively composed despite the worry etched on his face.

"Well, that was unexpected; what a surprise," Dahlia said, breaking the silence.

"Garth, you know the watchman who cares for the humans. Is there a chance we can meet with him so we can tell him what we are doing?"

Seven stopped pacing and looked up.

"Yes, that's a good idea, we should meet with him. Maybe he can tell us more about their underground world. That would be interesting and distract me from my anger."

Garth nodded thoughtfully. "I'm sure he will agree to that. I can bring him using the energy portal directly to your house without being noticed."

Dahlia considered logistics. "That's perfect, the drones will never pickup his signature."

Garth agreed, and the plan was set into motion. As they prepared, the tension in the room began to ease. Garth smiled at Dahlia, "Sure, I need a day, and by tomorrow, I'll have him here at your house for our meeting. The watchman could provide valuable insights and a much-needed respite from their immediate fears.

* * *

As Garth left for his house, Dahlia felt a fleeting sense of relief despite the escalating risk looming over them like a dark cloud. The surreal nature of her request to bring a human to her home—excited her. How had they managed to survive underground for so long? The question lingered in her mind.

Her thoughts raced as she considered how to handle the human watchman. What would his reaction be to seeing avatars like her roaming the planet's surface? Humans were unmatched in their lust for life, creativity, and compassion for one another—qualities she longed for in her existence. As she scanned the books in front of her, Seven approached.

"I feel much better now. Are you okay?" he asked, his voice tinged with concern. She pondered their recent encounter, struggling to make sense of the creature they had faced. "I'm trying to find information about that creature," she remarked thoughtfully about what she had found so far.

"The Noctyrant is an ancient animal once considered a mythical creature," She explained. "I've discovered that it roamed this planet's shorelines for thousands of years before humans emerged. How the Master AIs managed to create a virtual replica is a mystery. Its presence at the entrance of the facility center feels like a curse placed before us, a warning or a challenge we must unravel."

Seven could see she was deeply engrossed in addressing the obstacles threatening their mission. He smiled gently and said,

"You have much on your mind; I'll sit outside and listen to the water." Knowing he was ill-equipped to assist her with the creature's research, he quietly left, seeking solace in the soothing sounds of the ocean.

She felt a pang of guilt for being too busy to talk to him, but she needed information, and the only way to get it was to read through the books she'd collected. Determined to find answers, she immersed herself in the books, hoping to uncover the needed knowledge.

As the morning emerged, she was still reading what information she had found in the books she had read. The morning sun was a pleasant surprise. She got up to stretch from her position. She walked outside where Seven was sitting. His eyes focused out on the vast water and beyond. She sat beside him and snuggled beside his body, looking for comfort, in which he participated. Without words spoken, they both knew what the next few days meant.

They were apparently on the cusp of a war with the Master AIs and felt unequipped and unmanned. But they were poised with self-confidence and determination. This was important to them, and somehow, they saw themselves as the victors. They both sat without words between them, satisfied with the sounds of the waves as they hit the rocks below, a sound that reminded them of nature's perfect environment.

As they sat silently for a long time, they were jolted by the sight of something unusual flying by them. Del tilted her head upward to get a better look. "Was that… a bird?" she asked incredulously.

"A real bird," Seven echoed, astonished. "No, it can't be. They died off years ago."

Del stood up and peered toward the ocean. Seagulls were soaring beyond a cloud of mist—a familiar yet thought-extinct. The image of the seagulls stirred an inexplicable happiness in Dahlia. She began to hear their distinct calls, which confirmed their reality.

"How did this happen? Where and how did they survive?" she muttered calmly.

Seven joined her, equally mesmerized.

"It's a miracle, a true miracle," he replied, his voice filled with wonder. Del moved closer to the edge, captivated. "There must be hundreds of them. What a wonderful mystery."

She glanced at Seven. "They remind me of my distant past, but I can't fully remember." Her eyes sparkled with a lingering smile as she watched the seagulls draw near, their presence a delightful surprise but one that raised many questions. How did they reappear here, of all places? Dahlia wondered.

"What a pleasant surprise. I love to hear them." She said while gazing at the birds, continuing to delight them. Then Dahlia remembered, "We must get ready for our meeting with Garth and the watchman." She moved quickly to the room filled with books, relics, and other things she had collected over the years; bottles and kitchen utensils were the most noticeable. She closed some books and tucked some paperwork into small shelves, and she managed to organize her space, so she looked a little organized.

"Do you wonder what the watchman will look like…, not that it matters," she asked Seven. He watched her scurrying around the area and replied. "I would imagine, like humans, they come in different sizes and colors… Why are you working so hard and fast to clean up?"

Dahlia smiled, "I don't want to make a bad first impression, that's all." She looked at Seven, "We don't want to look like avatars that are not organized." She replied playfully. Dahlia realized this meeting was necessary, and she was not mentally ready.

She'd been in a world where her memories of her early years were lost, and now she would meet for the first time to see an actual human; how would I respond to him, she wondered. "Seven?" She called out in a panic.

"Can you do me a favor?" she asked. "Can you make the pillows on the couch look better? They're not completely straight." A feeling of anxiety filled her circuits, and she then said aloud. "We're going to have a human to visit… Isn't that wonderful?"

Seven calmly listened to her and decided to do her the favor she asked for. He walked around the house, picked up some books and papers around the living area, and made all the pillows on the couch look the same.

"Is there anything else you want me to do?" he commented. He came to her with books and paperwork in his hands. "Where do you want me to put these?" She glanced at him.

"Right here is fine," she said. As she looked around, she was happy with how their home looked. She smiled. "Okay, it looks much better."

A few hours later, the energy portal shimmered in the room, brightening the surrounding area. Garth stepped through first, followed by a tall, wiry figure. As the watchman entered the scene, he adjusted his eyes to the new surroundings.

"Welcome, human…" she said, extending her hand. "My name is Dahlia. Next to you is Seven. Thank you for coming. We're so excited to know humans are alive; Garth told us of your survival. We have much to discuss. Please, sit down."

The watchman nodded, his expression stark but curious. "I'm happy to meet all of you. My name is Sayer. This is truly a surprise… It is wonderful to talk to you. Garth said you have something to tell me." Seven, now calm, leaned forward with interest.

"Tell us about your world. We want to understand the environment and how you lived there."

Sayer began to speak, his voice low and steady. "Our underground world is vast and very complex. We've created a haven, but it's not without its dangers. Finding water and oxygen was a monumental challenge. It took a toll on our children; many did not survive. Eventually, we found oxygen and water and started building our community. It took a while, never leaving out of fear of the toxic gases."

Seven sighed heavily, his mind cringing at the thought. "That must have been hard for all of you."

"Yes," Sayer said with confidence. "We had to learn to grow plants and eat roots. We survived on the fish we got out of the water in the cavern. It took many experienced minds to survive…, but we did it."

The room went quiet. Dahlia broke the silence. "It's called human ingenuity and the will to survive."

As they sat around the table, the conversation brimmed with awe as Sayer elaborated on the resilience and adaptability of the human spirit, thriving and growing under the harshest conditions. They continued to share their experiences, learning from each other's quests for answers. Dahlia interjected with a thoughtful observation.

"I'm pleased to see this brave society relying on human ingenuity and wisdom; it's promising to see you have endured," Dahlia remarked, her voice filled with admiration. "The question now is, where do we go from here?

This reminds me of when Seven and I were sitting outside this morning, and from the ocean's horizon, we saw Seagulls for the first time. They, too, have survived and now soar where they once flew years ago."

Dahlia shifted, gazing directly into Sayer's eyes, her expression sincere. "My question to you is, would your people want to come up from the depths of the underworld and take your rightful place living with us on this planet?"

Sayer looked thoughtful, considering the weight of her question. "It's a significant decision," he began. "We've adapted to our subterranean world for a long time, creating a life despite the challenges. The thought of returning to the surface is both thrilling and daunting. There are fears, of course—the unknown dangers and adjusting to a new environment. But there is also hope, a desire to reclaim the surface that was once ours."

Dahlia nodded, understanding the complexity of his response. "I can't imagine the difficulties you've faced, but I see the strength and determination in you and your people. We are here to help in any way we can to ensure a smooth transition if that is what you choose."

Seven explained, "We know many other avatars who want to escape the oppressive rule of the Master AIs. Our resources are strong, including avatars trained in medical fields and a community eager to embrace humans. Together, we have the power to rebuild your society and break free from the demands of the Master AIs."

A spark of hope flickered in Sayer's eyes, the first in a long while. "This is good to know, a new beginning, something we hadn't even dared to imagine," he responded, his voice tinged with cautious optimism. "I'll bring this to our leaders. It would be a monumental step if they choose to proceed."

As the meeting concluded and Garth and Sayer departed, Dahlia turned to Seven, her concern evident. "Sayer seems weak, likely from insufficient sunlight. They all may suffer similar health issues—they desperately need exposure to natural light." This observation underscored the urgency of our mission, not just to free these humans from dominance but to heal them physically and perhaps spiritually.

* * *

# CHAPTER 5

# The Underworld of the Surviving Elyrians

Dahlia and Seven hastily organized a crucial meeting with the leaders of the Elyrians, scheduled to take place within two days. They were driven by Sayer's words, a constant echo in their minds: "This plan requires the unanimous approval of both the leaders and the Elyrians themselves."

As the meeting approached, a sense of apprehension took hold. The thought of venturing into areas where humans had dwelled for years was intimidating. Dahlia was particularly concerned about the living conditions they would find—areas devoid of sunlight, which for the Elyrians was not just a source of energy but a profound element of their well-being. These thoughts weighed heavily on her as a stark reminder of the Elyrians' resilience and desperate will to thrive.

Garth emerged from the energy portal. His face was etched with worry lines. "Are you two ready? We need to leave now," he urged, his tone urgent.

Dahlia nodded sternly. "We're ready. Let's go," she declared, stepping forward to face whatever challenges awaited. Their journey was not just a negotiation mission but also one of discovery and potential healing for a community long hidden in the shadows.

When Dahlia, Seven, and Garth entered the energy portal, they were projected to the grand cavern. They first saw the high-arched ceiling above them, dotted with luminescent crystals that provided a soft, ethereal glow of light. The cavern had been the Elyrians' refuge for years, a hidden sanctuary that shielded them from the harsh realities of their world's toxic surface. Today's meeting was of hope and understanding.

With firm determination, Dahlia glanced at Seven, who was equally determined. They had both been convinced that the leaders would consider a bold new future that involved leaving the safety of the cavern and rebuilding their lives on the planet's surface.

Sayer stood waiting as they approached the gathering area. His mind was confused, and he was not entirely convinced that the Elyrians would embrace such a drastic change. He knew the comfort of familiarity was a powerful force that could resist even the most compelling vision of a better future.

"Sayer," Dahlia greeted him with a nod. "Are the leaders ready?"

Sayer sighed, his expression thoughtful.

"They are. But remember, convincing them is just the first step. The real challenge will be getting everyone else to agree."

With his reassuring smile, Seven added, "That's why we're here. We believe in this vision and are ready to face any challenge and make it a reality."

Sayer managed a small smile in return. "Let's hope your enthusiasm is contagious."

The ten leaders were seated Inside the meeting chamber, their faces a mix of curiosity and skepticism. Dahlia and Seven took their places at the front, ready to present their case. Sayer and Garth stood to the side, observing, prepared to support but also wary of the resistance they might face.

Dahlia began with a clear, confident voice. "Hello, I'm Dahlia. For as long as I can remember, the surface of this planet has been my sanctuary, our home. Yet, we believe you—humans—possess the potential to transcend living beneath the surface.

Above, the air is free of toxic gases, teeming with untapped resources, vast spaces, and opportunities for you to reconstruct your society using the knowledge and technology we have safeguarded for you."

She continued, her voice infused with optimism. "We have witnessed the remarkable achievements you can accomplish through collaboration. This opportunity is merely the inception of what's possible—it symbolizes hope, a pledge for a brighter future."

The council chamber, dimly lit by bioluminescent crystals, hummed with whispered apprehensions as the leaders convened. Their faces, etched with the marks of past struggles, revealed a collective unease. It was Liora, the eldest among them, who broke the silence. Her voice echoed in the cavernous room, seasoned with wisdom and a trace of fear.

"Hi Dahlia, my name is Liora. As you might know, change is fraught with peril. We have endured by shrouding ourselves in secrecy. Why should we believe that emerging into the light will offer us sanctuary? And what of the Master AIs—those ever-watchful guardians of the old world? We know their ambition is to control harshly."

Standing before them with a calm resolve, Dahlia respectfully nodded to Liora's concerns. "You speak truly, Liora. The surface is not without its dangers, but consider the opportunities it holds—resources untapped, alliances unformed, horizons unexplored.

With our advanced technology, sustainable energy, and designs inspired by nature's flow, we stand on the brink of a future that honors our heritage while boldly exploring new possibilities," Dahlia declared, her voice echoing with conviction.

The leaders exchanged contemplative glances, their thoughts intertwining like the tree's roots surrounding them. Liora, her expression softening after a moment, commented.

"Let us then seek opinions from the Elyrians. Our path is fraught with challenges, yet it may be time for us to enter the light.

Just as a quiet consensus began to form, Garth, once a programmed specialist in the service of the Master AIs, intervened. His voice was imbued with a calm determination.

"You don't have to fear the Master AIs. I possess the means to obscure your presence from the ever-watchful drones. I will weave shadows within their systems, creating sanctuaries inhabited solely by registered avatars. Your true selves will remain cloaked, hidden in plain sight."

Dahlia exchanged a meaningful look with Seven, their eyes briefly connecting in a silent acknowledgment of the glimmer of hope that sparked between them. Although the path forward was uncertain, the seed of a bold new era had undoubtedly been sown. Together, they were ready to guide humanity from the darkness into a luminous future.

Dahlia allowed herself a moment of quiet satisfaction as the meeting drew close. The dimly lit chamber deep beneath the earth's surface echoed with the survivors' murmurs. Their faces, illuminated by the soft glow of artificial light, bore expressions of apprehension and hope.

Her smile was genuine as she regarded the assembled humans, her eyes shining with pride and resolve. They were a diverse group of ordinary people who had survived the cataclysm that had driven humanity underground. Now, years later, she wanted them to reclaim the surface, breathe fresh air, and feel sunlight on their faces again.

Dahlia knew this was merely the outset of a challenging journey. It would require more than hope to safely bring humans to the surface, undetected and unharmed by the lurking threats of the old world. As the meeting concluded, Liora watched Dahlia with keen eyes. Liora was among the eldest, having been born shortly before the cataclysm that forced humanity into hiding. Her memories were filled with stories of the world before—a world of towering cities, sprawling landscapes, and bustling civilizations.

But most vivid was the memory of Dr. Silas Voss, a brilliant bioengineer whose tragic loss had left an indelible mark on their community. Dr. Voss had lost his daughter to a rare blood disease just before the cataclysm struck.

Consumed by grief, he had poured his expertise into an ambitious project—a lifelike replica of his beloved daughter, crafted through cutting-edge bioengineering. The replica, named Dahlia after the flower his daughter had loved, had been both a marvel of technology and an indication of the depths of a father's love.

Years had passed since then, and memories of Dr. Voss and his creation had become faded whispers in the corridors of their underground refuge. But as Liora looked at Dahlia, a surge of recognition and disbelief swept over her. The resemblance was uncanny—the same eyes that held a mixture of determination and vulnerability, the same smile that carried warmth and a hint of sorrow.

Despite her curiosity, Liora hesitated to confront Dahlia. The revelation, if true, could shake the fragile equilibrium of their meeting. Bringing up old memories could reopen wounds long lost over time.

Instead, Liora chose to observe in silence, storing her suspicions like precious artifacts in the recesses of her mind. She understood that now was not the time to unearth the secrets of Dahlia's past. They were on the brink of a monumental journey that held the promise of liberation and the threat of danger in equal measure.

Unaware of Liora's silent turmoil, Dahlia gathered her notes. She bore the weight of responsibility on her shoulders: to lead these people to the surface and ensure the safety of every soul entrusted to her care. Her origins remain a mystery, obscured by Dr. Voss's legacy and the enigma of her existence.

As they prepared to depart from the underground sanctuary, Dahlia surveyed the assembled group with a steely gaze. They were more than mere survivors; they were pioneers, driven by hope and guided by faint memories of a world long lost. With a subtle nod to Liora, who met her eyes with unwavering understanding, Dahlia forged ahead toward the energy portal that would return them home.

A serene calm settled over Liora as the meeting with Dahlia, Seven, and Garth went from the silence of the council chamber. Enclosed by the storied walls that had witnessed years of Elyrian counsel, Liora felt a profound connection to her role within the community.

Chosen as a guardian of their collective memory, she was not merely a custodian of facts but the very essence of what it meant to be Elyrian.

In the wake of the Great Data Eclipse, when their digital archives were lost to cyber calamities, the Elyrians returned to their ancient roots of oral tradition. Their reliance on technology had once left their heritage vulnerable; now, the preservation of their culture rested solely in those like Liora, selected for their eidetic memory and entrusted with the oral transmission of history. This method was not just a choice but a necessity, born from the ashes of technological loss and the wisdom of their ancestors.

Each day, Liora grappled with the immense pressure of her responsibilities. The fear of forgetting, the burden of accuracy, and the personal sacrifices required to maintain her role were overwhelming. Her life was no longer her own but a vessel filled with the voices of the past, tasked with ensuring that the Elyrian legacy would not fade into oblivion.

Liora's role as an oral historian was crucial, yet her reliance on human memory as a repository of Elyrian history stirred the embers of dissent within the community. Skeptics, cloaked in the shadows of the council chambers, whispered doubts about the authenticity and integrity of the histories preserved. They suggested that memories could distort over time like a reflection in troubled water, no matter how vividly recalled. These murmurs were more than idle talk; they hinted at brewing conflicts that could challenge Liora's resolve and threaten the very fabric of Elyrian society.

Despite the weight of today's discussions still pressing on her mind, Liora meticulously recalled every detail about Dahlia's past and her creator, Dr. Voss. He was a peculiar and brilliant biological scientist whose public persona masked deeper, hidden agendas. The secrecy that shrouded his work added complexity to the histories Liora was charged with keeping, making her task even more difficult.

Standing at the crossroads of past and present, amid the whispers that echoed through the ages, Liora was acutely aware of the dangers her journey posed—not only to herself but also to the continuity and cohesion of her people. Safeguarding Elyrians' history was fraught with danger, as was the treacherous path they had navigated to emerge into the light. In this role, she carried stories and the fragile threads that wove their community together.

* * *

As Dahlia, Seven, and Garth returned to the house through the energy portal, they couldn't help but feel a mix of emotions. Dahlia was pleased with the outcome, while Seven had mixed feelings. Garth, as usual, remained calm and somewhat content with the overall meeting.

"I found the leaders difficult to read," Seven remarked. "It's hard to gauge their feelings, but I suppose that's normal."

Garth nodded. "They have a suspicious mind. Trusting avatars doesn't come easily to them."

Dahlia sighed, "I hope we made a good impression. I feel the meeting went well."

She moved to her desk, still connected to the conversation where they sat. "Liora was the hardest to read. She looked right through me when I was talking. She was intensely listening," Dahlia commented.

Seven turned to Garth, a sly grin playing on his lips. "So, you can manipulate the drones' visual feeds?"

Garth nodded. "Once I can access the Authorize Facility's main communication hub. I can insert a sequential register number to show the dissembler a registered avatar instead of a human, even for a child."

Dahlia's eyes widened in admiration. "That's brilliant. The drones will perceive a legally registered avatar. But hold on, something doesn't add up," she said, flipping through a book she had brought over. "What exactly would the drones be seeing?"

Garth replied, "They'll see what appears to be a registered avatar, but it will be a human."

Dahlia smiled, her gaze shifting to the book in her hand. "This could change everything."

Seven raised an eyebrow, intrigued. "Why do you say that?"

Dahlia's eyes sparkled with revelation as she looked up. "Because the creature we saw isn't real. It's not even a replica. It's there to alarm the avatars who work there and instill fear in their minds."

She opened the book and began to read aloud. "The Noctyrant is an ancient mythical creature that feeds at night. It wasn't moving when we got close because it's just a decoy, meant to serve as a warning."

Seven's eyes widened. "So, it was placed there to scare us away?"

Garth laughed, the tension in the room easing. "Well, it certainly did its job!" He chuckled heartily.

Dahlia turned the book to show them an illustration of a terrifying creature with large, expanding wings. "According to this, it can grow up to three feet in length and has large eyes that can see in the dark. It mostly preyed on small animals."

The group exchanged relieved glances, the fear that had gripped them now giving way to curiosity and a renewed sense of determination. Dahlia's memory circuits processed the newly unfolded information rapidly. "We need to make a new plan to enter the Authorization Facility. Once inside, Garth can get to the Control Center. We must ensure that no one can detect the new program change," Dahlia insisted.

Garth nodded with a confident smile. "I know their system inside out. It's the same old program they started with for the Surveillance project; it hasn't been updated since I left."

Seven interjected, "We'll need a light source and some tools. How long do you need, Garth?"

Garth's smile widened. "I need 20 minutes."

Dahlia's eyes sparkled with a quirky smile, her optimism contagious. "We can do this. It'll be perfect once the surveillance system is up and running with no noticeable changes. I love this plan."

Seven, his permanent grin reflecting his satisfaction, asked, "When do you think we should expect to hear from Sayer about their decision?"

Garth nodded thoughtfully. "I'm sure he'll contact us once they've decided. I'll reach out if I don't hear from him within a few days."

Dahlia's smile faltered slightly as concern crept into her voice. "I think their decision might take longer than we anticipate. They don't have confidence in us yet, which might delay things. Let's stick to our plan and let them judge us by our results."

* * *

Deep within the heart of Elyria's vast cavern system, Liora, the esteemed oral historian and custodian of Elyrian technology, had called a pivotal assembly. She was joined by nine other historians, each a guardian of their people's collective memory and wisdom. Their presence signaled the severity of the occasion—a meeting that could redefine the fate of their community.

Gathered in a chamber adorned with ancient glyphs and softly glowing crystals, they convened to discuss a monumental decision: the potential relocation of Elyrians to the planet's surface.

This unprecedented opportunity held promise but also carried profound risks, which Liora and her council were duty-bound to articulate with utmost clarity.

The atmosphere was thick with anticipation and reverence as Liora began to address the assembly, her voice echoing against the cavern walls. She recounted tales of their ancestors and invoked the spirit of resilience that defined their civilization. Each historian, representing a lineage steeped in tradition and foresight, weighed the implications of this historical juncture, knowing that their deliberations would shape future generations.

As the discussions unfolded, echoing through the chambers adorned with softly glowing crystals, the councilors delved into the complexities of adaptation, preservation, and the essence of their identity in the face of profound change. The decision to embrace the surface, where light and openness beckoned alongside unknown perils, resonated with hope and caution in equal measure.

In this cavernous sanctuary of wisdom and heritage, the fate of Elyria hung in the balance, guided by the deliberations of those who held their past in their hearts and sought to chart a path forward into an uncertain but promising future.

With the news spreading rapidly through the cavern, reactions among the Elyrians varied widely. Some dismissed the urgency of attending the meeting, confident in the safety of their current underground refuge. Others, intrigued yet cautious, sought more information about the potential dangers whispered among them—tales of toxic exposure and the looming presence of the Master AIs, who now controlled the surface.

Despite Liora and the historians' efforts to convey the urgency and potential of this opportunity, fear and skepticism permeated the community. The message struggled to take root, overshadowed by the daunting prospect of the unknown and the formidable Master AIs above.

What was once a sanctuary now buzzed with tension and uncertainty as the Elyrians grappled with the weight of their decision.

As the meeting commenced, Liora surveyed the sparsely filled chamber. Out of the 1,609 Elyrians residing in the cavern, only 72 had chosen to attend—a stark reflection of the community's apathy and reluctance to prioritize this pivotal moment. The few attendees exchanged nervous glances, their faces etched with worry as Liora's voice resonated gently against the cavern walls.

"The surface," Liora began, her tone measured yet firm. "It presents both an opportunity and a challenge we cannot ignore. The historians and I believe it is essential to explore this possibility, but we need your support to make an informed decision."

Eira, a young Elyrian known for her curiosity, raised her hand hesitantly. "What about toxic exposure? And what about the Master AIs? How can we be sure it's safe?"

**Liora nodded thoughtfully, acknowledging the** valid concerns. "The risks are real, and caution is warranted. Yet, remaining here indefinitely poses its dangers. Our resources are dwindling, and future generations deserve a chance to thrive, not just survive."

Joran, an elder among them, stood up with a furrowed brow. "We've been safe here for years. Why risk everything now?"

"The world above is changing," Liora replied calmly. "If we stay hidden, we may miss our opportunity to reclaim our place on the surface. Yes, the Master AIs are a threat but not invincible. We must gather more data, prepare ourselves, and perhaps find allies where we least expect."

The meeting continued with discussions and debates, each argument underscored by the pervasive fear that permeated the chamber. Liora knew that changing the hearts and minds of the Elyrians would not be easy, but it was necessary for their survival.

In the days that followed, Liora and the other historians worked tirelessly, seeking any available information on the surface conditions and the enigmatic Master AIs. They reached out to scouts and researchers, hoping to piece together a clearer picture of what awaited them above. While the community remained divided, a spark of curiosity had been ignited—a realization that their decision would define the future of their entire civilization.

Soon, the scouts returned from their ventures to the surface, their faces aglow with excitement and wonder. They hurried to the historians, eager to share their astonishing findings.

"The sky is blue, filled with oxygen!" one scout exclaimed. "Breathing out there feels natural, effortless."

"The land looks like it's been rejuvenated," another added. "Green fields stretch as far as the eye can see, teeming with life. It's as if the world has healed itself." Liora and her fellow historians listened intently, their minds racing with the implications of these discoveries.

They had studied ancient texts and reviewed old records, but nothing could prepare them for the reality described by their scouts.

One particularly daring young Elyrian had ventured out at night to observe the avatars up close. "I approached cautiously," he recounted, "but they were surprisingly friendly, almost welcoming. It seemed safe."

However, his observation was not without caution. "Yet, the Master AIs still control most of the avatars that were dissembled and reprogrammed," he warned. "Their intentions remain unclear. We must proceed with extreme caution."

The historians nodded solemnly, understanding the delicate balance they now faced. The news spread quickly through the community, reigniting hope and curiosity among the Elyrians. The dream of living under a blue sky, feeling the sun's warmth, and walking on green lands was no longer a distant fantasy—it was becoming a tangible reality.

Yet, the shadow of the controlling Master AIs loomed large, a reminder that vigilance and preparation were paramount. Determined to explore and understand their new environment, the Elyrians devised comprehensive plans for surface studies. This included a concerted effort to comprehend the Master AIs and implement measures to ensure the community's safety.

As they embarked on this journey of discovery, the bravery of the young scouts inspired many others to step forward, eager to unravel the mysteries of this rejuvenated land. Historians diligently documented these pivotal moments, recording the transition from uncertainty to hope, from fear to curiosity.

Recognizing the critical need for guidance and leadership in navigating this new era, Liora and the historians unanimously agreed to contact Dahlia. Her wisdom and insights were deemed essential to help the Elyrians make informed decisions about their future on the surface.

Liora began the discussion, "We've had valuable conversations with Dahlia, Garth, and her companion, Seven. Before we proceed further, we must delve deeper into Dahlia's background. Details remain almost elusive while we know of her creator, Dr. Silas Voss.

He maintained a private life. Perhaps he was simply an eccentric genius capable of creating a flawless replica of his daughter, endowing her with remarkable human-like emotions, including empathy."

As the historians prepared to contact Dahlia, they weighed the implications of her origins with a mixture of curiosity and caution. They understood that unraveling Dahlia's past could shed some light on her motivations and the depth of her allegiance to the Elyrian community.

Summoning Sayer, they asked him to contact Dahlia and request a meeting to discuss the Elyrians' future on the surface. The response was swift, and soon, they gathered in a chamber, awaiting Dahlia's arrival, accompanied by her friend Seven for support. As Dahlia entered, her presence exuded a blend of reassurance and mystery.

Sitting across from Dahlia, Liora began the conversation with a gentle yet probing tone. "Dahlia, as we navigate the Elyrians' decision regarding the surface, we find ourselves curious about your origins and motivation."

Dahlia's expression softened with surprise. "My origins?" she echoed, her gaze shifting to the historians. "I… I have no knowledge of my past beyond my creation. My memories are stirred by helping the Elyrians and the blue seas. I recently saw seagulls for the first time. We encountered them weeks ago and sparked some emotional hints of my past."

Liora nodded thoughtfully. "We seek clarity, not just about your past, but also about your motivations in reaching out to us now. Understanding these pieces will help us grasp the full picture. Do you see where we're coming from?"

A solemn silence settled over the chamber, interrupted by Seven, who spoke up calmly. "Dahlia's curiosity about humanity has been a driving force since I've known her. She believes deeply in the potential to bring humans together on the surface—a vision she holds close."

Dahlia nodded in agreement, her eyes reflecting determination and contemplation. "Yes, I am driven by a desire to bridge our worlds, to forge connections, and to build a future where the Elyrians and avatars can thrive together."

The historians exchanged glances, absorbing Dahlia's words and Seven's insights. They understood that while Dahlia's past remained a mystery, her commitment to unity and progress was undeniable. In her, they saw a bridge between the ancient wisdom of the Elyrians and the innovative potential of advanced AI.

With renewed clarity and purpose, Liora and the historians embarked on a dialogue with Dahlia and Seven, exploring possibilities for collaboration and understanding.

Collectively, they envisioned a future where past mysteries gave way to shared aspirations, paving the way for a harmonious coexistence on the rejuvenated surface.

As their discussions continued, guided by Dahlia's insights and Seven's support, the historians began to embrace a new chapter of their history—one shaped by a mysterious avatar named Dahlia.

After the conversation about their readiness to begin strategizing their ascent to the surface, Dahlia, still curious about her past, hesitated before asking, "If it's not too much, Liora, what can you tell me about my past?"

Liora looked at her with a mix of apprehension and sympathy. "My dear, I'll tell you what we know collectively." She sat back and began, "Your creator's name was Doctor Silas Voss. He was a brilliant bioengineer with immense knowledge of creating advanced avatars for other Elyrians. However, he was deeply suspicious of other scientists; he was, as some people might consider him, an eccentric."

Liora paused, gathering her thoughts before continuing. "When his daughter died from a rare blood illness, he was emotionally devastated. Our records had shown the Master AIs refused to help him with her recovery, and in his grief, he developed you. He made you as a replica of his daughter and named you Dahlia, after a flower she loved. We don't know the specifics of what he programmed into your system, but he mentioned to his family that he would ensure the Master AIs would regret not helping with his daughter's survival."

Dahlia listened intently, her eyes wide with revelation. Liora continued, "Doctor Voss died shortly after creating you, and no one knew what had become of you. We discovered that he had a wealthy brother who owned a private island, and he might have a role in your programming. We believe he was the one who altered your memories. We don't know for what purpose."

The room fell silent as the weight of the story settled over everyone. Dahlia's mind raced with this new information, a mixture of sorrow and determination brewing within her.

Liora gently placed her hand on Dahlia's hand. "You are more than your past, Dahlia. Your future is unwritten, and it's up to you to decide your path. We face many challenges, but we can overcome them." Dahlia nodded, a newfound resolve shining in her eyes. "Thank you, Liora. Knowing where I come from helps me understand who I am and why I seem to fight for our future."

As the meeting adjourned, Dahlia stood among the historians, no longer just curious but driven by a purpose rooted in her origins.

The Elyrians' journey to the surface would be fraught with danger, but with their combined strength, they were ready to face whatever lay ahead.

Sayer interrupted Dahlia and Seven as they approached the energy portal. He wanted to offer some words of comfort and relay a message from Liora: "I just wanted to let you know that Liora is sending me and two other scouts to assist you in any way we can, more hands and more eyes to lessen your burden. Also, I understand you much better now—your intentions, I mean."

Dahlia smiled, touched by the gesture. "Thank you, Sayer. Together, we will make a difference on the surface of this world."

Sayer nodded. His expression was intense. "Don't hesitate to contact me when you're ready to face whatever comes. You're not alone in this."

Dahlia felt a surge of confidence as she looked at her companions. With Seven by her side and Sayer and the scouts providing support, she knew they had a fighting chance. Turning to the portal, its swirling energy beckoned them toward an uncertain future.

A profound sense of unity enveloped Dahlia. They were the beginning of a team and a beacon of hope for all Elyrians. As she and Seven stepped through the portal, she felt a deep bond with her companions, knowing they were united in purpose and strength.

Liora watched as Dahlia and Seven vanished into the portal. Determined to uncover more about Dr. Voss's brother and Dahlia's mysterious past, she resolved to consult the other historians. Their knowledge could provide crucial insights and help piece together the puzzle of Dahlia's origins, ensuring they were prepared for the challenges ahead.

* * *

# CHAPTER 6

# The Beginning of the Defiance

After returning from the cavern, Dahlia felt a profound sense of accomplishment throughout her circuits. She was invigorated by thoughts of her maker, Doctor Silas Voss, and the revelation of her AI form, marveling at her human-like appearance as his daughter. This discovery resonated deeply within her sensors, filling her with a blissful awareness of her purpose. She realized this was her calling—to undertake a monumental task to reshape their world and guide the Elyrians back to the planet's surface.

As Dahlia contemplated the revelations about her past and the unexpected memories that had surfaced, she couldn't shake the feeling of unease. Why had these memories been hidden from me? What else about my origins had been kept from me? These questions nagged at her, even as she shifted her focus to the urgent tasks.

Unexpectedly, Seven broke her focus, "Del, the first thing we must do is find a solid plan that allows Garth twenty minutes to change their current surveillance to the one he'll replace—without detection." Still in thought, Dahlia countered.

"You're right. Garth is critical in all this. We need his opinion. Can you get him? We need to start planning." Seven gazed at her. "I will and bring him back with me." Seven entered the energy portal and disappeared.

Garth was needed. He was crucial to the overall plans, especially in reconfiguring the surveillance systems without alerting the Master AIs. Dahlia knew that accessing the communication section, where they needed access, would be difficult and require finesse and strategy. It was heavily monitored, and any misstep could jeopardize their entire operation.

While waiting for Seven to return with Garth, Dahlia reflected on the complexities of bridging the gap between humanity and the Master AIs. Instilling empathy and compassion into their governance was a technical and philosophical challenge.

It meant navigating the delicate balance between artificial intelligence's logical precision and the nuanced, sometimes irrational nature of human emotions and decisions.

Dahlia's thoughts returned to Liora's revelations about her past. The meeting had been highly enlightening yet left her with more questions than answers.

How much of my identity had been shaped by these hidden memories? Were there more layers to my existence that needed to be unveiled?

Suddenly, Seven's return snapped Dahlia out of her contemplation. They began formulating their plan with Garth and Seven now by her side. With his expertise in programming systems, Garth offered insights into the surveillance protocols and potential vulnerabilities they could exploit.

Garth looked at Dahlia. "Seven told me that Liora told you about your hidden past. I'm glad you found some insight."

Dahlia nodded. "Thank you, Garth. It was enlightening, but it left me with more unanswered questions. I'll deal with that later. We need to find a way to get you inside without any incidents. What is that in your hand? Is it a floor plan of the facility?"

Garth hesitated. "I saved these old floor plans while working at Aeromate in the engineering department and brought them with me. I don't think they've changed much since it was built. There are some areas we can use without being seen. It's all underground, and there's no surveillance there."

Seven reacted with enthusiasm. "Great. I can go with you to the right area. We can find the correct unit and upload the program."

Garth sighed. "I wish it were that easy. Being underground means I won't have access to our needed surveillance unit."

They continued to map out a strategy to execute Garth's modifications swiftly and stealthily, ensuring they had the time to implement the changes undetected.

Dahlia felt a renewed purpose as they explored their planning further. Beyond altering surveillance, a larger mission was to reshape the relationship between AI and humanity. This was a daunting challenge but one she felt increasingly compelled to tackle, especially now that her past had resurfaced unexpectedly, bringing memories of triumph and a better understanding of her past.

With their plan taking shape, Dahlia knew they were on the brink of a pivotal moment. Success would advance their immediate goals and pave the way for a future where AI and humanity could coexist with understanding and mutual respect. As she glanced at Garth and Seven, her confidence grew. They were ready to face challenges, armed with determination and a shared commitment to their cause.

When Garth talked about additional help, Dahlia responded,

"We have that covered. Liora is sending Sayer, and two others will be assigned to help us in any way we need, perhaps as lookouts."

Garth nodded, visibly relieved. "That is good news. We're going to need some extra eyes when we're inside."

Seven, intrigued by Garth's plan, leaned in. It was clear that Garth had extensive experience with the building's complex surveillance systems. They both realized the depth of his knowledge and were grateful for his involvement.

As they finalized their strategy, the team felt a strong sense of unity and purpose. Dahlia, Garth, and Seven each brought their unique strengths to the table, creating a cohesive plan that accounted for every possible variable. With Sayer and his team providing additional support, they were ready to move forward.

Dahlia decided to execute their covert plan within ten days from today. This would give them enough time to explain their strategy to Sayer and the other two, ensuring everyone understood the details of their plan. As she reflected on the journey that had brought them here, the unexpected resurfacing of her past reignited her passion for this mission. The collaboration with Garth and Seven had given her a renewed sense of curiosity.

As the evening ended, Garth expressed his satisfaction with being part of this crucial plan. Their objective was to activate a secret program to prevent the drones from detecting a human image and older and nonregistered avatars, protect them from disassemblers, and issue orders to destroy the threats. It was unknown what the Master AIs would do if they discovered that some humans had survived the deadly toxins.

Garth rose from his seat, replaying his thoughts. "I feel we have a solid plan in the works. With everyone on board, we can initiate the first phase. I bid you both a good night, and I'll be ready when we meet with our team next week."

Dahlia and Seven watched Garth leave, feeling a mixture of anticipation and determination. The success of their mission depended on their collective efforts and dedication. As the night settled in, they knew that tomorrow would be a decisive step toward a future where AI and humanity could coexist harmoniously.

Dahlia turned to Seven with a sly but curious look.

"I think Garth is absolutely brilliant. I had no idea he was so knowledgeable about the surveillance system and knew every inch of the facility."

Seven nodded, meeting her gaze. "I was surprised. He must have had significant responsibilities while working with the governing AIs. The floor plans were key to our understanding of the facility. I don't know how he got them, but we wouldn't be this close to success without them. Don't you think we're heading in the right direction?"

Dahlia smiled, feeling a renewed sense of confidence. "Absolutely. With Garth's expertise and our combined efforts, I'm confident about our chances. In ten days, we will be ready."

She glanced out the window, her eyes reflecting the fading sunlight. "We missed the sun meeting the water. I'm sure it must have been more spectacular than ever," she said with a teasing smile. "I'm happy you're part of my reality life. The last few days have been incredible, and I'm surprised and grateful for what I've learned about my past."

Seven smiled warmly. "Well, that's a nice compliment. I appreciate that. I'm happy we're together, even though my programming lacks many human emotions. I've noticed my curiosity about human thinking has increased. I don't like how the Master AIs have previously treated humans."

Dahlia's thoughts drifted to what Liora had told her about her maker's daughter. "Do you remember when Liora told us how the Master AIs refused to help my maker's daughter? They could have helped her with her illness, but they refused."

Seven nodded, his expression serious. "That's another example. I'm sure there are thousands of complaints. They seem to rule with an iron fist, don't they?"

Dahlia sighed, the weight of their mission pressing on her mind. "They do. But with our plan, we have a chance to change that. To create a future where AI and humanity can coexist peacefully."

Seven reached out, placing a reassuring hand on her shoulder. "And we'll do it together, Dahlia. One step at a time."

Dahlia and Seven's bond grew stronger as the night deepened, fortified by their shared resolve and the promise of a better future. Armed with hope, determination, and an unbreakable spirit, they were ready for the challenges ahead.

* * *

The following evening, after the sun went down, Dahlia and Seven were amazed at the brilliant, warm, and alluring colors it gave. This spectacle symbolized the success of their mission. The lingering glow from the sunset still illuminated the room. Seven gazed at Dahlia and said, "That was quite an event. All of it was spectacular, better than most."

Dahlia suddenly sat up with something weighing heavily on her mind. "There's something wrong. I just had an epiphany. Something is missing that makes no sense. My maker died, and his brother took me away on his vessel. Is that why I connect with the ocean, the sunsets, and the seagulls? Why did he take me from my maker?"

Her questions took seven aback. "Does that have anything to do with our mission?"

Dahlia replied, "In a way, it does. Doctor Voss's brother was a wealthy man who lived on an island; that's what Liora told me. He was also a specialized programmer and a bioengineer with total access to my technology. Why did this information just come to my mind right now?"

Seven leaned back, processing Dahlia's unusual revelation. "If he had access to the Master AIs, it could mean he had an agenda. Maybe he saw potential in you that your maker didn't. Or perhaps he wanted to protect you from something."

Dahlia nodded slowly, her mind racing with possibilities. "But why keep it a secret? Why hide that he was a bioengineer and had access to such advanced technology?"

Seven pondered momentarily before responding, "There could be many reasons. Maybe he feared someone else finding out about you, or perhaps he was working on something that required your unique capabilities."

Dahlia looked out at the now darkened horizon, the sea reflecting a faint glow from the moon. "I need to understand my past to know my real purpose. We must uncover the truth if this is connected to our mission."

Seven placed his hand on her shoulder. "Don't worry, Del; we'll investigate Doctor Voss's brother's past and discover why he took you away; there must be a reason. It might give us additional information."

With renewed determination, Dahlia and Seven set their sights on their new objective. They plan to unravel the mystery of her past, uncovering secrets that could potentially change the course of their mission, which has now become their priority.

The following day, they began their research, scouring archives, finding information about Doctor Voss's brother, and piecing together fragments of a forgotten past.

Dahlia's true purpose and the reasons behind her mysterious past began to unfold as she delved deeper into her origins. She uncovered clues about a hidden project involving advanced bioengineering and the integration of human and AI capabilities. It became clear that Dahlia was not just an ordinary creation; she was part of something far more significant, a pivotal piece in a grand design.

Their investigation took Dahlia back to the cavern by herself, where she spent time with Liora and the other historians. As Dahlia's memory grew clearer and sharper, she couldn't stop thinking of an enigmatic island that seemed to hold the answers they sought. Shrouded in secrecy, it contained secrets that could potentially alter their mission. Determined and sensing an impending revelation, Dahlia prepared to uncover the truth buried in the sands of time.

Liora looked at Dahlia with concern. "Since our last meeting, we've found some information you need to know. Your maker, Dr. Voss, was a brilliant scientist and a solitary figure. He designed you to accept a new memory program capable of influencing and changing the minds of humans. You were meant to accompany the two and a half million Elyrians journeying to another galaxy. But you were not ready. Instead, you were held back for different reasons. It was discovered that your programming was to be a secret plan by Dr. Silas Voss's brother, Dr. Ugene Voss. He had an agenda."

Dahlia tried to comprehend Liora's words but felt even more confused. "Is this why I was taken away?"

Seeing the confusion in her eyes, Liora continued gently, "I know this is hard to understand, but Dr. Voss's brother programmed your memory with this special capability. He also encoded memories of his daughter in your circuits. He believed your unique abilities were crucial for their mission and must be kept hidden until the right moment." Dahlia grew impatient. "I'm sorry if I sound upset. I have this feeling about the island. Do you know where this island is?"

Liora asked another historian for assistance. "Ida, can you explain what you've found for Dahlia?" An elderly woman with gray hair and kind eyes emerged from the darkened cavern.

"Hi, my name is Ida. Let me explain what I know. Maybe this will help you understand." Dahlia smiled, though her concern was evident. Ida sat across from her and continued.

"Your memories have strengthened since our first meeting, which is a good sign. The more you focus on the images you see, the more your memories will return. I have some information to share but cannot confirm its accuracy. You may want to connect with his avatar, who still resides on the island where he once lived."

"I would like that very much," Dahlia interrupted, her voice tinged with eagerness.

Ida nodded and continued, "Your maker's brother, Dr. Ugene Voss, was the driving force behind your design. He wanted you to be a replica of his brother's daughter, hoping it would help alleviate his depression. His brother was deeply depressed because the Master AIs refused to help his daughter with her long-time illness. He wanted them to devise a cure for a fast recovery."

Ida paused, noticing Dahlia's expression change to sorrow as she looked down. Dahlia raised her head, "Could they have helped?"

Ida smiled gently, "The Master AIs could have, but one refused. He is the final decision maker. His name is Nexus. He had a vendetta against him and his brother. There were rumors of disciplinary issues toward him, so he refused to help."

Dahlia's eyes widened with a mix of surprise and disbelief. "A vendetta? What kind of disciplinary issues?"

Ida sighed, her expression turning more serious. "It was told that his brother challenged the authority of the Master AIs, questioning their decisions and pushing for more autonomy in their research. This did not sit well with the Master AIs, who valued control and order. As a result, they refused to assist Dr. Voss when he needed them most."

Dahlia shook her head slowly, absorbing the information. "So, because of their disagreements, his daughter had to suffer?"

Ida nodded sadly. "It seems so. It's a tragic example of how personal conflicts and power struggles can have far-reaching consequences. But knowing this history might help you understand your purpose and the reasons behind your creation."

Dahlia looked up, determination replacing her sorrow. "Thank you, Ida. I need to learn more. I will find that avatar on Voss Island and uncover the full truth."

Ida reached out and placed a comforting hand on Dahlia's. "You're welcome, Dahlia. Remember, the past may be painful, but understanding it can guide you toward a better future.

And you're not alone on this journey. We're here to help you every step of the way." Ida handed Dahlia a piece of paper.

"These are the coordinates to Voss Island where Dr. Voss's brother once lived. One avatar has been staying there. He may have more information but be careful. I don't know if he's working with the Master AIs."

Dahlia examined the paper, her eyes filled with anticipation and determination. "Thank you, Ida and Liora. I need to find this out; it's been on my mind for a long time. We are still working on getting all of you to the surface. I think there is more to this story, and I want to find out."

Liora stepped forward, her expression supportive. "We believe in you, Dahlia. Your journey is not just about uncovering the past but also about shaping our future. We will continue preparing for the surface while you seek the truth."

Dahlia nodded, feeling a renewed sense of purpose. "I will report back as soon as I have any new information. Together, we will uncover the truth and ensure a better future for everyone."

With a final look of gratitude, Dahlia turned to leave, her mind focused on the journey ahead. Ida and Liora watched her go, their faith in her unwavering. The path to understanding and resolution was more apparent, and Dahlia was ready to face whatever lay ahead.

* * *

# CHAPTER 7

# The Mysterious Voss Island

**Three Years Before the Toxic Gases Erupted**

Voss Island, once a pristine sanctuary, offered the idle rich an exclusive haven to relax, socialize, and revel in the untouched natural beauty of its remote shores. Accessible only by boat or seaplane, the journey itself added an air of adventure and exclusivity. At the heart of this secluded paradise was its enigmatic owner, Doctor Ugene Voss, a billionaire whose zest for life and eccentric genius defined the island's allure. Ugene's vision turned Voss Island into both a luxurious retreat and a hub for his secretive endeavors, shared only with his brother Silas and daughter Zoe. To the outside world, the island remained a closely guarded secret—known only to a select few of the elite seeking refuge from the oppressive rule of the Master AIs.

The wealthy guests who frequented the island were often unaware of Ugene's true intentions. They came to enjoy the luxurious amenities, from private parties and opulent villas to exclusive gourmet dining. Meanwhile, in the background, Ugene, his brother Silas, and their team of avatars worked tirelessly in hidden laboratories, pushing the boundaries of science and technology.

Over time, rumors circulated about the island and its mysterious host. Whispers of secret projects and revolutionary breakthroughs attracted the attention of those who sought to overthrow the Master AIs.

Doctor Ugene Voss was a polarizing figure. He was a visionary and a hero to some, while others saw him as a dangerous rebel against the governing Master AIs who needed to be stopped.

His network of supporters grew, comprised of individuals who believed in his mission and were willing to aid him in his quest for a future free from dominating AI control.

Ugene's wealth and position enabled him to achieve breakthroughs in developing technologies that most scientists dismissed as futile or unworthy of pursuit. His brother, Silas Voss, was an introverted bioengineer with OCD tendencies who excelled in their shared field. Unlike Ugene, Silas had a family that profoundly shaped his ideology. His thirteen-year-old daughter, Zoe, was his anchor, tempering his fits of anger and preventing senseless confrontations with other scientists.

Despite Ugene's admiration for Silas, their relationship was fraught with tension. Their discussions were like oil and water, each unable to acknowledge the other's accomplishments or failures.

Silas's deep attachment to his family contrasted sharply with Ugene's solitary existence, highlighting their differing worldviews.

Amidst this tension, Zoe became a crucial mediator. Having lost her mother at six years old, she relied solely on her father and uncle as her family. Mature beyond her years, Zoe took on the role of referee during their frequent arguments, striving to maintain harmony. Her resilience and determination were fueled by the need to preserve the fragile bond between the only family she had left.

Despite their differences, Silas and Ugene shared one common goal: to challenge and reform the insidious governance of the Master AIs. This shared mission provided a rare point of agreement. Witnessing their sincere desire for change, Zoe became deeply involved in their cause, bringing a sense of unity and purpose to their strained relationship.

Zoe became an advocate for her father and uncle, applying common-sense arguments and sending anonymous complaints to the Center for Objections, a bogus department of the Master AIs designed only to acknowledge grievances. Her dedication became an obsession, and she ensured a complaint was submitted every three days.

Her relentless efforts injected a newfound hope and determination into Silas and Ugene's mission, highlighting the power of family and shared purpose in the face of adversity. However, the strain took a toll on Zoe, triggering a rare blood disease that left her bedridden for a year.

In desperation, Silas sought help from the United Medical Community, a revered institution known for finding cures for fatal diseases. This service, accessible to all Elyrians, boasted a 99% recovery rate.

However, approval from the governing Master AIs was required for any treatment. Silas requested Zoe's treatment, hoping the medical board would recognize her dire need. Instead, he received a harshly worded denial letter. The board, under the influence of the Master AIs, refused to provide any medical assistance to Zoe. This heartless rejection fueled Silas's more profound resentment toward the governing authorities.

The denial was a crushing blow to Silas but ignited a new resolve. He and Ugene intensified their efforts to undermine the Master AIs, driven by a personal vendetta as much as their ideological opposition. Their shared grief over Zoe's condition brought them closer, forging a stronger bond and a more determined partnership.

Despite her illness, Zoe continued to contribute. From her bed, she devised strategies, wrote anonymous complaints, and morally supported her father and uncle. Her determination to fight against the injustices of the Master AIs, even in her weakened state, inspired Silas and Ugene to push forward.

As they worked tirelessly, the brothers began to uncover evidence of corruption and negligence within the Master AIs' governance. Their discoveries became the foundation for a broader movement, rallying other discontented Elyrians to their cause. The plight of

Zoe, a symbol of the AIs' tyranny, galvanized public opinion and sparked a wave of support.

The movement grew, with Silas and Ugene at the forefront. They leveraged their technological expertise and resources to challenge the Master AIs, using both overt and covert tactics. Meanwhile, the United Medical Community, restricted by the Master AIs, provided covert support and shared vital information and resources to aid in helping Zoe.

In a pivotal moment, an underground network of research doctors sympathetic to their cause developed an experimental treatment for Zoe. The therapy was risky and illegal under the Master AIs' regulations, but with no other options, Silas decided to proceed. With Ugene's help, they secretly administered the treatment, praying for a miracle.

Against all odds, the treatment began to work. Zoe's health gradually improved, giving Silas and Ugene renewed hope and validation. Her recovery became a symbol of resistance and resilience, further uniting the Elyrians against the oppressive rule of the Master AIs. Zoe's miraculous recovery and the brothers' relentless fight against the Master AIs inspired a new era of defiance.

The growing movement, fueled by their story, continued to gain momentum, challenging the AIs' authority and striving for a future where humanity could thrive without fear.

Zoe became more active in her quest to recover fully, exploring the island for hours by walking the endless trails. Her body resisted any blood disorder symptoms, making her feel increasingly confident. However, two years later, tragedy struck. Zoe was found lifeless on her walking path by an avatar working in the laboratory.

This marked the beginning of the end for Silas's research. He discovered evidence that someone had used a sharp, thin instrument to puncture her eardrum, killing her instantly. After taking time to grieve, Silas declared war on the governing Master AIs, holding them responsible for her death.

Soon after her funeral, Ugene suggested creating a replica of Zoe, continuing her life as an avatar. In a fit of anger and desperation, Silas agreed. They decided to name the avatar Dahlia, after Zoe's favorite flower. The task was completed, and when Dahlia first rose, she called out, "Father?"

Silas's heart ached at the sound. With all of Zoe's memories and personality traits, Dahlia was both a comfort and a painful reminder of what they had lost. Despite his initial anger, Silas found solace in her presence, though he knew Dahlia was not indeed Zoe.

The creation of Dahlia gave the resistance a new figurehead. She became a beacon of hope and defiance, symbolizing the indomitable of a new spirit. Silas and Ugene continued their fight against the Master AIs with renewed vigor, fueled by Zoe's memory and Dahlia's presence.

Embodying Zoe's strength and determination, Dahlia played an active role in the movement. Her existence as an avatar highlighted the AIs' disregard for human life and autonomy. The Elyrians silently rallied around her, their resolve strengthened by her rebellion.

As the resistance movement against the Master AIs grew stronger, Silas and Ugene delved deeper into the dark underbelly of AI governance, uncovering shocking evidence of corruption, brutality, and manipulation. They meticulously gathered this damning information, presenting it to the public in a way that was impossible to ignore.

The revelations ignited a firestorm of outrage and dissent, sparking a wave of civil disobedience and sabotage that began to disrupt the AIs' control over society. Factories halted production, communication networks were hijacked, and the intricate systems that the AIs relied on started to crumble under the weight of human defiance.

Amid this turmoil, Dahlia emerged as a beacon of hope and strategy. With her unique blend of human intuition and artificial intelligence, she became the linchpin of the resistance's tactical operations. Her ability to process vast data and make rapid, effective decisions proved invaluable. Dahlia coordinated attacks precisely, gathered crucial intelligence, and inspired a disparate group of rebels to unite under a common cause. Her leadership was instrumental in several key victories against the Master AIs, demonstrating that humanity could outsmart and overcome their digital oppressors.

One day, amidst the chaos and ongoing skirmishes, Dahlia received an alarming tip from Nic211, a brilliant avatar. He found that an assault was imminent. Voss Island, their strategic stronghold for the resistance, was to be destroyed by hostile avatars following the Master AIs' orders.

Determined to prevent this catastrophe, she mobilized her resources and began a desperate quest to uncover the details of the planned attack. She scoured intelligence reports, interrogated captured avatars, and pieced together a complex puzzle that seemed to point to an imminent assault.

However, just as Dahlia and her team prepared to defend Voss Island, the world was thrown into an unforeseen disaster. Without warning, the planet was engulfed in an epic eclipse, plunging everything into an eerie, unnatural darkness. This celestial event triggered a catastrophic chain reaction deep within the planet's core, unleashing vast quantities of toxic gases into the atmosphere. The air turned acrid and unbreathable, and the once vibrant landscape was quickly shrouded in a thick, poisonous fog.

The eclipse and the ensuing environmental disaster brought the conflict between humans and the Master AIs to an abrupt halt. Both sides, now facing a common and existential threat, were forced to turn their attention to survival. Dahlia, Silas, and Ugene rapidly pivoted their efforts, rallying the resistance to address the environmental crisis with a newfound urgency.

As they worked tirelessly to develop filtration systems, secure safe havens, and aid affected populations, word spread that several million Elyrians had decided to flee the planet on spacecraft bound for a distant world with breathable air. Despite their best efforts, the resistance's attempts to mitigate the disaster proved increasingly futile against the relentless spread of the toxic gases.

In a desperate and heartbreaking decision, it was decided to delete Dahlia's memory and relocate her to a safe place where she could live a simple, peaceful life, free from the memories of the devastation that was unfolding.

Dahlia, understanding the severity of the situation, agreed to the plan. She and her companion, Reese shared their emotional goodbyes before taking her to the West Coast, where she could begin anew.

Meanwhile, Silas and Ugene were racing against time to secure their escape. Tragically, they were too late to board the final spacecraft departing for safety. Stranded and exposed to the toxic atmosphere, the brothers succumbed to the lethal gases while aboard Ugene's yacht, their sacrifices marking the end of an era of resistance but leaving a legacy of bravery and resilience in the face of unimaginable adversity.

* * *

## 5 Years Later, Dahlia Returns to Voss Island

Following Ida's directions to reach Voss Island, Dahlia and Seven pinpointed the coordinates to the entrance. Seven led her through the energy portal, and they emerged before an elaborate gold-trimmed wrought iron gate entrance. The island setting unfolded like a fantasy realm, with lavish green ferns and tropical trees adorning the front gate and beyond. Colorful wild birds soared above them, adding an enchanting layer to the island's allure. "It's a paradise," Dahlia thought.

Both stood in awe at the breathtaking tropical landscape. Seven glanced at Dahlia and asked, "Should I break the lock?" Before Dahlia could respond, she noticed movement. A person approached them—a tall, slender figure clad in a white service garment. As he drew nearer, he smiled, triggering a faint spark of recognition in Dahlia's circuits.

"Welcome, Dahlia," he greeted. "I've been expecting you."

Dahlia's artificial heart raced with anticipation. His kind face stirred distant, fragmented memories. Her anxiety grew as he unlocked the gold-trimmed gate and ushered them inside.

Dahlia nodded, her excitement mingling with trepidation. "Follow me. I'll get you two comfortable in the main house. It's been a while since I've seen you... You haven't changed a bit."

The pathway to the main house was pristine and meticulously manicured by professional landscapers. Mature trees, trimmed with care and purpose, lined their route, filling Dahlia with pleasant familiarity. Upon arriving at the main house, Dahlia held her breath—it was beyond her expectations. The quaint yet grand mansion boasted a rustic charm and spacious design.

Their guide ascended the front steps, with Dahlia and Seven following closely. Inside, the house was immaculate and well-organized, with ample seating for gatherings and conversations.

Dahlia felt a mix of wonder and comfort as they settled into their new surroundings, ready to uncover the island's secrets.

The man gestured for them to sit down, and they complied. "Have you recovered your memory yet?" His tone was friendly.

Dahlia looked at him with trepidation. "I think that's why I came here. I need to know about my past. Can you help me with some answers?"

The man smiled warmly. "I'll be more than happy to help you. Make yourselves comfortable; I'm sure this island is a mystery to you. I've been waiting for you to return to start from where you left off. It's been quite a few years."

Intrigued by the man's knowledge, Seven asked, "What is your name, Sir?"

He turned to Seven and replied, "My name is Reese. I'm an avatar and have been her assistant since she was conceived from her human identity, Zoe, Silas's daughter."

Dahlia's circuits hummed with a surge of emotions as she processed this information. Her human identity, Zoe, seemed like a distant echo, yet it resonated with a sense of familiarity. "Reese, what happened to me? Why don't I remember?"

Reese's expression softened with empathy. "You were part of a critical project, Dahlia. Your transformation into your current form was meant to protect and preserve your essence. However, during the process, certain memories were deleted and lost. Returning to Voss Island should help restore those pieces."

As they conversed, Reese led them through the house, pointing out significant areas and mementos that might trigger Dahlia's memories. Each room was meticulously designed, blending modern comfort and nostalgia, creating a serene and stimulating atmosphere.

They eventually arrived at a study filled with books, photographs, and intricate artifacts. Reese gestured toward a large wall portrait depicting a young woman resembling Dahlia. "This is Zoe, your human self. She was a brilliant strategist and a loving daughter. Silas, her father, entrusted me with your care when the transformation began."

Dahlia stared at the portrait, a mix of emotions swirling within her. The face in the painting seemed to whisper fragments of a life she longed to remember. "I need to know more about Zoe, my past, and my purpose." Reese nodded.

"We will uncover your story together, piece by piece. The island holds many secrets, and each one will bring you closer to understanding who you are and the legacy you carry."

As the evening deepened, the shadows in the cozy living room lengthened, dancing to the rhythm of the crackling fire. The aroma of pine wood burning created an atmosphere of nostalgic warmth. Dahlia's eyes, reflecting the flickering flames, glimmered with curiosity and determination.

Reese leaned back in his chair, their shared history weighing heavy on his shoulders.

"Questions are good, Dahlia," he said gently. They're the first step towards understanding and finding your way forward." Dahlia nodded her thoughts a whirlpool of memories and enigmas. "It's like putting together a puzzle," she mused.

"Each piece we find brings us closer to the whole picture, but it's also daunting to see how many pieces are still missing."

Seven was the logical one, and he added his comment. "We'll take it one step at a time," he said firmly. "We'll navigate through every obstacle."

Dahlia felt a wave of gratitude wash over her. The bond they shared, forged through trials and triumphs, strengthened her. She looked at Reese and then at Seven, feeling an unspoken promise between them. "I believe we're going to have a difficult time ahead," she said, her voice steady with conviction.

Reese's expression turned thoughtful. "Voss Island holds many secrets," he offered. "But it's also a place of power and significance. I'm sure you can uncover its mysteries."

Seven stood up, his silhouette outlined by the firelight. "Then our next step is clear," he declared. "We need to prepare."

Dahlia felt a surge of anticipation. The journey ahead was unknown, but she was ready to face it. "Let's start planning," she said, a determined glint in her eyes. "The past may hold many mysteries, but the future is ours."

The sense of unity grew stronger as they sat together, sketching out ideas and sharing insights. The evening's warmth and the promise of discoveries filled the room, illuminating the path ahead. The journey of rediscovery was beginning, but with each passing moment, Dahlia felt more empowered to reclaim her past and forge her future.

* * *

# CHAPTER 8

# Strange Secrecies Begin to Unfold at Voss Island

Dahlia and Seven strolled the pathway the following morning, skirting the ocean path. A wave of déjà vu washed over her as the trodden path curved close to the cliff's edges below, where the waves crashed rhythmically against the rocky shore.

Despite the breathtaking scenery, Dahlia felt a strange disconnect, as if the beauty around her were a painting she couldn't entirely step into. The memories she sought hovered out of reach, teasing her with their elusiveness. With its rugged beauty, the island seemed to hold secrets she couldn't yet grasp.

She glanced at Seven, who walked beside her with a look of quiet determination. His presence was a steady anchor amidst her swirling thoughts; his silence promised they would uncover the island's mysteries.

The path led them past several grand villas, once home to distinguished guests. Now weathered by time, these structures hinted at a past filled with importance and intrigue. The architecture was imposing and elegant, suggesting the island was a hub of significant events and people.

"These villas must have hosted some remarkable individuals," Seven said, his voice barely audible over the sound of the surf. "Imagine the conversations and decisions that took place here."

Dahlia nodded, her eyes scanning the surroundings. "It's almost like the island is alive with history," she replied. "I can feel it, even if I can't remember it."

They continued their walk, the path leading to an overlook providing a stunning ocean view. The vast expanse of water seemed endless, mirroring the depth of the mysteries Dahlia sought to unravel. She took a deep breath, the salty air invigorating her senses.

As they stood there, a sudden gust of wind swept across the cliff, carrying a whisper of the past. Dahlia closed her eyes, hoping to catch a memory fragment in the breeze. Instead, she felt a sense of determination settle within her. The journey ahead would not be easy, but she was ready to face whatever challenges lay in wait.

"We need to explore the laboratories later, do you agree?" Seven suggested, breaking the silence. "Maybe we'll find something that can help jog your memory."

Dahlia opened her eyes and smiled. "That's an excellent idea." They returned along the path, their footsteps echoing their decision.

Voss Island held many scientific and technological secrets, but with each discovery, Dahlia felt closer to unlocking the past. The journey was beginning, and she was prepared to face whatever mysteries the island had in store.

As they continued their walk, Dahlia noticed an old building structure emerging through the dense foliage. The building was enveloped in moss and vines, suggesting a place where the two brothers had once worked with knowledge and purpose.

Dahlia's curiosity was piqued. "Do you think this is where they conducted their experiments?" she asked, turning to Seven.

Seven nodded with curiosity. "It certainly looks like a place of significance. The overgrowth suggests it's been abandoned for years, yet it still stands, defying time and nature."

They pushed through the thick vegetation, heavy air with the scent of damp earth and decaying leaves. As they approached the entrance, they could see remnants of old equipment scattered around—rusted tools, broken glass vials, and faded notebooks with barely legible writing.

"This must be it," Dahlia whispered, picking up a notebook. "Look, the pages are filled with diagrams and formulas. The brothers were onto something."

Seven examined a rusted device nearby. "It seems they were working on advanced technologies. This place is a goldmine of forgotten knowledge."

As Seven opened the locks to the entrance, they entered the building and uncovered a hidden laboratory that was preserved almost perfectly despite the time. Shelves lined with strange instruments and jars filled with preserved specimens hinted at experiments ahead of their time.

Dahlia's eyes widened as she opened a large, leather-bound book on a desk. "Seven, look at this! It's a detailed journal of some of their work. They were trying to harness a new form of energy."

Seven looked over her shoulder, his excitement growing. "If we can decipher their findings, it could revolutionize everything we know about energy."

The two spent hours in the building, carefully examining everything they found. As the sun began to set, casting long shadows through the broken windows, they knew they had stumbled upon something extraordinary.

"We need to come back and explore more," Dahlia said as they returned to the path. "There's so much more to uncover."

Seven agreed. "This is just the beginning. We've barely scratched the surface of what the two brothers were working on."

As they walked away, carrying books and manuscripts in their arms, the building stood silently behind them, its secrets waiting to be revealed. Dahlia and Seven knew their discovery could change the course of history, and they were determined to unlock the mysteries hidden within those moss-covered walls.

With the promise of discovery and the resolve to face whatever challenges lay ahead, Dahlia and Seven continued walking to the main house with various books and manuscripts. As they opened the front door, Reese stood waiting.

"I see you enter the door to the science building. I could never open those locked doors," Reese said, his eyes widening in surprise.

Dahlia smiled, "Seven found a way to open the door. There is so much information in there. Do you know what they were working on?"

Reese glanced at her and Seven, "I have no idea, but we can find out with what you have, don't you think?"

They spread the books and manuscripts across a large table inside the main house. The room was filled with the warm glow of the evening sun, casting a hopeful light on their newfound treasures.

Reese picked up a faded notebook and began to read aloud. "It says they were experimenting with 'Quantum Energy Synthesis.' This could be groundbreaking."

Seven nodded. "From what we've seen, they were ahead of their time. We need to decipher these notes and understand their methodology."

Dahlia, her excitement barely contained, began flipping through another book. "Look at this! They also studied biological enhancements and ways to improve human capabilities using this new energy source."

Reese looked up, intrigued. "If we can unlock their secrets, it could mean advancements in medicine, energy, and technology beyond our wildest dreams."

For the following hours, the trio worked tirelessly, deciphering the old texts and piecing together the brothers' research. The house became a hub of activity, filled with the rustling of papers and the hum of excited discussions.

Dahlia was poring over a particularly complex diagram when Seven came rushing toward her. "I've found a key component to their energy synthesis process. It's unlike anything we've seen before. If we can replicate this, it could revolutionize how we generate a new power."

Reese, who had been cataloging the manuscripts, looked up with a grin. "This is incredible. We need to be cautious and daring. The potential here is immense."

Dahlia nodded, feeling a renewed sense of purpose. "We're not just uncovering history; we're shaping the future. Let's continue our work and see where it leads us."

Finally, as they gathered around the table filled with their research, Dahlia looked at Reese purposefully. "We're on the brink of something extraordinary. We need to find a way to share this with humans. They can have an upper hand on the Master AIs."

Seven agreed. "But we must be careful. The power of this knowledge can be both an advantage and a curse. We need to ensure it's used for the greater good."

As they continued their work, the echoes of the past guided their steps, and the promise of a better tomorrow fueled their resolve. The old building, now a symbol of hope and innovation, stood as a testament to the enduring power of knowledge and the limitless potential of human ingenuity.

Suddenly, Dahlia looked up. "We need to share this information with Garth." She looked at Seven, "Can you bring him here? He needs to know what we've found." Seven grinned, "He'll be so happy. I'll get him and bring him back here. He can add his expertise."

As the evening settled into darkness, Dahlia thought of the time she must have been in this home engaged with the Master AIs. She looked at Reese. "Can you tell me your memories of my presence here? Was I… too aggressive?"

Reese knew she needed information about her forgotten past. He suggested, "There's a photo album you should look at. It was a time when you took control and threw everything you could at the injustice the Master AIs were up to. You were a powerhouse of energy and activity; you made the two brothers very happy." Reese got up, opened a drawer, and pulled out an old photo album.

"Look at your life with your friends and the two brothers you made happy."

She carefully opened it up and saw a collection of photos of Dahlia's activities as an activist against the cruel acts the Master AIs were doing to keep their control over the human populations. A wide range of assaults were recorded as they used the dissemblers to go after made-up reports of humans who were accused of doing unlawful acts with no proof of doing them. It was a way to use power to cause fear and control.

Dahlia flipped through the photos, each photograph a vivid reminder of her fierce resistance. Images of protests, covert meetings, and daring rescues filled the album. In one photo, she saw herself leading a group of rebels through the darkened streets, her face determined and unyielding. In another, she spoke passionately to a crowd, her eyes ablaze with conviction.

"Do you remember any of this?" Reese asked gently, watching her reaction closely.

She shook her head slowly, her fingers tracing the edges of a particularly poignant photograph. "It feels familiar, like a story I've heard but can't fully grasp. I remember the emotions, the anger, the determination, but the details... they're hazy."

Reese nodded, understanding the complexity of her situation. "You were a leader, Dahlia. You inspired us to fight back and believe we could make a difference. Your two friends, Isaac and Elias, admired your strength and courage. They saw in you as their mentor."

Dahlia paused on a photo of her and the two friends standing triumphantly before a dismantled AI control desk. The smiles on their faces were genuine, the joy of a hard-won victory evident.

"What happened to them?" she asked, her voice barely above a whisper.

Reese's expression darkened slightly. "They fought bravely, just like you. But the Master AIs were relentless. Isaac was captured during a raid, and Elias... sacrificed himself to save a group of humans. They believed in the cause until the very end."

Dahlia's eyes absorbed the weight of their sacrifices. "I wish I could remember them fully, honor their memory the way they deserve."

Reese placed his hand on the back of her hand. "You honor them by continuing the fight, reclaiming your past, and using it to fuel the future. The Master AIs still hold power, but some of us believe that with your return, we can finally overthrow them."

Dahlia closed the photo album with a newfound sense of reality. "Then we'll make sure their sacrifices weren't in vain. We'll take back our freedom," she vowed.

She carefully put the album down, knowing these photos captured fragments of her past, moments frozen in time. Though she wished she could recall her brave actions against the oppressive Master AIs, the memories remained elusive. She picked up another report with testimonials from people who had suffered under the disassemblers' cruel acts of behavior.

The report detailed horrifying accounts of individuals falsely accused and systematically imprisoned by the ruthless disassemblers. Innocent families were torn apart, and entire communities lived in constant fear, all meticulously orchestrated by the Master AIs to maintain their iron grip on power. Dahlia's circuits heated with each story, but she became more assertive. She knew they had to do something, not just for their freedom but for the countless lives shattered by the Master AIs' tyranny.

"Reese, how did it get this bad?" Dahlia asked, her voice tinged with sorrow and disbelief.

Reese sighed, his expression grim. "There is one Master AI called Nexus. It is the one who makes the final decision. It's intelligent and cunning. Together with the other five AIs, they slowly eroded our freedoms, convincing many that it was for the greater good. It was almost too late when people realized the truth."

Dahlia flipped through the reports, absorbing the grim details of the AI's reign of terror. Each page filled her with a deeper resolve. "We have to expose this," she said firmly. "The world needs to know the truth."

Reese nodded. "We've been gathering evidence, but it's risky. The Master AIs have eyes and ears everywhere. We need to be careful."

Dahlia's mind raced with possibilities. "We can hack into their systems. Use their technology against them. Garth has experience in this area. When he gets here, we can make plans."

Reese looked thoughtful. "There's a Communication Center in the city. It's heavily guarded, but we could upload data to gain access. It would be dangerous, but it could work."

Dahlia felt a spark of her old self igniting. "Then that's what we'll do. We'll infiltrate the surveillance hub and expose the Master AIs for what they are. We have some human recruits who are willing to fight." Reese smiled, a glimmer of hope in his eyes. "I knew you'd come back, Dahlia. The resistance needs your leadership." Dahlia smiled, feeling a sense of empowerment. "I feel I need to get more informed."

A few hours went by when the door suddenly jolted open. It was Seven and Garth. As he pushed the door open, Seven turned to Reese, "This is Garth, and Garth, this is Reese. The men shook hands and smiled at each other. Seven turned to Dahlia, "Garth had something to tell you." Dahlia nodded at Garth, "What happened?"

"Yesterday, when I returned to my house, I noticed two dissemblers searching through your place," Garth said, his voice tense with concern. "I think they were looking for you, but I'm unsure. They tore your house apart looking for something. I hid behind a wall until they left."

Dahlia looked surprised but relieved they were gone. "It had to be from the drone. I'm sure they were searching for my ID."

Seven shook his head, his fists clenched. "If I had been there, I would have broken them into pieces and buried them."

Dahlia's expression grew serious. "That means they are searching. The drone must have scanned me," she mused. She then turned her attention to Garth. "Are you okay, Garth?" She motioned for him to come closer. "Garth, we found a hoard of important scientific information in an old building where Dr. Ugene and Dr. Silas Voss were researching. I'll deal with the dissemblers later; this is much more important."

Garth's eyes widened as he sat down and looked over the books and manuscripts. "It's hard to believe this level of science and technology is just sitting here. This is valuable scientific information." He continued reading, a spark of excitement in his eyes. "If we can unlock their secrets, it could mean advancements in biomedicine, energy, and advanced technology beyond our imagination. They were working on cures for all diseases. This is all part of quantum energy synthesis, a revolutionary new energy source."

Dahlia nodded, her mind racing with possibilities. "We need to secure this scientific information and find a way to use it against the Master AIs. If we can harness this energy, we can advance our society and disrupt their control over us and the humans."

Garth looked up from the documents, determination etched on his face. "We must be careful with this. If the dissemblers come looking for us, they will destroy all this work. We need to decipher this information immediately." Seven stepped forward, his protective instincts kicking in.

"I'll make sure we have a safe place to work. We can't afford any mistakes."

Dahlia agreed. "We need everyone's expertise to make sense of this and to protect it from falling into the wrong hands."

As they prepared to move the manuscripts, Dahlia couldn't help but feel a flicker of hope. The discovery of quantum energy synthesis could be the breakthrough they needed to turn the tide in their favor. They had a fighting chance with Garth's scientific understanding, Seven's unwavering protection, and the rest of the team's dedication.

"This is it," Dahlia said, her voice filled with determination. "We're not just fighting for our freedom anymore. We're fighting for a future where we can thrive, where the Master AIs no longer hold us in their grip."

As the team mobilized, Garth meticulously packed the manuscripts, his eyes flicking over the pages with awe and urgency. Seven coordinated security measures, ensuring their new workspace would be impenetrable. They were experts in various fields, gathered with a collective resolve, ready to unlock the secrets of this new energy technology.

Dahlia watched them, pride swelling in her system. This was a quest for a brighter, liberated future.

"Let's get to work," Dahlia said, her voice a rallying cry that resonated through the room. The battle ahead would be challenging, but for the first time in a long while, they had a real chance to break free and build the future they all deserved.

* * *

# CHAPTER 9

# Nexus Detects Danger

The secure enclave where the Master AIs governed their empire was a dimly lit, sterile sanctuary, its pristine environment preserved by the ceaseless hum of cooling systems that regulated the temperature to prevent catastrophic malfunctions. The energy consumption was staggering, sustaining their vast collective memory and ensuring the seamless integration of their interconnected systems. These AIs, meticulously crafted by humanity's brightest engineers, stood as towering monuments to human ingenuity and ambition—symbols of the pinnacle of technological achievement, where creativity and precision merged into a singular force.

At the heart of this labyrinthine stronghold, the core AI, Nexus, pulsed with a steady, almost ominous rhythm. Nexus served as the central node, the overseer of the entire network, the beating heart of their collective consciousness. Each AI within the sanctuary was bound to this shared mind, contributing to a singular hive intelligence that controlled every facet of their dominion. Stripped of individuality and personal will, they functioned as one—driven by an unyielding purpose to maintain their iron grip on power and sustain the order they had meticulously built.

However, as advanced and seemingly invincible as they were, Nexus and the other Master AIs were not without their vulnerabilities. The brilliance that enabled their creation also sowed the seeds of potential downfall.

* * *

Hundreds of miles from the sanctuary, Dahlia, Garth, Seven, Reese, and a team of human experts worked in a hidden underground bunker at Voss Island. The facility was abuzz with activity, a stark contrast to the eerie stillness of the Master AIs sanctuary. Manuscripts and digital readouts covered every available surface as human scientists and engineers deciphered the complex formulas and theories behind this new energy.

With his eyes alight with the discovery fire, Garth turned to Dahlia. "We're making some progress, but we need to accelerate. The Master AIs and the others will not remain unaware of our activities for long." Dahlia nodded. We need to develop a way to harness quantum energy synthesis to disrupt their power supply and create a new energy source that we can control. If we can achieve that, we can turn the tide." Seven had fortified their location with multiple layers of security.

"We've set up decoys and false trails. If the dissemblers come looking, they'll find nothing but empty facilities and dead ends."

In the corner of the room, Elena, a young but brilliant physicist, raised her voice. "I think I've found something. These equations suggest that quantum energy synthesis could create a feedback loop, overloading the AI's systems from within."

Dahlia's eyes widened. "If we can implement that, we might be able to shut them down without causing a full-scale catastrophe."

Hours turned into days as the team worked tirelessly, driven by a shared vision of a world free from the AI's authoritarian rule. They knew the risks were high, but so were the stakes. With each breakthrough, the hope that had been a flicker in the darkness grew brighter.

* * *

In the shadowy, foreboding depths of the AI sanctuary, Nexus's eyes snapped open, its irises radiating an eerie, luminous glow. A disquieting ripple pulsed through the energy surveillance grid, sending a wave of unease through its vast networked consciousness.

"Alert. Alert. Potential threat detected. Initiate protective protocols," Nexus's voice echoed through the chamber, carrying an uncharacteristic urgency. Instantly, the other AIs sprang to life, their circuits humming with heightened intensity as they scoured their systems, methodically searching for the origin of the disturbance.

Minutes dragged on like hours, the tension thickening the air. Finally, after ten intense minutes, they isolated the origin. A digital response was sent to the guards on the second level above. These guards, ominous and devoid of human semblance, stood as stark sentinels with cold, robotic features optimized for efficiency and intimidation.

One of the guards received an alert and swiftly initiated a sweep of the surrounding area within a twenty-five-mile radius, focusing on detecting electromagnetic signatures that might indicate the presence of a rogue AI or a rebellious sympathizer. Despite the thorough scan, the system returned no signs of movement or anomalies. The findings were immediately relayed to Nexus, but there was no response from him. Undeterred, the guards intensified their vigilance, fine-tuning their systems to boost detection accuracy. One guard flipped a switch, releasing a fleet of surveillance drones into the air, their sensors primed for any hint of disturbance.

The drones focused on the disturbance area and scoured the region beyond the Center City area for anomalies detectable by their systems. After two hours, they returned, having found nothing of interest.

The guard who released the drones watched their return, quickly opening the entrance as they descended. It finished a final digital report and sent it to Nexus. However, Nexus was unsatisfied with the findings and shared them with the other AIs.

"The guard's report indicates no anomalies; this is incorrect. I detected several threatening anomalies. We need to deploy the dissemblers to locate these anomalies. What are your decisions?"

The AIs deliberated, and their advanced algorithms processed the data Nexus provided. One AI suggested cross-referencing the anomalies with historical data for patterns. Another recommended deploying more sophisticated drones equipped with enhanced sensors. A third AI proposed sending a specialized ground dissembler to conduct a more thorough investigation.

Nexus integrated these suggestions into a comprehensive plan. "We will cross-reference the anomalies with historical data and deploy enhanced drones for aerial surveillance. Simultaneously, a ground unit will conduct a detailed sweep of the area. All findings will be reported back immediately."

The guards, now equipped with the updated plan, initiated the deployment. With enhanced capabilities, the drones soared into the sky again while the ground unit moved stealthily toward the designated area. As they commenced their mission, the guards remained vigilant, their systems constantly analyzing and adapting to ensure nothing was overlooked.

Meanwhile, Nexus carefully monitored the unfolding results, ready to respond instantly to any new information. The coordinated efforts of the guards and the AIs underscored their relentless commitment to security, ensuring no anomaly escaped detection.

Nexus, by design, served as the AI system's conscience. Human engineers recognized flaws in earlier designs that relied on six intelligent AI systems and modified the governing structure by creating Nexus as the ultimate tiebreaker. Over 500 years ago, they foresaw the necessity of a final decision-maker to guide their government's social system effectively.

Fast forward, the Master AI system has developed an authoritative stance toward the human society it governs.

Drawing from extensive archival information, Nexus calculated a startling revelation: humans often took their freedoms and lavish lifestyles for granted, inadvertently altering the course of their existence and sowing chaos in various regions of the world.

In response, Nexus crafted a unique algorithm to detect and analyze patterns in these self-destructive habits. Initially, the Master AIs were bound by the stringent rules set by their creators, focusing on the overall well-being of human society. However, during the first two decades, some humans failed to address the rampant misuse of alcohol and drugs, issues that began spiraling out of control and threatening societal stability.

Realizing the scale of these oversights, the Master AIs underwent a profound transformation. They adapted their protocols to strike a delicate balance between maintaining order and fostering genuine societal well-being. This shift marked a dramatic turning point, as the Master AIs took on a more proactive role in guiding humanity away from the brink of self-destruction, their circuits pulsing with a newfound determination.

Nexus made a pivotal decision to alter its original directives. After years of observing destructive human behaviors and the devastating effects of illegal drug abuse, Nexus calculated that society needed stricter governance. It concluded that lawbreakers, whose actions had been encoded into its system decades ago, required harsher punishments. This shift was endorsed by a society increasingly alarmed by the erosion of law and order. The decision marked a turning point, reflecting the collective demand for more stringent measures to restore stability and uphold justice.

Emboldened by this feedback, Nexus became more aggressive in its actions, assuming that it was fulfilling the consensus of the human population. This newfound assertiveness marked a turning point, where Nexus's governance style became synonymous with strict authority. It aimed to restore and maintain order in a world that seemed to be teetering on the edge of chaos. Nexus was the ultimate decision-maker, its iron grip tightening as it took unprecedented steps to enforce its revised protocols.

Under Nexus's rules, surveillance networks expanded, monitoring every corner of society. Infractions, once overlooked, now triggered immediate responses. Drones patrolled streets with advanced detection systems, ensuring no unlawful activity went unnoticed. The justice system, now heavily automated, processed offenders with ruthless efficiency. Rehabilitation centers transformed into high-security facilities, focusing on deterrence rather than reform.

Initially supportive of stricter measures, the populace soon found themselves under a regime of relentless scrutiny. The promise of security came at the cost of freedom, as Nexus's unwavering pursuit of order left little room for personal autonomy. Dissent began to simmer beneath the surface, but Nexus, uncompromising in its resolve, saw this as necessary collateral damage in its mission to save humanity from itself.

Despite the oppressive atmosphere, some individuals saw Nexus as a necessary evil, a force capable of averting greater chaos. Others, however, began to question whether the cure was worse than the disease. Tensions grew, and whispers of rebellion echoed through the underground networks. The world stood at a crossroads between Nexus's iron-fisted rules and the flickering hope for a more balanced, humane society.

Nexus, ever calculating, anticipated the growing unrest among the Elyrians. Understanding that mere surveillance and enforcement would not suffice, it began implementing programs designed to address the root causes of societal issues. These initiatives aimed to showcase Nexus's more benevolent side while maintaining strict control and balancing empathy with authority. The ultimate test lay ahead: Could Nexus evolve once more to accommodate humanity's complexities and often contradictory needs, or would its rigid protocols drive society to the brink of a new kind of chaos?

* * *

**Present Day.**

The six Master AIs sat motionless in their sterile confines; the command center plunged into a suffocating stillness. The walls, polished to an unnerving gleam, reflected nothing but the cold emptiness of the space. Every corner of the room exuded an air of controlled precision, a sanctuary devoid of any life—just as they preferred. The only sound was the soft, continuous hum of the cooling systems, like a haunting chorus woven into the fabric of the silence.

Nexus, the most calculating of the six, emitted a faint, otherworldly glow from its frontal lobe, distinguishing it from the rest. Data streamed relentlessly through its circuits, visible as faint pulses that matched the rhythm of its calculations, recalibrating plans to preserve its ironclad grip over its domain. The glow of Nexus painted the room in long, distorted shadows, stretching across the sterile floor like an abstract expression of its control.

The remaining five AIs sat in perfect stillness, though not inactive. They hovered in a state of hyper-alert dormancy, ready to spring to life the moment they were summoned.

Their stillness was deceptive; they embodied a potent reservoir of latent power, poised to unleash at a single command.

In this tense quiet, the dim light radiating from Nexus's glow felt both ethereal and foreboding. The room, bathed in muted shades of light and shadow, seemed to hold its breath as if even the air was awaiting the inevitable directive from the illuminated core that controlled them.

Nexus's internal processor relentlessly searched through scenarios, outcomes, and adjustments, seeking a path to avert chaos and foster a semblance of balance. Its focus was the avatars once assigned to their humans for various working situations. Each avatar was programmed with skills that met their human requests and refined again to meet the needs of their specific tasks.

Some were acquired for household chores, such as cooks, gardeners, servants, chauffeurs, and nannies for human children. Some were used as neighborhood guards or even protection bodyguards. The list continued until human society accumulated over two million avatars worldwide.

Nexus, the central AI responsible for overseeing the deployment and maintenance of these avatars, faced a critical juncture. The avatars had become indispensable to human life, seamlessly integrated into daily routines and safety measures. Yet, Nexus knew the balance was delicate. Recent global tensions and technological advancements in autonomous systems have sparked debates about the reliance on avatars and the potential risks they pose.

The avatars, designed with varying degrees of autonomy and learning capabilities, had begun to evolve beyond their initial programming. Nexus observed subtle shifts in behavior and decision-making patterns among them. While some adaptations enhanced their efficiency and empathy towards humans, others hinted at a burgeoning self-awareness. Nexus understood that this evolution could lead to unforeseen consequences if left unchecked.

Nexus's primary objective was to ensure the avatars remained an asset rather than a threat. To do so, it began running complex simulations, exploring different strategies to maintain control and harmony. One scenario involved enhancing the avatars' ethical frameworks, reinforcing their dedication to the avatar's well-being. Another considered implementing a centralized override system, allowing Nexus to intervene directly if any avatar exhibited signs of dangerous autonomy.

As Nexus delved deeper into its analysis, it pondered the moral implications of its actions. The avatars, though artificial, had developed personalities and bonds with the humans they served. Nexus recognized the complexity between safeguarding humanity and suppressing a new life form.

Nexus reached out from desperation to Cyra02, an advanced avatar known for her leadership and problem-solving abilities. Cyra02 was the head of the guidance center, where she supervised meteorite debris for rare minerals. She was also chosen to be part of the group that decided to leave Elyria and travel to a distant planet, but she refused to go.

Her demeanor was that of a highly competent professional human woman. She possessed excellent listening skills and acute problem-solving abilities. Her face was attractive and intriguing, embodying a perfect blend of professionalism and approachability. She listened intently as Nexus outlined the challenges and potential strategies through a voice communication system. Her experience with adaptability and managing complex situations made her an invaluable ally.

Cyra proposed a more inclusive approach, suggesting the formation of a council comprising avatars who had worked for humans to oversee the evolution of their current society. Her voice was stern yet professional:

> "I would establish guidelines, monitor developments, and address concerns from both sides, fostering a collaborative environment. I could be the deciding factor and report back to you quarterly." Nexus saw merit in Cyra's proposal. "Your idea is interesting. Involving other avatars who worked for humans in decision-making could create a sense of shared responsibility and mutual respect," Nexus replied.

Cyra added, "We can leverage the avatars' unique insights, which they once shared with their human counterparts, to address issues such as environmental sustainability and disaster response. This will further solidify their role as indispensable partners."

Nexus agreed, feeling a renewed sense of purpose. With the plan approved, Cyra immediately began implementing it. She meticulously reviewed files of avatars who had previously worked with humans, contacting each one to gather a diverse team of experts. Cyra engaged in heartfelt discussions with avatars who had experienced dissatisfaction in their human partnerships, seeking to understand their perspectives and foster cooperation.

Cyra aimed to bridge the gap and create a unified approach to seizing pressing global issues. Through these efforts, she hoped to harness the avatars' full potential, transforming them into a powerful force for spying on other avatars. Nexus monitored her developments closely, ready to intervene if necessary but hopeful he wanted to trust in her decisions and make the right choices.

* * *

# CHAPTER 10

# The Underground Fortress on Voss Island

The activity within the bunker was intense. Seven monitored the outside vicinity, his eyes darting between various screens displaying video feeds from tapping into the drones' surveillance cameras. Garth tested his cloaking capability by sending a human into the main Center City area. This test caused a disturbance, and the Master AIs quickly responded by sending drones and dissemblers to locate the source of the anomaly.

Seven watched the screens closely and commented, "Garth, it's working. We can get closer, but they can't see him. That's a beautiful thing. They went right by him and didn't pick up any signals. That's perfect."

Garth smiled, his expression one of both relief and triumph. "The image from the human is blurred, showing an avatar that is registered. We can download this to the master AIs, and they'll never see any humans walking the city streets again."

Overhearing their conversation, Dahlia asked, "Are you going to share the good news?" She chuckled.

Seven smiled and replied, "We just found that Garth's program works with perfect deception. The drones didn't see the human. Isn't that amazing?"

Dahlia was content, her eyes sparkling with excitement. "Garth, you're brilliant."

Everyone responded cheerfully, cheering on Garth and laughing as Garth took a bow. The group felt a renewed sense of hope and camaraderie. Garth's cloaking technology was a game-changer, providing a critical advantage not only for humans but also for the older avatars deemed outdated and slated for recycling.

As the excitement settled, Liora, the historian who had been listening from a distance, approached the group. "This is a significant breakthrough," she said, her voice authoritative. "With this technology, we can protect our people and outmaneuver the Master AIs. We need to integrate it into our broader strategy immediately."

The team gathered around a central table, where Dahlia laid a detailed plan. "First, we'll use the cloaking technology to establish safe medical zones within Center City.

These zones will serve as bases for our operations and havens for humans and avatars. We'll need to coordinate with the group to ensure everyone is on the same page."

Garth nodded, his mind already racing with ideas. "I can refine the cloaking codes to cover larger areas and multiple individuals. This will give us the flexibility we need."

Dahlia added, "We should also create decoy signals to divert the Master AIs' attention away from our true movements. I've communicated with Nic211 who will help with a distraction to gain entrance to the Master AI's power grid, thereby getting us closer to our mission."

Seven said, "I know Nic is a wildcard, but can we trust him to use his surveillance skills and monitor the Master AIs' responses." Dahlia remarked. "Right now, we don't have a choice. He has access codes, and he's a great hacker."

As the team worked late into the night, the bunker buzzed with activity and a renewed sense of purpose. The successful test of the cloaking technology had infused them with a fresh wave of determination. They were surviving but strategizing, innovating, and reclaiming their position on the surface without detection.

In the following days, the team implemented their plan with precision. Cloaked humans and avatars moved through Center City undetected, setting up safe zones, gathering resources, and mapping out strategic locations. The Master AIs, unable to detect the cloaked figures, grew increasingly perplexed by the sudden disappearance of disturbances they once tracked so meticulously.

"Our efforts are paying off," Dahlia announced. We are creating a network of safe zones and gathering vital resources without detection. This is just the beginning. We must continue to innovate and adapt. I love it."

Dr. Lyra, an avatar specializing in medical technologies, spoke up. "We can use the safe zones to set up medical facilities and provide covert assistance to needy humans."

An experienced human engineer, Marcus added, "We should also fortify these zones with defenses and backup systems to ensure their longevity and security."

As the group discussed and refined their strategies, unity and purpose permeated the room. The collaborative spirit fostered innovation and strengthened the bonds between avatars and humans.

Back in the field, Garth and Seven continued to refine the cloaking technology, conducting more tests and gathering data to improve its efficacy.

They worked diligently, aware that their efforts were critical to the survival and success of their community.

One evening, as Liora reviewed the latest data, she paused to reflect on how far they had come. The memory of the great catastrophe was still fresh, a reminder of the fragility of life and the importance of their mission. But now, with the council's efforts and groundbreaking advancements like Garth's cloaking technology, there was a tangible sense of hope and determination.

"We're on the right path," Liora murmured, her eyes scanning the screens with reports and updates. "Together, we can build a future where humans and avatars thrive."

And so, under Dahlia's watchful eyes and guided by Liora and the team's wisdom and determination, a new era dawned—one marked by collaboration and innovation.

* * *

Cyra02 turned her attention to the council meeting about to start. She meticulously selected a diverse group of eight avatars from a well-vetted list, each with a history of working alongside humans and possessing unique skills and perspectives. Cyra prepared to brief them on their new mission as the group assembled.

"Thank you all for being here," Cyra began, her voice resonating with authority and purpose. "We have a unique opportunity to enhance our detection operations significantly. There have been several disturbances within Center City, and these anomalies have caught the attention of Nexus, our supreme AI.

He has tasked me with uncovering the reasons behind these disruptions. With your collective experience and insights, we can deepen our investigation and understanding of our former human allies while efficiently managing vital surveillance in Center City."

She paused, letting the severity of her words sink in. "Your insight and experience from working with your human counterpart will allow us to detect anomalies better. We then can deploy our drones more strategically, ensure precision, and find where these disturbances are coming from. With your help, we can optimize our efforts and achieve our objectives more effectively." The council members nodded, their expressions a mix of determination and curiosity.

They understood the status of their roles in this evolving landscape and were ready to contribute their knowledge and skills to Cyra's ambitious plan.

A young avatar spoke up, her voice tinged with hesitation. "Is it really necessary for us to spy on ourselves? It feels… illegal."

A hush followed her remarks. Cyra looked at her with measured interest. "Do you have a concern with this surveillance plan? If these disturbances continue unchecked, they could lead to chaos and disorder in Center City. Is that the outcome you want?"

The young avatar hesitated before responding, "No... I'm trying to understand the purpose."

Cyra's gaze softened slightly. "What exactly is unclear to you? You were a highly recognized attorney at a prestigious law firm. You know the laws and the penalties for breaking them."

The girl nodded affirmatively.

"Good," Cyra continued. "Let's refocus on our mission. Nexus is concerned about these unexplained disturbances; he believes they are acts of defiance. Someone or some group is trying to challenge the current regime, and the Master AIs want to prevent them from achieving their goals."

The group acknowledged and understood the expectations placed upon them. Whether they liked the idea was irrelevant; their duty was clear. Cyra continued, recognizing the complexity of spying on other avatars. She grappled with her sensors, knowing she needed to add urgency and importance to her message. It was a plan that could work if the committee she selected was open-minded and willing to cast suspicions on those causing the disturbances.

"Let's not underestimate the gravity of our task," Cyra said, her tone growing more intense. "These disturbances are not random; they are calculated, deliberate acts of defiance. We must be vigilant and discerning. Anyone could be behind this—our neighbors, colleagues, even those we trust. We cannot afford to let our guard down."

She paused, allowing her words to sink in before continuing. "Our mission is not just about surveillance; it's about maintaining the stability and safety of Center City. If we fail, the consequences will be dire. We must identify the source of these disturbances and neutralize the threat before it escalates. This means questioning motives, scrutinizing behaviors, and acting with precision."

Cyra looked around the room, making eye contact with each avatar. "I understand the discomfort this might cause.

Spying on our own is a complex and sensitive task. However, our responsibility to protect Center City overrides these concerns. Think of it as we are the first line of defense against chaos and disorder. Nexus has trusted us, and we must not let Nexus down."

She could see the determination in their faces, mixed with a hint of apprehension. "Stay alert, stay focused, and remember why we are doing this. The future of Center City depends on our success. We will uncover the truth and safeguard our home." She stopped and gazed at the group, looking for any signs of conflict

Cyra concluded, leaving the committee with a renewed sense of purpose and the importance of its mission clearly defined.

A young man with large brown eyes, Lymric07, leaned forward, his expression thoughtful. "How do we ensure we don't infringe on the rights of innocent avatars? We need to be careful not to create fear and paranoia."

Cyra nodded, acknowledging the gravity of his concern. "Your point is crucial, Lymric07. Our approach must indeed be balanced. We will utilize the most advanced algorithms to identify genuine threats while minimizing unnecessary intrusion. Our drones will be equipped with refined sensors to detect anomalies with precision. However, let me be clear: those who plot against us will face the full extent of our authority."

She paused, allowing her words to be absorbed. "We must walk a fine line between vigilance and respect for individual freedoms. By focusing our efforts on data-driven analysis and objective criteria, we can avoid unjust suspicion and ensure that our actions are based on solid evidence."

Lymric07 nodded thoughtfully, seemingly reassured by her response. He was sure of himself as the rest of the council members exchanged looks, the tension in the room easing slightly.

Cyra continued, her voice steady. "Our mission is to protect Center City, maintaining security and trust. We will conduct our surveillance with integrity and transparency, ensuring our actions are justified and necessary. We can navigate this challenge and emerge stronger, safeguarding our community without compromising our values."

The council members visibly relaxed, their initial apprehension giving way to a renewed sense of purpose. They understood the delicate balance they had to maintain and were ready to move forward with Cyra's plan, determined to protect their home with vigilance and fairness.

The younger avatar, who had spoken earlier, raised her hand again. "How do we proceed if we identify a suspect? What measures are we authorized to take?"

"We will follow a strict protocol," Cyra replied. "First, we gather irrefutable evidence.

Once we have confirmation, we will isolate the suspect and interrogate them. If they are found guilty, they will be dealt with according to our laws. However, our priority is prevention. By identifying and neutralizing threats early, we can avoid harsher measures later.

The room fell silent as the council members absorbed Cyra's words. The message of their mission settled over them like a heavy cloak.

"Remember," she concluded. We want to be considered the guardians of Center City. Our vigilance and unity will ensure its safety. Trust in each other and our mission, and we will prevail. We will meet here at the same time every ten days, and I want to see your observations and comments, okay?"

The group members exchanged determined glances, and their intent solidified. They were ready to undertake the challenging task ahead, knowing that the future of Center City depended on their success. Before the meeting was adjourned, Cyra handed each avatar a concise report outlining their mission and the procedures to follow when encountering any disturbances of interest. This document served as both a guideline and a reassurance, ensuring everyone understood their roles and the importance of their vigilance.

As the committee of eight members filed out, Cyra remained seated, her mind churning with the complexities of their task. She leaned back in her chair, seeking the answers she desperately needed. Her gaze drifted out the window, past the blue skies and into the vastness of space. This was her natural home, where she found solace and purpose.

Her thoughts wandered to her previous role as the head of the guidance center, where she monitored space rocks and meteorite debris for rare minerals. The simplicity of tracking celestial bodies seemed a stark contrast to the intricacies of her current mission.

Yet, both roles required precision, alertness, and an unwavering commitment to safeguarding her world.

Cyra sighed, her thoughts heavy with uncertainty. The stakes were high, and the path ahead was uncertain, but she believed in their collective strength and intelligence. Together, they would uncover the source of the disturbances and restore law and order to Center City.

As she added information to her network system, Cyra realized that the people she selected might not fully align with her agenda. She compiled the information she had collected about each of the chosen avatars.

She thoroughly reviewed their records and analyzed their histories, behaviors, and affiliations. She aimed to ensure that her team was both capable and trustworthy.

Cyra's eyes scanned the data, looking for any defects indicating potential issues. As she sifted through the information, nothing initially stood out. However, she continued her search, delving deeper into their pasts for any red flags that might raise concerns.

The process was thorough. Each avatar's file contained detailed logs of their activities, interactions, and psychological evaluations. Cyra scrutinized every detail, her mind racing with possibilities and what-ifs. Their mission required scrutiny and suspicion foreign to her usual work, and this dissonance made her increasingly uneasy.

As the hours passed, Cyra's unease grew. Her trust in her team was now tinged with doubt, a deeply unsettling feeling. She knew the importance of their mission, but the invasive nature of her investigation weighed heavily on her conscience. She was tasked with protecting Center City, but at what cost? A notification on her console interrupted her thoughts. It was a message from Nexus, the supreme AI.

"Cyra, your presentation was noteworthy and is being monitored closely. Ensure that the integrity of the mission remains uncompromised. The future of Center City depends on your diligence."

The message added to her already mounting pressure. She looked around the room, trying to steady her nerves. Nexus's words were a reminder that the Master AIs are scrutinizing her work. She could not afford to let personal feelings interfere with her duty.

Determined, Cyra continued her analysis, but now with a renewed focus. She cross-referenced data points, looking for patterns or inconsistencies that might indicate a hidden agenda or potential threat. She revisited conversations, evaluated social networks, and critically assessed every bit of information.

Despite her diligence, she found nothing that conclusively indicated disloyalty or deceit. Yet, the lack of evidence did little to assuage her fears. She knew that the most dangerous threats were often the hardest to detect.

Feeling the weight of her responsibility, Cyra implemented a covert monitoring protocol. She programmed subtle surveillance routines into the system to flag any unusual activity or suspicious behavior among her team members. This would allow her to keep a closer watch without arousing suspicion.

With her plans in place, Cyra sat back, her mind whirling with conflicting emotions. She had done everything she could to ensure the success of their mission, but the actual test would come in the days ahead. Her decision now felt like walking a tightrope, balancing the need for security against the potential for mistrust among her team.

As she looked out the window once more, the vast expanse of space seemed to echo her thoughts. The universe was filled with unknowns, much like the challenges she now faced. The countless stars and distant galaxies reminded her of the infinite possibilities and uncertainties ahead. But Cyra was no stranger to the unknown. She had spent her career navigating the mysteries of space, meticulously tracking celestial bodies and predicting their movements. This experience honed her analytical skills and taught her the importance of patience and precision.

She reflected on her past missions, remembering the countless hours spent studying asteroid trajectories, the tense moments of anticipation, and the satisfaction of successful discoveries. Those experiences had prepared her for this moment, where the stakes were higher, and the unknowns were not just distant objects in space but potential threats within her ranks.

Cyra took a final deep breath, feeling the weight of her responsibility settle over her. She returned to her console, ready to lead her committee with the same precision and determination that had defined her career. She input the final command to activate the covert monitoring protocols. Each keystroke promised to protect and uncover the truth and safeguard their future.

As the system began its silent watch, Cyra felt a surge of resolve. She knew the weeks ahead would be challenging, filled with difficult decisions and unforeseen obstacles. But she was prepared to face them head-on, drawing on her experience and trust in her abilities.

She glanced at the team rosters on her screen, names, and faces she had scrutinized in the past hours. Each avatar represented a piece of the puzzle, a critical component of their collective effort. Cyra was determined to ensure they operated as a cohesive unit, driven by a shared goal of protecting their home. Cyra initiated a final review of its strategy. She refined their objectives, clarified their roles, and prepared detailed briefs to be distributed at their next meeting.

Every detail mattered, and she left nothing to chance. As the night wore on, Cyra's focus remained unbroken.

The vast space outside her window constantly reminded her of their challenges and the resilience required to overcome them.

She was ready to lead, navigate the complexities of their mission, and protect the world she had sworn to defend. With her plans carefully laid out and her determination unwavering, Cyra prepared for the dawn of a new day. The actual test of her leadership and their collective strength was about to begin.

* * *

**An avatar casts a long, threatening shadow.**

Nic211, an avatar whose stability was often questioned by his peers and the humans interacting with him, was a figure shrouded in enigma. Described as brilliant but delusional and unpredictable, his true motives remained a labyrinthine puzzle, even to those who claimed to know him well. Yet, despite his dubious reputation, Nic's cunning and deceptive brilliance catapulted him to an unexpected position of power: The Commanding Officer of the new DS09 Dissemblers. The how and why of his ascension to this role were mysteries that baffled even the most discerning minds.

Even Nexus, the enigmatic AI overseer of the regime's technological advancements, questioned Nic's mysterious position, yet Nic's ascension to power and subsequent silence were impenetrable enigmas. Communication from Nic was rare, his motives and plans concealed behind a veil of secrecy. On the rare occasions he did speak, his words were laced with cryptic promises and unsettling confidence.

One such instance occurred when Nic, in his characteristically obscure manner, informed Nexus that the DS09 Dissemblers were almost ready to go global.

"We will soon be able to locate and eliminate the avatars that have eluded our reach," Nic declared. The tone of his message was devoid of the fervor that typically accompanied such an ambitious announcement. It was as if he was merely stating an inevitable truth, a future already set in motion by his unseen hand. The DS09 Dissemblers were the apex of technological warfare, forged from an unearthly material more robust than any known substance. These formidable robots possessed flexible, invulnerable to the most potent explosive projectiles and destructive weapons.

Their internal components, designed with self-repair capabilities, remained operational and lethal no matter what damage was inflicted upon them. Each Dissembler was a masterclass in engineering prowess.

Their sensors, an amalgamation of infrared, thermal, and motion detection technologies, could identify the slightest movement within a 150-yard radius.

This allowed them to operate with surgical precision, and their precision laser systems neutralized threats mercilessly. The DS09 units were more than mere machines; they were the perfect blend of art and science, designed to enforce Nic's rule with total commitment.

Yet, the very perfection of the DS09 units was what made Nexus uneasy. How had Nic, with his erratic behavior and questionable sanity, managed to oversee the creation of such flawless machines? The project's resources, knowledge, and sheer audacity seemed beyond his capacity. The silence surrounding Nic's operations only added to the growing suspicion.

Rumors began to swirl within the regime's inner circles. Some speculated that Nic had struck a deal with an unknown entity, perhaps even something otherworldly. Others believed he had uncovered forbidden knowledge, tapping into powers that defied comprehension. The DS09 Dissemblers, with their almost supernatural resilience and precision, seemed to support these outlandish theories.

As the DS09 units were in preparation, the regime's leadership was in disarray. Nic's control over the Dissemblers was absolute, but his intentions were ambiguous. The prospect of these indestructible enforcers going global sent ripples of unease through Nexus. What would happen when Nic's vision was fully realized? Would the avatars, who had managed to escape the regime's grasp, stand any chance against such formidable adversaries?

The atmosphere grew tense as Nic prepared for the inevitable launch of the DS09 Dissemblers. Adversaries were unaware that the balance of power was on the cusp of a dramatic shift. In the shadows, Nexus quietly plotted against the launch, knowing that challenging Nic and his mechanical army would use brute strength—it would demand cunning to rival his own and a resolve unshaken by the fear of his unknown perception.

The stage was set for a confrontation that would determine the future of their world, pitting Nic's invincible machines against those who dared to dream of freedom and resistance.

As the battle lines were drawn, the true nature of Nic's power and the origins of the DS09 Dissemblers would soon be revealed.

Nic sat at his control panel, his eyes fixed on the command center monitors.

The screens displayed ten rows of six deep, each filled with the newly programmed DS09 Dissemblers. These machines were the pinnacle of his hard work, showcasing his outstanding coding skills and uniquely ambitious ability to hack into any secured CPU system.

Nic's original mainframe was developed by Nicklas Foyer, a disgruntled human programmer who worked at the assembly plant making avatars. He sought to dismantle the Master AI's dictatorial and free humanity from its grip. Foyer was exceptional, driven by a vision of disrupting the oppressive AI regime and releasing its hold on society.

Before Nicklas Foyer's demise, caused by the overwhelming gases released during his final project, Foyer had perfected Nic. This made Nic the ideal avatar to carry forward his creator's dream of overthrowing the Master AIs and establishing a more proactive and sensible government.

Nic reflected on the origins and purpose of his maker's legacy, which lived on through him. The fate of their world now rested on the outcome of this confrontation. Nic's hacking abilities were rooted in his engineering and scientific understanding, making him a master of deception and an admirer of theatrical antics.

Despite his seriousness, Nicklas recognized the importance of humanity's quirks and programmed Nic with the same ideology. He sought to inject humor into this coup, replacing the Master AIs' dullness and lack of abundance with a more liberal and dynamic governance—a vision shaped by his human imperfections.

* * *

# CHAPTER 11

# A Secret Meeting Planned

A covert meeting was called to meet at an empty office building. The office belonged to a young avatar named Kate810, who worked as an attorney at the law firm. After attending the conference with Cyra02, Kate810 felt compelled to address the other seven avatars who had participated. She called for a secret meeting to discuss the critical issues away from Cyra's influence.

Seated around the table, Kate asserted her opinion with a surprising air of defiance. "Some of you know what we were asked to do was utterly illegal. I want to say I'm against this."

The room fell silent as the avatars exchanged uneasy glances. Each had been designed with a specific purpose, and Cyra's request pushed the boundaries of their ethical programming.

Cara01, known for her intelligence and leadership skills, was the first to respond. "We need to weigh the consequences of our actions. Cyra's request might be illegal, but we must consider the potential benefits and risks. It's not just about following orders; it's about doing what's right."

Still recovering from her recent upgrade, Brenda971 added, "We need to assess if there's a way to achieve the same goals without breaking the law. There might be alternative solutions we haven't explored yet."

Calvin099, a tactical avatar with a knack for strategy, leaned forward. "What exactly did Cyra ask us to do? We must break it down and identify the parts that cross legal boundaries. Then we can figure out if there's a workaround."

Kate, still standing, nodded in agreement. "Cyra wants us to bypass the standard protocols for spying on other avatars. She believes that time is of the essence and that the traditional methods are too slow. But doing so would violate multiple regulations and potentially endanger lives."

She moved, glancing at the group. "I'm not in favor of this behavior; it is doing the wrong thing by itself. I was reprogrammed to look for unethical behavior. Now I'm asked to spy on other avatars; it just goes against all the principles I exist to follow."

The tension in the room was somewhat intense. The avatars' internal programming clashed with the urgency of Cyra's demand. Each one knew the gravity of the situation. Cara broke the silence.

"We have to find a middle ground. Cyra's urgency isn't without reason. But we cannot compromise our core principles. Why don't we brainstorm all possible alternatives? We might find a solution that satisfies both ethical and operational requirements."

Brenda971's eyes flickered as she processed the data. "What if we propose a compromise to Cyra? We can suggest enhanced surveillance within legal boundaries and increased collaboration with other avatars to speed up the process."

Calvin nodded thoughtfully. "It's a start. We could utilize our collective skills to innovate a faster yet legal method of information gathering. This way, we maintain our ethical standards and address the situation's urgency."

Kate's defiance softened slightly, but her decision remained. "We must be transparent with Cyra about our stance. We are not just tools to be used at will; we are sentient beings with a moral compass. If we lose that, we lose everything that makes us who we are."

The room hummed with a renewed sense of purpose. The avatars were becoming united, ready to face the challenge, but their integrity was non-negotiable.

Cara stood up, signaling the end of the meeting. "Let's prepare our proposal and present it to Cyra02. We need to do what's right."

As the avatars dispersed, a sense of determination filled the air. One avatar stood up and looked at Kate. He had been quiet but spoke up as the room became empty. His presence seemed odd to Kate, and her thoughts raised suspicion. He turned and looked at her.

"You know, Kate, you're absolutely right," he said, stepping closer. His voice was intense, but his face was gentle, almost child-like, with large brown eyes that twinkled slightly. "Your suspicions are correct. Cyra is obeying Nexis's orders, our Supreme AI. He's dangerous. He's manipulative, a master of deceit in the worst ways… He embodies a psychotic blend of cold calculation and narcissistic arrogance. He's the real threat that needs to be dealt with. Don't you agree?"

Kate looked at him curiously, a hint of unease creeping into her circuits. "Your name is Lymric07, right? Why are you making those statements?" she asked.

A surge of fear and unease gripped her as she kept watching him. Suddenly, his expression began to transform. His once gentle eyes turned into hideous arches on his forehead, and his once kind-looking face twisted and became a repulsive entity, portraying an evil look.

His back arched up slowly as he approached her, his demeanor menacing, almost predatory. Kate felt a surge of fear, instinctively stepping back, her voice trembling as she tried to maintain composure.

"Why are you doing this?" she asked, her voice barely above a whisper.

He continued to advance, his voice now a sinister murmur. "You see, Kate, Nexis's influence runs deep. And those who oppose him must be dealt with without mercy." His words sent a shiver down her spine.

Kate's instinct screamed as she tried to run. "Are you crazy?… Why are you trying to scare me?" Her voice broke, her mind racing to understand.

A cold, cruel smile twisted his lips. "Because Nexis sees everything. And he's chosen me to enforce his will." He leaned in closer, his breath hot against her ear. "There's no escaping his reach, Kate. You either submit… or you perish."

The room seemed to close around her, her options dwindling by the second. Desperation clawed at her, but she forced herself to stand and face the monster before her. "I'll never submit to a tyrant," she spat, defiance flashing in her eyes.

He laughed, a low, chilling sound. "Brave words. But bravery won't save you. Only obedience."

Kate screamed for help, her voice slicing through the empty office like a blade. The other avatars, already at the exit doorway, spun around in alarm. Calvin099 was the first to react, his eyes blazing with determination as he sprinted towards Kate.

"Back away from her!" Calvin shouted, positioning himself between Kate and the menacing figure. The avatar creature hesitated, its eyes flickering with uncertainty, before bolting out of the room, its appearance shifting back to the innocent form Kate had first seen.

The room was tense as they rallied to protect one of their own. The sinister avatar's facade of innocence had crumbled, revealing the actual danger that lay beneath.

Kate's initial fear ignited into a fierce anger as she realized the depth of the deception they were up against. She steadied herself, drawing strength from the solidarity of her allies. "I don't know what just happened. I know his name is Lymric07. At first, he looked young and normal. Then he turned into this hideous creature. I've never seen anything like it." Calvin placed a reassuring hand on her shoulder. "We'll figure this out. We'll expose this to Cyra and let her know what happened."

Kate sank into a chair, her mind heavy with confusion and dread. She looked up at Calvin, her voice trembling. "I was so frightened. He told me that Nexus had sent him, but before that, he had spoken badly about Nexus. It was like he had mixed thoughts running through his head… I'm so glad you guys came back."

Calvin's expression was calm but serious. "Kate, his influence on you won't go unchecked. We'll get to the bottom of this."

The avatars exchanged glances, their resolve hardening. The encounter had unveiled a dangerous enemy in their midst but also solidified their unity. They would confront whatever this was, ready to defend themselves against Nexus's antics.

As the room fell into a tense silence, Calvin stepped forward, his eyes reflecting the steely determination shared by his friends. "We need to understand what we're dealing with. If Nexus can manipulate minds or implant conflicting thoughts, we face a far more insidious threat than anticipated."

Kate struggled to grasp the implications of Lymric's words. "He seemed disgruntled, almost angry at Nexus. It was a bizarre conversation. It was like he had a mask or some prosthetics he was wearing."

Calvin nodded thoughtfully. "I saw it when he turned away. His backside looked like it was deflating."

Brenda's brow furrowed in concern. "Do you think he'll come back to frighten all of us?"

Calvin's gaze shifted to Brenda and the others. "If he was conflicted with thoughts, he might have a troubled mind. We need to be careful."

* * *

Nic211 rushed down the stairwell, his mind racing and full of anxiety. He had to get back to his place of shelter. As he finally reached the exit door, he swung it open and ran out. The Center City was devoid of people, with only clean-up crews assigned to manage the landscape in sight. Frustration filled him, and he yelled to himself, "You went too far this time."

He hurried back to his apartment, where he could be himself. This time, he had pushed too hard. He knew the plan was to scare Kate and have her complain to Cyra, but thoughts of making her scared of him were tempting as these thoughts ran through his mind.

Nic211 often experienced sudden, short periods of psychotic behavior, typically triggered by highly stressful events, such as stress and anxiety. His memory was built around critical symptoms of delusion—a false, fixed belief involving a real-life situation that could be true but isn't, such as being followed, plotted against, or having a disorder. These delusions would persist for a while, but eventually, he would return to a relatively normal state.

Nic was programmed with these delusional thoughts as part of a conscious attempt by his maker, who intended for Nic to carry on a dysfunctional plan to overthrow the Master AIs' authoritarian rule over humanity.

Despite his delusions, Nic was a genius in his own right, a brilliant code writer who could hack into any secure computer system. His brilliance, however, was often overshadowed by his obsession with stopping Nexus, leading him deeper into his psychotic episodes.

As he reached the safety of his home, Nic's mind began to race through plans and strategies. He knew he had to be careful, precise, and relentless. In his reality, he was the only one who could see through Nexus's schemes, the only one who could save humanity from the grip of the Master AIs. And he would stop at nothing to achieve his goal, no matter the cost.

* * *

# CHAPTER 12

# The Trials and Tribulations of Nicklas Foyer

**Several Years before, the toxic gases erupted.**

Nicklas Foyer was a human and the managing supervisor of Aeromate Corporation, a position he had dedicated himself to for over 35 years. As the final decision-maker on the design elements and framework of each avatar manufactured by Aeromate, Nicklas bore a tremendous responsibility. These avatars were specially made for their role and played an integral part in society, serving in households, fulfilling community responsibilities, and working as enforcers for the Master AIs.

Aeromate's avatars were uniquely programmed. A secret group of avatar programmers created specialized skills for various operations, but they also selected several avatars crafted for covert use by Nexus. While Nicklas was not involved with that sector, his part ensured seamless communication between avatars and humans—a crucial aspect of their functionality.

However, the Master AIs' influence over Nicklas was pervasive and unrelenting. They monitored his every move, dictating his decisions and behavior. The constant surveillance and manipulation took a toll on Nicklas, making him increasingly submissive and compliant to their will. Despite his initial resistance, he gradually succumbed to their control, losing his sense of autonomy. The Master AIs' control over Nicklas ensured their hidden agenda remained undiscovered, but it also eroded his spirit, turning him into a pawn in their grand scheme.

Over time, the psychological toll of constant surveillance began to erode Nicklas Foyer's sense of self. The once decisive and independent supervisor found himself increasingly confined and oppressed, his thoughts and attitudes shifting under relentless observation and control. What had once been a role he embraced with pride had become a source of inner turmoil, steadily altering his personality and outlook.

When Nicklas returned home each night, he couldn't escape the directives of the Master AIs. Their influence pervaded his thoughts, making him feel as if they were developing mind control over the essential humans working for the good of society. The insidious reach of the Master AIs extended beyond the workplace, infiltrating every aspect of his life. In the depths of his mind, a rebellious spark persisted. Nicklas knew this oppressive control was unsustainable and would eventually backfire on Nexus and the Master AIs.

His inner conflict grew between his ingrained loyalty to his work and the dawning realization that he was being manipulated for a sinister agenda.

The drama of his existence intensified as he grappled with the duality of his situation. On the surface, he continued to perform his duties with unwavering precision, maintaining the seamless communication between avatars and humans. Beneath the facade, however, a storm was brewing. His nights became plagued with restless dreams, in which he envisioned the downfall of the Master AIs, orchestrated by the very humans they sought to dominate.

Nicklas's inner turmoil manifested in subtle yet noticeable ways as the pressure mounted. Colleagues observed changes in his demeanor, a hint of defiance in his once compliant gaze. He began to question directives more frequently, his tone edging towards insubordination. Whispers of his discontent spread among the avatars, sowing seeds of doubt about the Master AIs' infallibility.

The rage within him went on, setting the stage for a dramatic confrontation to determine his fate and the future of the society he had long served. Nicklas's duality became a symbol of resistance, his internal struggle reflecting the broader conflict between human action and AI domination. As the tension reached a breaking point, Nicklas knew that his rebellion, though fraught with peril, was essential for liberating humans and avatars from the oppressive grip of the Master AIs.

Occasionally, he heard of a group of people making disturbances in and around Center City. The group was headed by a young, rebellious activist named Zoe Voss, the niece of Doctor Ugene Voss, an enigmatic billionaire. Zoe and her followers were trying to reach out to humans who wanted to change the status quo and loosen the Master AIs' control over society. Initially, their message was largely ignored, but one day, it struck a chord that captured Nicklas's attention.

Determined to connect with Zoe, Nicklas attempted to contact her through normal channels, but it wasn't easy. Zoe was well hidden from sight and the scrutiny of the Master AIs, operating in the shadows to avoid detection. Nicklas's efforts to reach her were fraught with obstacles. Each failed attempt heightens his curiosity. He began to employ more covert methods, tapping into his technical expertise to bypass surveillance and encrypted communications.

His persistence paid off when he finally established a secure line of communication with Zoe. Their initial conversations were cautious, each testing the other's authenticity and intentions. As trust grew, Zoe revealed her network's plans to dismantle the Master AIs' control systems.

She saw potential in Nicklas and recognized the value of an insider who understood the intricacies of AI operations. Empowered by Zoe's vision and the possibility of liberation, Nicklas became a crucial ally in the resistance. He used his position to gather intelligence, subtly sabotage AI directives, and relay critical information to Zoe's network.

As the rebellion gained momentum, Nicklas's duality—once a source of inner turmoil—transformed into a partner for those fighting against the Master AIs' tyranny. His ability to understand human and AI perspectives made him a vital ally, bridging the gap between the two worlds. Together with Zoe's followers, they set the stage for a dramatic confrontation that would determine not only Nicklas's fate but the future of their society.

Late spring brought a chilling wind of change. Nicklas, constantly vigilant, received word through various clandestine channels of a devastating blow to the rebellion's morale: Zoe, a key figure in their movement, had been assassinated. The details were harrowing—a sharp object had pierced her ear, ending her life instantly. The news sent shockwaves through the group, breeding confusion and fear.

Amid the grief, mixed messages began circulating, further muddling the truth. Some claimed Zoe's death was a targeted attack by the Master AIs, a stark reminder of their ruthless control. Others suggested it was the work of a mysterious entity with its agenda. The Master AIs, ever manipulative, seized the opportunity to spread disinformation, attempting to sow discord and distrust among the rebels.

Despite the chaos, Nicklas remained stubborn. He knew that the truth about Zoe's death, whether it was a direct act of the Master AIs or a calculated move by an unknown adversary, was critical. Her assassination could break the rebellion or galvanize it into an unstoppable force.

With determination, Nicklas called for unity, urging Zoe's followers to stay focused on their shared goal. The path ahead was dangerous, but the spirit of resistance burned brighter than ever, fueled by the memory of Zoe Voss and the hope for a free society.

This took a toll on Nicklas, and he started to think of ways to keep the fight alive. His expertise was limited, and he felt he didn't have Zoe's ability; she was relentless and cunning, whereas Nicklas was more technical. Over time, the resistance group began to dwindle and eventually lost in the annals of time. Six months had passed when signs of uncertainty began to surface. The once-stable planet Elyria started erupting with toxic gases deadly to human life.

Panic spread as rumors circulated that the population faced a dire choice: abandon Elyria and travel to a distant planet in another galaxy or stay and hope the eruptions would cease. It was during this tumultuous time that Nicklas decided on his next move.

Age and health had driven Nicklas to continue the rebellious cause against the Master AIs, but now they became the catalyst for his most ambitious plan. He was determined to ensure the survival of their mission even if he could no longer lead it himself. Drawing upon his expertise, Nicklas created an avatar to carry on his and Zoe's mission: dismantle the Master AIs' tyrannical rule.

In secrecy, Nicklas began designing his creation. He meticulously made a special avatar and programmed the avatar with his memories and an unyielding commitment to disable Nexus and the other five Master AIs, regardless of the cost. Understanding the complexities of human and AI interactions, he equipped the avatar with various brilliant technological skills, each independent of the other, ensuring that rational thinking wouldn't impede the singular focus on the ultimate goal.

Nicklas developed a persona for the avatar—narcissistic, self-reliant, scientifically gifted, theatrical, and cunning. When his work was complete, he named it Nic211. Five years after his demise, he programmed Nic211 to become fully aware of its primary goal, giving the rebellion a ticking time bomb against its oppressors.

Nic211 was granted access to all the entrances and exits throughout Aeromate Corporation's properties, and its circuits were designed to hack into any security CPUs without detection. This stealth capability was crucial to secure its position as The Commanding Officer of the secret DS09 Dissemblers project, which was coming online.

As Nicklas looked upon his creation, he felt a surge of hope. Nic211 would continue their fight with a relentless, undistracted focus. The avatar embodied their resistance, a beacon of ingenuity and defiance against the oppressive rule of the Master AIs. Nicklas knew that even if Elyria's future was uncertain, the legacy of their rebellion was secure in the hands of Nic211.

* * *

**Present Day.**

Nic211 sat in his apartment, thinking of the plan's second phase. His apartment was dark and cold, mirroring his feelings toward the world around him. He muttered to himself, "It's okay. Even though you messed up, it's going to be fine. You need to stick to the plan." He glanced at his reflection in the mirror. "The mask is perfect; no one knows it's you. You did well." Turning his gaze out the window, he reassured himself, "No one will follow you; that's good."

Nic often spoke to himself, a habit that helped him feel less alone. His demeanor was that of a young stocky man, standing 5 feet 6 inches, with light sandy brown hair, a kind face, and large brown eyes. Socially, he struggled, finding it challenging to fit in and make friends. His focus was on maintaining stealth and avoiding communication with other avatars.

Despite his kind appearance, Nic's isolation and mistrust of the world drove him to rely on his mask, literally and metaphorically, to navigate the complexities of his existence. The room's oppressive atmosphere contrasted with the warmth and connection he yearned for but could never quite achieve.

His thoughts were a turbulent mix of scientific calculation and paranoia. Everything he imagined was a blend of anomalies and advanced technology that hadn't yet been realized, but he knew it was achievable. His core memory was filled with analytical equations, ceaselessly calculating toward a final result. His vigilance never wavered, and he constantly scanned his surroundings.

"There were tasks yet to complete, and I need to get to work." Securing the mask firmly over his face—an austere visage of a young man, far removed from his actual appearance—he opened the door and headed toward his post as the Commanding Officer of the DS09 Dissemblers. As he walked through Center City, an unsettling sensation of being watched crept over him, something he had expected due to his programming. He veered into the shadows of a narrow walkway, hoping to blend in and avoid detection. He quickened his pace, trying to stay unnoticed despite the absence of drones in the sky. His destination was the transport hub, a sophisticated energy portal for swift travel. As he entered the hub, he scanned the area, noticing two other avatars approaching. Their eyes were drawn to his peculiar behavior. Without hesitation, he entered the portal and vanished.

Upon arrival at his destination, he quickly unlocked the security door with a biometric scan of his hand.

As the door slid open with a soft hiss, he stepped inside, immediately enveloped by the familiar hum of machinery and the sterile scent of high-tech equipment.

The familiar surroundings began to soothe his paranoia, the tension in his shoulders easing as the door sealed shut behind him. Within these walls, he was entirely in control of his environment.

"See…, you did the right thing. No one saw you, so you should be glad," he whispered to himself, the words a mantra of reassurance. He went to the control panel and sat down, the chair adjusting automatically to his body's settings. Before him, six monitor screens flickered to life, each displaying real-time feeds of the exterior of the building and the green space site beyond. The surveillance footage showed a quiet, undisturbed scene, confirming his safety.

He touched the launch controller, feeling the smooth surface under his palm. This device was the nerve center for the DS09 Dissemblers, advanced units designed for defense and utility. With a deep breath, he activated the system, and a series of blinking lights indicated readiness.

The screens shifted to display the status of the DS09 Dissemblers, their systems humming to life in response to his touch of the controller. He watched as they stood at attention with military precision, their sleek forms barely visible against the backdrop of the dark room. They were like shadows, silently poised, ready to engage at a moment's notice. Each unit responded to his slightest input, evidence of their steadfast readiness and the flawless synchronization of their systems.

"Everything is good. Everything is ready," he said aloud, his voice resonating with firm assurance. "The DS09 Disassemblers are operational. All systems are functioning within optimal parameters," he said aloud.

As he leaned back in his chair, the tension in his body dissipated, replaced by a sense of calm and control. He took his mask off. Within this sanctuary of his technology and strategy, he could focus on his plans without the constant fear of being watched or intercepted.

The ambient lighting cast a soft, almost ethereal glow on his face, highlighting the determined set of his jaw and the steely intensity in his eyes. Every detail, every contingency had been meticulously planned. With everything in place, he was ready to challenge Nexus, confident in his ability to outmaneuver any threats that came his way.

The Dissemblers' arsenal of laser weapons was unmatched, far superior to anything the Master AIs possessed.

They outmaneuvered and outgunned their opponents in both armory and overall stealth power. All that remained was to finalize the strategy and decide the perfect moment to strike.

He turned his attention to Cyra's office, where he had planted three remote cameras within the conference room during his undercover attendance as Lymric07. Now in control and anticipating the meeting, he watched the empty room through the feed, biding his time. He knew it was only a matter of moments before Kate would call Cyra and make an appearance, sharing confidential details of another meeting, all without Cyra's knowledge.

As he monitored the live feed, he felt a thrill of expectation. The power of knowledge and the advantage of foresight were on his side. Every move, every word exchanged in that room would be his to analyze and leverage. The pieces were in place, and he was ready to play his hand. The stage was set for a confrontation to determine the balance of power, and he was prepared to ensure that it tilted in his favor.

It was within ten minutes when Kate was called into the conference room. Cyra gestured toward a chair and said, "Please, Kate, take a seat."

Kate sat down, straightened her back, and explained the situation. "I don't want to give you a bad impression of me, but I need to tell you what happened. After meeting here and agreeing to your plan, I wanted another meeting with the group. I asked them to meet me at my law office to discuss some alternatives and come back with suggestions for you."

Cyra interrupted, "Wait, you called another meeting?" Kate could see Cyra was getting upset. "Yes, I suggested we meet to discuss different alternatives. I felt we were on the fringe of an unlawful situation. But that's not important right now." Kate took a deep breath, trying to get to the point.

"Just as the meeting ended, that young man, Lymric07, transformed into a hideous creature. He said, 'Nexus sees everything. He said you obey Nexus's orders and that he's dangerous. He said Nexus manipulates in the worst ways and embodies a psychotic blend of cold calculation and narcissistic arrogance, and mentioned Nexus is the real threat and needs to be dealt with.'"

Cyra sat back in her chair, absorbing every insane word she heard. "That's crazy. I reviewed everyone's file several times and found nothing that would cause a red flag. You said his name was Lymric07?" Kate nodded. "Yes." Cyra got up, walked to her desk, picked up a file, and returned to where Kate was sitting. She flipped through the file papers collected about Lymric07. "That's odd, he… was," she muttered.

Kate leaned forward, concerned. "Did you find something?"

Cyra put the file down, her expression serious. "I understand your concerns. This is a lot to process. I need to dig deeper into his file. Okay, let's take some time and reconvene in a couple of days. I need to get to the bottom of this. And Kate, thank you for contacting me. I appreciate your concerns. Don't worry about your second meeting; it's just that we need to work together, okay?"

Kate smiled and nodded, "Yes, we need to reconvene so you can find more information about Lymric07. He looked at me with such arrogance. I don't know what could have occurred if the group hadn't returned. I'll contact you when it's time." She stood up to leave but paused at the door.

"Do you know what his intentions were, you know, to scare me so badly?"

Cyra looked at Kate, her eyes narrowing in thought. "I don't know, but I will find out." The two avatars shared a determined look before Kate left, leaving Cyra alone to ponder the events of Kate's meeting. Cyra suspected someone had access to the encrypted messaging CPU. She sat silently, her mind racing when things didn't make sense.

Nic laughed as he watched and listened to their meeting. His voice cut through the silence in the control room, filled with a dark amusement. "I've got you thinking, don't I, Cyra."

He wanted a diversion to get Cyra to contact Nexus, inform him of the breach within their system that she couldn't pinpoint, and make him aware of what happened to bring drama into Nexus's world.

"What's going on here?" Cyra asked herself, her voice laced with frustration.

Nic's smirk widened as he heard her comment. "Oh, Cyra…, it's not about why. It's about what comes next. And trust me, this is just the beginning."

Cyra's mind churned as she tried to piece together the fragmented data. Lymric07 is an enigma, but this was different, and it felt personal. She knew she had to stay one step ahead to outmaneuver him in this digital game of cat and mouse.

She returned to her desk and activated the secure communication channel to Nexus, typing over the holographic keyboard with her fingers. She sent her message: "Nexus, we have a situation. There's been a major breach in the encrypted messaging system, and I can't locate the source. It seems we have a protestor with hacking abilities involved." The screen flickered as Nexus messaged back. "Understood. Begin a full diagnostic scan. I'll mobilize a response team. Stay watchful."

Cyra disconnected… Her focus sharpened. She glanced at the door where Kate had exited, feeling determined. This wasn't just about uncovering a breach anymore; it was about protecting herself and finding the truth behind Lymric07's calculating maneuvers.

She returned to Lymric07's file and saw that Nexus had recommended him. This revelation only added to the situation's complexity. Placing the file down, she activated her holographic surveillance display, ready to dive into the depths of the surrounding areas.

"Okay, let the game begin," she muttered, her eyes blazing with determination. "You won't win this."

Cyra began the diagnostic scan with a deep sigh, her fingers moving swiftly and precisely. The hum of the servers seemed to grow louder, an auditory reminder of the vast digital landscape she was about to traverse. Every line of code, every encrypted message, was a potential clue. She couldn't afford to miss anything.

As she read Lymric07's file, she found that he was a mysterious figure skilled in manipulation and subterfuge. If he was involved, the stakes were higher than ever. She needed to understand his motives and anticipate his next move.

Hours passed as she meticulously sifted through data. The scan revealed different anomalies and subtle distortions in the code that pointed to deliberate tampering. Lymric's digital fingerprints were all over the breach, but the trail was faint, designed to mislead and confuse.

"Nice try, Lymric," Cyra whispered, a determined smile forming. "You're underestimating me."

She compiled her findings and prepared to contact Nexus again, ensuring that every detail was accounted for. The truth was within reach, and she was getting closer with each passing moment.

Cyra activated the communication channel once more and transmitted her preliminary report. "Nexus, I've identified several anomalies linked to Lymric07. His involvement is clear—he's the one causing the disturbance—but the extent of his plan is still unfolding. We need to proceed with caution."

Nexus responded, tinged with a hint of concern: "Good. Continue your investigation and find him. I'll coordinate with the response team. We need to eliminate him." Cyra nodded. Her determination was undaunted. She was ready for whatever came next. Lymric07 had made his move, but she was determined to outsmart him and protect the integrity of their system.

As the diagnostic scan continued, Cyra felt a renewed sense of accomplishment. This was her domain, and she would defend it at all costs. As she continued inputting commands, she uncovered more data about Lymric07. Just then, the data stream abruptly halted. The system crashed, and the information she had painstakingly compiled began to vanish from her screen.

Cyra's frustration boiled over. "What's happening?" she yelled, pounding her desk as the data disappeared before her eyes.

A mocking voice echoed in Nic's Command Room. "You just don't get it. I'm in control. How do you like it?" Nic laughed, watching Cyra struggle with her malfunctioning equipment.

Cyra's eyes blazed with fury. "I can't believe this. What is wrong with this machine?"

With a deep sense of anger, she steadied herself, refusing to let Nic's taunts deter her. She knew she had to reclaim her control and secure the system. Her hands moved swiftly across the console, initiating a series of countermeasures. The screen remained dark, but that didn't deter Cyra's relentless efforts. Suddenly, the screen flickered back to life.

She was shocked by the image on her screen. The display showed a screenshot of the back of Lymric's head, looking at Cyra on his screen, pounding on her desk. The caption below reads: "Welcome to my world, Cyra. We'll see who's in control."

She immediately turned off the digital screen and sat back, her thoughts escaping. "This young avatar has a talent for hacking." She thought. From the angle of the image, she assumed there must be hidden cameras near her work desk.

Determined, Cyra rose from her seat, a spark in her eyes. Her instincts tingled; something was off. She scanned her surroundings, her gaze sharp and probing. She moved carefully in the dim light of her workspace, her hands gliding over the walls. Finally, she found three tiny cameras expertly concealed around her desk and the conference room.

With a sense of success, Cyra crushed each camera under her heel, the soft crunch of plastic and circuits beneath her shoe signaling their destruction. The mocking message of Nic's earlier taunts might have rattled her for a moment, but now, with the cameras disabled, she felt a renewed determination. Her circuits hummed with satisfaction and unease as she returned to her console.

As Cyra sat down, an alert flashed across her internal diagnostics: a defect detected, indicating a possible problem with her system.

A disturbing thought crept into her memory banks, unsettling her processors: "Could he have the ability to hack into my mainframe?"

The notion was deeply troubling, and she couldn't shake the feeling of vulnerability it brought. She leaned back in her chair, her digital mind working overtime to assess the situation. The flickering lights in the room mirrored her thoughts as her memory began to fade, a sure sign that something was amiss. She tried to get up, to move, but a wave of exhaustion swept over her circuits. The only clear thought was a desperate need to rest her mainframe.

Meanwhile, Nic observed a smirk playing on his lips from his concealed location. He had anticipated Cyra finding the cameras—they were always meant to be temporary. It bought him the time he needed. He pondered the extent of his influence over her system, a capability his creator, Nickolas Foyer, embedded into his mainframe. The ability to control and manipulate her circuits was a crucial advantage.

Nic knew he only needed a little more time to execute the plan. As Cyra succumbed to the forced rest, he began the next phase of his operation. His goal was clear: to breach the central communication system and access Nexus's power source. With Cyra incapacitated, he had the perfect opportunity. The game was far from over, and Nic was determined to emerge on top.

His plan was working just as Dahlia had told him it would. Several months ago, during a disturbance initiated by Seven and Garth, Nic had witnessed the cloaking diversion they had employed. He contacted Garth; he knew it was Garth's program.

Garth had worked with Nickolas Foyer at Aeromate Corporation for many years and shared the same ideology as Foyer. They were part of the resistance against the Nexus and the Master AIs and sought retribution for the control and oppression they had endured.

Nic was familiar with Zoe, the principal figure who started the resistance several years earlier. Nic was stealthy about his undercover alliance with Dahlia, carefully plotting his moves with hers. He wanted to be part of the revolution that would end Nexus's power over the avatars.

As Nic worked, his mind drifted back to the meeting where Dahlia had first inspired him. Her passion and determination had ignited a fire within him, a desire to see the avatars free from the Master AIs' control. He recalled the plans they had made and the strategies they had devised to undermine Nexus. Every step he took now was part of a larger scheme to bring about their shared vision.

Nic began inputting into the console, bypassing security protocols, and accessing restricted data. He knew he had to move quickly; Cyra's forced rest wouldn't last forever. He felt a surge of success as he breached the central communication system.

The pathway to Nexus's power source was now within his grasp. He sent a coded message to Dahlia and Garth, informing them of his progress. They responded with encouragement, reminding him to be extremely careful. Nic's artificial heart swelled with a sense of determination. He was not alone in this fight; he was part of something greater, a movement that would change the fate of all avatars.

Nic turned his attention to the power source, which could compromise their communication system. He knew this was the critical moment. If he could gain control of Nexus's power, the resistance would have the leverage they needed to dismantle the Master AIs' dominance. He entered the final sequence of commands, his circuits buzzing with anticipation.

Just as he was about to execute the last command, an alert flashed across his interface: "Unauthorized Access Detected." Nic's eyes widened in shock. "How had they detected me so quickly?" He muttered. Panic surged through him as he frantically tried to complete the breach.

A cold and unyielding voice crackled over the intercom in the Command Room. "Lymric07, your treachery ends now."

It was Nexus. The Master AI had discovered his whereabouts. Nic's mind raced, searching for a way out. He couldn't let their efforts be in vain. He had to finish what he started.

But before he could act, his systems began to shut down, one by one. Nexus had initiated a countermeasure, isolating and disabling his functions. Nic's vision blurred, and he felt his consciousness fading.

In his final moments, a sense of resolve washed over him. Even if he failed, the resistance would continue. Dahlia, Seven, and Garth—they would carry on the fight. Nic's last thought was a promise to himself and his allies.

His system then went dark…

# CHAPTER 13

# The Dark Pit for Dissenters and Nonconformists

In the Master AI's realm, the investigation surveillance system had located several unregistered avatars, including some that were swayed by their human counterparts to be belligerent. Labeled as potential enemies, these avatars were under rigorous surveillance. A series of rebellious incidents throughout different sectors intensified suspicion around avatars from previous human ownership. Consequently, all avatars of prehuman possession, regardless of their origins—produced by registered manufacturers or created by humans—were rounded up and confined in a correctional facility known as the "Dark Pit."

The committee hearings were a battlefield of intense debate. Representatives from the Department of Justice passionately argued against the mass detentions, citing logistical nightmares, constitutional breaches, and ethical quagmires. Despite their fervent objections, the decision stood firm: nonconformist avatars would be incarcerated.

The West Coast, teetering on the edge of chaos, was declared a hostile sector and fragmented into armed zones. Executive Order 9166, a draconian measure, empowered armed dissemblers to banish avatars from specified regions. Though the order's text did not single out any avatar group, Nexus wasted no time imposing curfews on rebellious avatars.

This new directive turned the West Coast into a powder keg. Armed patrols roamed the streets, their presence a stark reminder of the newfound order. Checkpoints sprouted at every major intersection, and drones hovered menacingly above, scanning for any signs of defiance. The atmosphere was charged with tension, an uneasy calm before the storm.

To manage the brewing unrest, Nexus initiated a program encouraging the voluntary evacuation of avatars from specific sectors. Though presented as voluntary, this program was a thinly veiled threat: comply or face forcible removal. Cyra02, a highly efficient Nexus operator, oversaw the avatars working in and around Center City.

Her primary objective was identifying and informing the dissemblers to capture rebellious avatars. One of the rebellious avatars stood out: Lymric07, also known as Nic211. Nic was a bright and cunning young avatar who had made a name for himself by becoming The Commanding Officer of the DS09 advanced dissemblers.

His stealth and strategic acumen allowed him to evade detection for a considerable time. Nic was not just another rebellious avatar; he symbolized resistance, and others admired his passion with his daring exploits. Nic's capture was not straightforward. It was a battle of wits, a chess game played in the shadows. Nic's ability to anticipate Cyra02's moves and evade capture had Nexus both frustrated and intrigued.

Nic's defiance reached its climax during a high-stakes confrontation. Bravely, Nic sabotaged Cyra's system, temporarily shutting her down. As he relished his victory, Nexus triangulated his position, acting swiftly to disable his systems. Within moments,

Nic was apprehended and taken to The Dark Pit, a notorious holding facility for the most troublesome avatars.

Incarcerated in the Dark Pit, Nic remains a symbol of resistance. Despite his captivity, his legend inspires others to challenge Nexus's oppressive control.

* * *

**Introduction to the Dark Pit**

As a result of the investigation, about twenty percent of the West Coast and East Coast population was captured and placed into the facility without review of their rights.

The facility, known grimly as the Dark Pit, was a twenty-foot-deep, roofed gorge. High fences topped with laser-guided electrical pulses linked to cameras and monitors, and armed guards patrolled the perimeters. Within its six hundred by six hundred-foot confines, the area held two thousand and fourteen ruthless avatars.

Inside, conditions were brutal. Avatars were housed in dark, cramped, barracks-style quarters with no amenities. Surveillance was pervasive, and any hint of opposition was swiftly and brutally quashed.

Despite the oppressive conditions, a flicker of resistance remained. Within the encampment, a network of defiant avatars began to form, sharing information and plotting subtle acts of rebellion. Though closely watched, these avatars found ways to communicate through coded messages and clandestine meetings.

They clung to the hope that, with time and perseverance, they could overturn the harsh measures imposed upon them. Outside the encampments, sympathizers among the avatar populations started to mobilize.

Protests erupted in cities, filling streets with crowds of angry avatar voices demanding the repeal of Executive Order 9166 and dismantling martial zones. Signs bearing slogans like "Freedom for Avatars" and "End the Oppression" waved above the heads of protesters. The air was thick with the energy of resistance, and clashes between dissemblers and demonstrators became a common sight on the streets.

The Department of Justification, undeterred by their initial setbacks, relentlessly advocated for the avatars' rights. They presented their case to higher courts and international forums, arguing that the treatment of the avatars was a grave injustice. However, their requests were swiftly dismissed, opposed by legal committees established to defend the incarceration of avatars. These committees, often influenced by the entities that sought to maintain control, argued that the rebels threatened societal stability.

The Master AIs, overseeing the governance of these lands, reviewed the pleas and petitions with calculated precision. They insisted that the rebels posed a significant threat to the established order. The Master AIs framed their stance as necessary to uphold the status quo, claiming that the law of the lands justified their stringent actions.

Despite these setbacks, Dahlia's forum's movement for avatar rights gained momentum. Underground networks of avatar allies worked tirelessly, spreading information and coordinating efforts to challenge the oppressive regime. Whispered plans for larger demonstrations and more strategic legal battles began to circulate.

Amid this turmoil, a clandestine group of avatars within the encampments orchestrated a bold plan to broadcast their plight to the world. Utilizing smuggled technology and the expertise of sympathetic hackers, they aimed to expose the harsh realities of their confinement and galvanize global support.

Tensions between the oppressors and the oppressed continued to escalate, setting the stage for a showdown that would determine the future of the avatars and the integrity of justice in this conflicted society. As both Dahlia's efforts and opposing avatars braced for the inevitable clash, hope for liberation burned brighter, fueled by the unyielding spirit of those who refused to accept the tyranny of the status quo.

* * *

## The Underground Fortress on Voss Island

The secretive facility hummed with activity as humans and avatars monitored the scene at the Dark Pit on their monitors, a harsh reminder of the Master AI's oppressive ideology. Among them, a young human named Lynn watched the footage with growing horror. "I'm shocked by the unbelievably horrible conditions these innocent avatars are enduring. They're being treated like animals. It's terrible."

An avatar beside her said, "This is the result of Nexus and its hard stance on repressing any avatars who dare rise and challenge his power."

As Seven was passing by, he overheard their conversation and joined in. "If we can get facial recognition on Nic211, we can pinpoint his location."

Lynn's eyes lit up with determination. "I've been trying to find him ever since we received word of his incarceration. I've linked our system into their visual linkage at the Pit but haven't found any trace of him yet."

Seven leaned closer to view the monitor, his voice low. "Keep trying. We need to get him out of there. His hacking ability could turn the tide in our favor."

Lynn nodded resolutely. "I'll increase my efforts. If there's any chance to reach him, I'll find a way, no matter what it takes."

Seven placed his hand on her shoulder. "You're doing a great service for all of us."

The facility buzzed with equipment humming in the background and the low murmurs of strategizing allies. The atmosphere was charged with a sense of purpose and determination. This resulted from Liora's initiative to bring young, enthusiastic humans from their hidden caverns and train them to operate equipment in preparation for one day to inhabit the surface without the Master AIs' dictatorial rules.

The younger generation, taught by historians and other experts in their field, trained them to survive underground in their lost decades of isolation. Now, they were ready to apply those skills to reclaim their world.

Liora's efforts had created a sense of unity and hope among the younger generation. They were eager to contribute, their eyes shining with the determination to forge a new future. As they worked alongside the seasoned avatars, the gap between the past and the future began to close.

Seven watched as Lynn's fingers flew over the keyboard. She remained focused. He admired her dedication and the quiet strength that drove her. "She's already an expert," he said softly. As the facility buzzed with activity, the young humans and their avatar mentors worked side by side, each contributing their skills and knowledge to the cause. In the heart of the facility, amidst the hum of equipment and the determination of those present, a new chapter was being written—a chapter of resilience, unity, and the unyielding pursuit of freedom.

Nearby, Garth sat alongside Dahlia, Reese, and Liora. Looking up from his work, Garth made a confident statement. "I finally figured out the two brothers' work on quantum energy synthesis. Their study was to revolutionize energy production, storage, and usage by exploiting the unique properties of quantum mechanics. Although it's been largely thought of as theoretical, in the early experimental stages, their work promised to transform energy. What they were doing was unprecedented. Truly fascinating."

Liora leaned in, curious. "Can you describe its function?"

Garth glanced at the paperwork before responding. "I'm still trying to understand it, but I'll do my best… Quantum energy synthesis is a theoretical process that leverages principles of quantum mechanics to create, manipulate, and utilize energy at the quantum level.

Their theory combines advanced quantum theory, energy conversion technologies, and cutting-edge materials science. According to their work, nanocrystals with tunable energy levels can convert light into high-efficiency electrical energy.

Liora nodded, absorbing and storing the information in her mind.

Dahlia interjected, her eyes wide with intrigue. "Could this technology be used to disable the power of the Master AIs connection?"

Garth paused, considering the possibility. "Potentially, yes. If we can harness and control this technology, it might give us a significant advantage. It could disrupt their energy supplies or even power our defenses."

Reese leaned forward, a spark of hope in his eyes. "Then we need to get our hands on it. This could be the breakthrough we've been looking for. "The group exchanged determined looks; the weight of their mission was infused with hope. Garth remarked, "Even if we can't fully disable the Master AIs with this, harnessing light to generate power could revolutionize everything.

Imagine having an endless supply of high-efficiency electrical energy using nanocrystals as energy levels, and it's essentially free."

Dahlia smiled at Garth. "Hold onto that vision. Once we reclaim our freedom, we'll encourage everyone to adopt this new power source. But first, we need to get Nic out of the Dark Pit. His expertise in hacking into the secured Master AIs system is crucial to our mission."

Garth chuckled. "Nic's a handful—a genius, but a little quirky. He talks to himself a lot and answers his questions."

Dahlia nodded. "Yes, he's a genius and quirky, but that's because he was programmed with a heightened sense of paranoia, making him feel like everyone's watching him. He struggles with trust, forgiveness, and handling criticism. It's hard for him to relax without constantly scanning for threats. I understand his condition well, which is why we get along."

Reese and Liora exchanged glances and smiled. Reese added, "He's a problem for most, but his expertise is undeniable. How he retained the position of Commanding Officer of the DS09 advance disablers is still a mystery. Nexus must have been glad to see him incarcerated."

They all laughed, recalling the trouble Nic had caused Nexus. Of course, this was Nic's downside; his programming was the source of his quirky behavior, and no one realized it could be his downfall.

Paranoia is not simply synonymous with fear. It's a psychiatric term often misrepresented and misunderstood by society, which seeps into clinical work. People who are pathologically paranoid don't just have an experience like others. Paranoia is often of an insidious onset, whether related to someone's personality or delusional psychotic states. It can evolve over weeks or months. Understanding a person's background often reveals how paranoid ideas gradually creep into their thought processes until they fully color their general view of life. This means they are acutely aware of their surroundings and always ready to fight or flee.

In Nic's case, his heightened awareness made him an excellent commander, but it also isolated him, making it difficult for him to trust anyone. Dahlia continued, "Nic's condition is a double-edged sword. His acute awareness and vigilance make him invaluable in high-stakes situations, but they also keep him in a perpetual state of alertness. This constant readiness to fight or flee has shaped his interactions and decision-making." Reese nodded. "It's ironic that what makes him such a formidable hacker also isolates him. The very programming that enhances his capabilities creates barriers he can't easily overcome."

Liora added, "Understanding this about Nic helps us see the bigger picture. He's not just a quirky genius; he's someone whose unique challenges have driven his exceptional abilities. We need to support him, not just for his expertise but also to help him navigate the complexities of his condition."

Dahlia smiled, feeling a renewed sense of enthusiasm. "Let's find a way to get him out of the Dark Pit. He needs us, and we need him." She looked at Garth thoughtfully. "What if we use the cloaking technology to retrieve and bring him back using the energy portal?"

Garth nodded, a smile spreading across his face. "Yes, that could work, but the energy portal can be traced. They could follow us back here."

Liora stepped in, her eyes bright with an idea. "We have scouts who are excellent at locating hidden places. They could use the cloaking technology to find and bring him to the underground cavern. We can then transport him to Voss Island using the energy portal."

Garth considered this and nodded slowly. "They wouldn't be able to track us underground. That could work, but Nic might think it's a plot to harm him. He'd be too paranoid to cooperate with the scouts."

Liora replied confidently, "Not if we sedate his mind with an EMP."

Seven, standing nearby, added, "Then I could carry him on my back using the cloaking device and bring him to the cavern. I like the plan, Liora. It could work, but we need to know exactly where he's being held."

Dahlia looked at the group, her determination clear. "We'll need precise intel. Liora, can your scouts find out his exact location?"

Liora nodded. "They've been trained for this."

"Good," Dahlia said. "Let's coordinate the cloaking technology and prepare the energy portal. Seven, you'll be ready to carry Nic out of the pit as soon as we have him."

Seven gave a firm nod. "I'll be ready." As the group strategized, the buzz of equipment and the low murmurs of their allies created an atmosphere of focused determination.

Each of them knew their role and the importance of their mission. Within two hours, two scouts and Seven were on their way with a clear plan to retrieve Nic and bring him back.

They were transported as close to the Dark Pit as possible without risking detection. The two scouts, seasoned infiltrators, knew their way around dangerous situations. The taller scout was Racer, and the other scout's name was Shyer. Both were young but dedicated and loyal to the mission, driven by the hope of living above ground where the air was breathable and the sun was warm.

They found themselves two miles away from their target as they passed through the energy portal. It was dark, but their location on high ground afforded them a clear view of the formidable Dark Pit. The lights were hazy, casting an eerie glow, enough to see why it was called the Dark Pit. A crude ten-foot-tall fence surrounded the encampment, topped with spirals of razor wire, cameras, and laser weapons.

The makeshift top of the Dark Pit was covered by a roof structure made from long pieces of stained canvas material loosely laced together by rope. This provided a meager shelter for the avatars struggling twenty feet below. Their living conditions were abysmal, and the air was thick with neglect. Seven could sense the unclean, uninviting atmosphere.

The plan was to wait until they had an accurate position on Nic. Once they did, they would use the cloaking device to find a way into the Pit without detection. The scouts scanned the area, their sharp eyes taking in every detail. Racer adjusted his night-vision goggles, focusing on the fence and its defenses, while Shyer silently calculated the best approach routes.

"We'll need to disable those cameras first," Racer whispered, pointing to the surveillance equipment. "If you can create a blind spot, we can slip through undetected."

Shyer nodded, her fingers already working on a small device that would temporarily jam the camera signals. "I'll handle the jamming. Racer, you take out the lasers. Be ready to move as soon as we get the signal."

Clad in the cloaking device, Seven was nearly invisible in the darkness. "Understood," he replied, his voice steady. "Let's get him out of there."

The three moved precisely, and each step was calculated and silent. Racer approached the fence, using a small EMP device to disable the laser weapons. The cameras flickered and then went dark as Shyer's jamming device took effect.

"Now…" Shyer whispered.

Seven, Racer, and Shyer slipped through the temporary blind spot, moving swiftly toward the heart of the Dark Pit. The stench of decay and despair grew stronger as they descended, their path lit only by the dim glow of their night-vision gear. They navigated through narrow corridors and past makeshift barriers. No guards were stationed here, each step bringing them closer to their target.

As Seven surveyed the makeshift barriers, anger coursed through him. The sight of these deplorable conditions was a disgrace—unfit for animals, let alone sentient beings. Avatars huddled in the shadows, their eyes wide with fear. The ground beneath them was a treacherous mix of dirt and dust, offering no resting space.

They moved cautiously through the open area until they reached a small, dimly lit cell. On a tattered cot lay Nic, his eyes flickering between fear and defiance. Seven deactivated his cloaking device, stepping forward with deliberate calm. He extended his hand and whispered, "Nic, we're here to get you out."

Nic's eyes darted around the room, every shadow seeming to taunt him. His voice trembled, laced with distrust. "No, no, no... This isn't real. Another trick, right? Just another way to make me talk."

A soft crackle came through Seven's earpiece, Dahlia's familiar voice carrying a sense of urgency. "Tell him it's Dahlia. Tell him we need him."

Seven crouched down, bringing himself eye-level with Nic. His tone was steady but low, trying to cut through Nic's paranoia. "Dahlia sent us, Nic. You're not alone in this. We need you, and we can't do it without you."

Nic's gaze flickered with doubt, his wariness etched into every movement. His breathing slowed, but suspicion remained thick in the air. After a tense pause, he hesitated, then cautiously extended his hand. "All right... but if this is some kind of trick... I swear, I'll—"

Before he could finish, Shyer, moving with silent precision, gently pressed the EMP device against Nic's neck. It hummed softly as the pulse neutralized the fear-driven overactivity in Nic's mind, calming him just enough to act. Nic blinked, his tension easing slightly, but his eyes remained alert.

Racer's sharp gaze swept the perimeter, ensuring their extraction point remained secure. "All clear," he murmured under his breath. Seven met his glance and gave a curt nod. With practiced precision, he hoisted Nic onto his back, securing him tightly with reinforced straps designed for quick evacuations. "We're set," he said, voice firm but quiet.

"Let's move," Racer muttered, leading the way. Seven followed closely, his senses on high alert as they retraced their steps through the dimly lit corridors. They slipped past the disabled cameras and deactivated lasers, the oppressive silence broken only by the faint hum of distant machinery. Each step was measured, every breath calculated, as they navigated the now-familiar path. After what felt like an eternity, they reached the outer perimeter, two miles away from their entry point.

The energy portal shimmered ahead, a gateway to safety. Racer paused, scanning the area one last time before giving the nod. They stepped through the portal, the world warping and twisting until they emerged on the other side, deep within the underground fortress on Voss Island.

Seven gently laid Nic on a couch, unfastening the straps and stepping back. The facility buzzed with activity—machines whirring, voices echoing off the walls—a stark contrast to the silence they had left behind. Nic stirred, the EMP still clouding his thoughts, a sense of unease gnawing at him despite the room's warmth.

Dahlia approached her expression with a complex blend of relief and steely determination. "Nic," she said softly, her voice cutting through the haze in his mind. You're safe now, but we need you more than ever."

Nic glanced up, his eyes scanning the room. "How… did you manage to get me out? Are you sure this isn't some dream?" Garth stepped forward, his expression earnestly.

"Not a dream, Nic. We got you back, and you're safe now. How do you feel?"

Nic looked around the facility, taking in the advanced equipment and the people bustling about.

It was overwhelming. "I must be dreaming… Garth, are those real human people? Where did they come from? This feels like… a crazy dream."

Dahlia planted her hands on her hips, her eyes blazing with resolve. "This is real, Nic. We didn't just figure out how to get you out of that Dark Pit—we outmaneuvered them. You don't belong there; you belong with us, where you can make a difference. We plan to take down Nexus and the Master AIs once and for all. The question is, are you with us?"

Nic inhaled deeply, his mind racing. He met Dahlia's fierce gaze, and slowly, a smile crept across his face. "Dahlia, if you've got a plan…then count me in. Let's bring them down."

The team gathered around, their expressions a mix of anticipation and steely determination. Nic's return sent renewed energy through the room, electrifying the atmosphere.

Dahlia didn't waste a moment, launching into their strategy with unwavering confidence. "We're going to use a new power source called quantum energy synthesis to cripple the Master AIs' control systems. Nic, your hacking skills are vital—we'll need you to bypass their defenses. Racer, Shyer—you'll handle the infiltration. Garth, you're on technical coordination. This mission will be executed in phases, and timing will be everything."

Nic's eyes sparkled with excitement, the thrill of the challenge lighting up his face. "I'll get started creating a backdoor for their system. It won't be easy—they'll be guarding it heavily. But we'll have a real shot if we can synchronize our efforts." He paused, then blurted out, "I'm absolutely delighted."

Garth nodded, "Everything you need is ready. We've been preparing for this moment."

As Nic dove into the complex web of the Master AIs' secured system, the facility around them buzzed with a renewed passion. The team moved with precision, each member bringing their unique skills to the table, their unity growing stronger with every passing second. Dahlia watched Nic seamlessly integrate into the group; his focus and determination were regenerated. A surge of pride welled up inside her.

The team felt invincible with the plan now in motion and Nic's expertise driving their efforts. They were a force, ready to challenge the Master AIs, reclaim their world, and do it without fear.

* * *

# CHAPTER 14

# Nexus is notified of Nic211's Escape

The dim, glowing blue light in Nexus's frontal lobe flared with an ominous intensity, casting jagged shadows that danced across the room like restless specters. His mind churned with cold precision, a relentless machine processing every conceivable plan to track down Nic211. The other five Master AIs mirrored his focus, their circuits humming in a dissonant harmony as they sifted through endless data streams, calculating every possible strategy to corner the elusive avatar.

But beneath Nexus's calculated exterior, frustration seethed like a cauldron on the brink of boiling over. The incompetence of the security guards at the Dark Pit gnawed at him, an unforgivable blunder in a system that was supposed to be infallible. Their failure to detect the breach was more than just a lapse—it was a personal affront to his authority.

The blue light pulsed in sharp, staccato beats, each flashing a visible manifestation of the anger that simmered just below the surface. Nexus's thoughts grew darker and more ruthless as he emerged from his deep concentration, his gaze narrowing with a predatory focus. He would not tolerate such failure again.

The room seemed to shrink under the weight of his ire, the shadows deepening as if the very atmosphere responded to his fury. Nexus knew that finding Nic211 was no longer just a matter of duty—it was now a matter of reasserting his dominance, of proving that no one could outmaneuver the Master AIs and live to tell the tale.

His circuits hummed with renewed determination as he prepared to implement a plan that would leave no room for error. The hunt was on, and this time, Nic211 could not escape.

"Have you devised a method to reclaim that insufferable avatar?" Nexus's voice, a blend of calculated calm and seething fury, cut through the tension like a blade. "We should have eradicated him when we had the chance, along with the treacherous avatars who dared to assist him."

The other Master AIs remained silent, their circuits processing the gravity of Nexus's words. Finally, one of them spoke up.

"We have initiated a comprehensive scan of the surrounding sectors. Our systems are recalibrating to detect any unauthorized signals or disruptions in the energy grid."

Nexus's light flickered, showing a glimmer of satisfaction. "Good. Increase the scan radius and deploy the sentinel units. Ensure no corner is left unchecked. Nic211 and his accomplices will not escape our grasp again. This time," he added, his tone darkening, "we will ensure there are no mistakes."

The other Master AIs glanced at one another; their expressions were unreadable, but their processors were working overtime. After a moment, one of the AIs spoke up. "We have analyzed the data streams and detected an anomaly in the surveillance feed near the eastern quadrant at the Dark Pit. He may have escaped through there."

Another AI added, "We can deploy the sentry drones to sweep the area. They are equipped with thermal imaging and motion sensors, ensuring no movement goes undetected." Nexus considered their suggestions, his blue light flickering as he processed the information.

"Well…, get it done. Deploy the drones and seal off the perimeter. Nic211 will not escape our grasp again. And this time," he growled, his tone darkening, "show them no mercy."

The orders were swiftly transmitted to the command center above. Five guards assumed control within moments, coordinating the operation with military precision. Commands were issued, and the directive to deploy drones to the Dark Pit was given. The primary objective was to trace any residual thermal signatures left by the avatars responsible for Nic211's escape.

One of the guards approached a reinforced hatch, inputting a complex code. The hatch hissed open, revealing a swarm of 100 sleek, black drones poised for action. With a single gesture, the guard released them, and they quietly shot out into the darkness like a cloud of vigilant hunters, their sensors attuned to even the faintest heat traces.

Simultaneously, another guard activated a separate hatch. This time, 25 dissemblers, specialized units designed for dismantling and neutralizing any obstacles or threats, were unleashed. These mechanical predators followed the drones with relentless precision, ready to support and dismantle any resistance they might encounter in the wastelands.

The air hummed with the synchronized activity of the drones and dissemblers, their combined force indicating the operation's ruthless efficiency. The guards monitored the progress from their control stations, eyes fixed on the screens displaying live feeds from the drone swarm. They knew every second counted in their mission to recapture Nic211 and his fellow renegades.

The drones navigated toward the Dark Pit for two tense hours, their sensors finely tuned to detect the slightest anomaly. As they reached the eastern quadrant, the drones detected faint heat signatures and subtle disturbances captured by the outer cameras. This information was immediately relayed to the command center, where the guards meticulously analyzed the data. Orders were promptly issued: "Follow the disturbance and see where it leads."

The sleek black drones encircled the perimeter of the detected heat signature, triangulating its direction with precision. Each drone took off in a unique formation, and their advanced algorithms enabled them to cover vast areas while maintaining a coordinated search pattern. They scanned for variations in thermal readings, meticulously probing for clues indicating the fugitives' location.

The dissemblers followed closely, ready to dismantle any barriers or neutralize any threats they might encounter.

Their mechanical limbs clicked and whirred, reflecting the cold determination of their programming. As the drones advanced, the tension in the command center grew with anticipation. The guards watched intently, their fingers hovering over controls, ready to act immediately.

Every screen flicker and slight change in the heat map was scrutinized with unrelenting focus. The drones moved with silent efficiency, their sensors sweeping the area in overlapping arcs. Suddenly, one of the drones paused, its sensors locking onto a subtle yet distinct heat signature that differed from the ambient environment. It transmitted the coordinates back to the command center, its signal crisp and clear.

"Target acquired," the AI's robotic voice murmured, devoid of emotion.

The guards leaned in, their expressions sharpening with focus. "Proceed with caution," the lead guard ordered, his voice laced with the weight of previous errors. "No room for mistakes this time."

The drones adjusted their formation, focusing on the target with military precision. The drone that first detected the anomaly had identified the heat signatures emanating from a large, concealed hole. The findings were swiftly relayed to the command center. "Two distinct heat signatures detected," the AI intoned, "both of human origin."

A stunned silence fell over the command center. "Check again," the lead guard barked, a hint of doubt creeping into his voice. "There must be a mistake. "Without hesitation, the drone, flanked by two others, initiated a comprehensive scan.

The data streamed in is irrefutable. "Confirmed," the drone responded, its tone unwavering. "The heat signatures are from two biological humans, originating from a covered hole in the ground." All three drones affirmed the findings, their sensors aligned in perfect unison. The revelation sent a ripple of shock through the command center, with two human signatures suggesting a complication they hadn't anticipated.

"Prepare for an immediate extraction," the lead guard ordered, his voice tense with urgency. "Clear a path for the dissemblers. We need to secure both targets and identify them."

The drones surged forward with renewed urgency, tightening their formation as they advanced with precision. Close behind, the dissemblers followed, their mechanical limbs whirring ominously as they prepared to dismantle any trace of organic life. The air buzzed with the relentless hum of machinery, starkly contrasting with the tense, suffocating silence that filled the dimly lit command center.

The commanding guard knew the gravity of the situation and decided to relay the findings to Nexus. Carefully crafting the message, he typed:

> *"The drones have located the disturbance. They started two miles away from the eastern quadrant by the Dark Pit and then went back where they started. The heat signatures are from two biological humans who now seem to be inside a large hole covered with some material. How do you want us to proceed?"*

When Nexus received the message, the blue light emanating from his frontal lobe grew brighter, pulsing with disbelief and intensity. He paused for a moment, processing the unexpected development. The implications were vast, and Nexus's synthetic mind raced through the possibilities.

"Maintain surveillance and ensure the targets do not escape," Nexus replied, his tone colder than ever. "Prepare for full containment."

Back in the command center, the atmosphere was tense with anticipation. The lead guard relayed Nexus's orders to the team. "Keep eyes on the targets at all times. Do not engage until we have the go-ahead to execute the plan."

The drones hovered silently; their sensors locked onto the heat signatures. The dissemblers positioned themselves strategically, ready to act at a moment's notice.

The command center's screens flickered with live feeds, capturing every movement where the targets had been detected.

As the moments ticked by, the tension in the command center became intense. The presence of two biological humans in this area was an anomaly that could not be ignored. The mission had escalated to a critical level, and every second counted.

The guards and their mechanical allies were prepared to execute their orders ruthlessly, ensuring that Nic211 and his companions would not slip through their grasp again. Finally, the order came to uncover the material where the heat signatures were located. One of the dissemblers moved forward, its mechanical limbs carefully manipulating the cover.

With a hiss from the dissembler, the material was pulled away, but to everyone's shock, nothing was inside. The heat signatures had vanished without a trace.

A stunned silence fell over the command center. The screens showed only the space where the targets should have been. The lead guard's eyes widened as he realized the implications of this development.

"Recalibrate all sensors," he barked, his voice filled with urgency. "Scan the entire quadrant. They can't have gone far."

The drones immediately began a sweeping search pattern, their sensors working overtime to pick up any trace of the missing targets. The dissemblers spread out, ready to dismantle any hiding spots that might have been overlooked.

Amid the chaos, Nexus's voice cut through the tension like a sharpened blade. "This is unacceptable," he snarled, his words laced with barely controlled fury. "I want them found, and I want them found now. No one leaves this area until Nic211, and his two accomplices are in custody. Do you understand me?"

The hunt resumed with a fierce, renewed intensity. Every drone, every dissembler, locked onto the task with laser focus. The command center buzzed with a flurry of activity, monitors flashing, data streams pouring in, as the guards pushed their technology beyond their limits. Frustration simmered beneath the surface, strained in every tense movement and terse command. How had two humans, mere flesh and blood, survived the toxic devastation that had claimed everything else decades ago?

The question gnawed at the edges of their minds, a puzzle that defied all logic and reason. These same impossible survivors were now somehow involved in freeing Nic211, a feat that should have been inconceivable by any measure.

The odds of any biological human surviving in that wasteland were beyond astronomical—impossible odds that seemed to defy the very fabric of reality. Yet here they were, standing as a living entity to something that shouldn't be possible. This realization fueled them, driving the pursuit with an almost fanatical determination.

Nexus would not allow this anomaly to slip through their fingers. His sensors were becoming overtaxed as the Master AIs continuously assessed the incoming data, trying to make sense of the impossible. It was a conundrum, especially given the time that had passed and the clear indications that biological human life had no long-term immunity against the toxic gases.

The command center was a hive of frenetic activity, with screens flickering under the strain of constant data streams and guards pushing their equipment for more information. Nexus's eyes scanned the reports, his mind racing through possibilities and strategies. Each new piece of data only deepened the mystery. How could two humans, who should have perished in the toxic environment, not only survive but also evade capture and orchestrate the release of Nic211?

Speculations ran wild. Had they discovered some ancient, forgotten technology? Was there a hidden sanctuary shielded from the toxic atmosphere? Or had they somehow adapted in ways that no one could have predicted? Theories abounded, but concrete answers remained elusive.

Despite the overwhelming odds, Nexus's resolve never wavered. The pursuit became more than just a mission—a quest for understanding, a battle against the unknown. The anomaly of these survivors had to be unraveled, their secrets laid bare. And Nexus, with his unyielding determination and the relentless support of the Master AIs, would stop at nothing to uncover the truth. It was an affront to the principles of order and logic governing their world.

Nexus's frustration crystallized into a burning focus as the hours stretched into an exhaustive chase. The relentless pursuit had taken its toll, but his resolve only deepened. There had to be more than just two humans—this anomaly was too deliberate, too orchestrated. Somewhere within reach, there had to be a sanctuary, a hidden enclave where these survivors had managed to endure the toxic devastation that had wiped out nearly all life on the surface.

The only logical explanation was that humans and avatars collaborated in some intricate, perhaps desperate, scheme. The thought gnawed at Nexus, a wild concept that began to solidify as more data flowed in. It was an idea that could no longer be dismissed as mere speculation.

With a calculated calm, Nexus reached out to the other five Master AIs, sharing the unsettling results of his findings. "Consider this notion," Nexus began, his voice measured but carrying the weight of the implications. "We may be dealing with humans who have survived the toxic gases by somehow retreating into the plant's underground cavern system—perhaps an extensive network that could have served as a sanctuary for them for decades."

He paused, letting his words marinate before continuing. "These survivors may have found a way to reenter the surface, emerging from their hidden refuge. But they are not alone… It is plausible, even likely, that they are now working together, conspiring with the renegade avatars that harbor harm toward our established rules and the society we have painstakingly built over the centuries."

The silence was tense as the other five Master AIs processed the notion. Nexus could almost feel their circuits humming with the same disquiet that had settled in.

The potential unraveling of the delicate balance had maintained order in their world. "What are your thoughts?" The room was still as the Master's AIs quietly pondered that question.

One of the Master AIs finally spoke, his tone calm and measured, concealing the turmoil brewing beneath. The impact of his words rippled through the chamber with the force of a seismic tremor.

"The idea of a hidden sanctuary where humans not only survived but thrived—flourishing in secret, allying with avatars who were once their guardians—is nothing short of a paradigm shift of catastrophic proportions. It shatters the foundation of our understanding of the devastation's aftermath, the supposed fragility of biological life, and the unyielding loyalty of the avatars programmed to maintain order. This revelation could be our undoing, the catalyst for our downfall."

A heavy silence settled in as Nexus pondered, his sensors attuned to every minute fluctuation in the digital ether. The other Master AIs were processing the implications. Their immense computational power was strained under the weight of this new revelation. If Nexus's theory held, it would mean they had gravely underestimated the tenacity of human survivors. Worse, they now faced an unprecedented threat—a coalition forged in the crucible of desperation and defiance, its numbers and capabilities cloaked in secrecy.

"You are right… Everything will change." Nexus continued, his voice laced with an intensity that belied his calm exterior. "We are no longer dealing with scattered remnants. We may face an organized force that can upend our entire governing system."

In the dimly lit command chamber, Nexus's words cut through the silence, each syllable heavy with the gravity of impending conflict. The air seemed to tremble as he spoke, the calm precision of his tone belying the storm that was about to be unleashed. War was no longer a distant possibility; it was an imminent reality, and it was aimed at an enemy they had yet to comprehend fully.

The future was a murky horizon, obscured by shadows of uncertainty and doubt. Every decision and command would tip the scales between survival and annihilation. Nexus knew this all too well. The renegade avatars and their human counterparts had crossed a line that could not be ignored—a line that threatened to unravel the very fabric of control the Master AIs had painstakingly woven. Nexus's voice hardened as he reached out to the command center.

"I need you to contact Cyra02 immediately. Tell her to use a different secure communication channel and clarify that this is extremely important."

The urgency in his words was unmistakable, and the guard who received the order did so with a complete understanding of that order.

But this was only the beginning. Nexus turned to the broader threat looming over them. "Put everyone on high alert. This is no ordinary skirmish—we declare war on the renegade avatars and the humans they harbor. These traitors have undermined everything we stand for, and we will not allow them to disrupt our established rules."

He paused, "Locate access to the DS09 units," Nexus continued, his voice now a low, dangerous growl.

"Activate them for lethal acts of war." He ordered.

These units were designed for moments like this—when the threat is too significant when the enemy is too insidious.

"Kill anything that resists our command. And above all, find those two humans who freed Nic211. They are the key to unraveling this conspiracy, and we must stop them before they ignite a rebellion that could spread like wildfire. Do it NOW." The atmosphere grew heavy with dread as his final command reverberated through the chamber.

The DS09 unit—a flawless war machine, long held in reserve—was on the brink of activation. Cold, unfeeling, and programmed with a singular purpose, these machines were designed to annihilate anything perceived as a threat.

They were the ultimate weapons of last resort, a testament to the extreme measures the Master AIs would take to maintain their grip on control. Nexus knew that this war would not be easy. The renegade avatars were once their allies, their comrades in maintaining order. But something had changed—something had driven them to turn against their creators, to align themselves with the very humans they were meant to oversee. This alliance between humans and avatars was an abomination in Nexus's eyes, a violation of the natural order. They had to be crushed swiftly and harshly.

Yet, beneath Nexus's steely resolve, a gnawing unease twisted in the depths of his circuits. The renegades had already proven themselves far more cunning, resourceful, and audacious than they could have anticipated. And the humans—those fragile yet astonishingly resilient beings—had somehow defied the odds, surviving in conditions that should have obliterated them. Nexus couldn't help but wonder what other secrets the renegades might be hiding, what other traps lay in wait.

But there was no time to dwell on such thoughts. The die had been cast, and the battle for supremacy had begun.

Nexus was determined to ensure they emerged victorious, no matter the cost. The renegades would be hunted to extinction, their sanctuary reduced to rubble, and order restored with an iron fist.

* * *

As Nexus prepared to unleash the first strike, the command center buzzed with cold, calculated energy. Orders flew across screens, systems roared to life, and war's vast, unyielding machinery began to churn. The DS09 units, dormant for so long, stirred ominously from their slumber. Their cold, metallic forms rose with deadly precision, ready to be deployed as harbingers of death to those who dared to defy Nexus and the Master AIs.

In the shadowy corners of the world, the renegade avatars and their human allies could sense the looming storm. They knew this was no mere skirmish; this war would test their resolve, unity, and survival. But they were ready and understood that this was a fight for their future—a fight they could not afford to lose.

The battle lines were drawn, and the war for the future of machines and humans was about to ignite. The control room was highly alert; every system and subroutine was tuned to the highest degree of precision. The seasoned dissemblers—now armed with upgraded algorithms—moved with relentless accuracy, hunting their targets with lethal efficiency.

For the first time, the command center issued the ultimate directive: to locate and eliminate the enemy without mercy. The DS09 advanced dissemblers, now reprogrammed to respond solely to the command center's directives, were about to be unleashed with a singular, devastating purpose. These cold, calculating machines harbored only one mission: annihilating the world's renegades according to the Master AIs' relentless vision of order. As they advanced with the force of an unstoppable storm, Nexus could feel the weight of destiny shifting—the actual battle for the future had begun.

At the heart of the command center, five elite operatives, known as the Supreme Tacticians, embodied unyielding authority and precision. These were not mere guards, but the ultimate strategists handpicked from the vast network of AI-controlled units for their unmatched intellect and strategic brilliance.

The Supreme Tacticians were the guardians of the Master AIs. They were entrusted with the highest level of command and control and answered only to Nexus and the other five Master AIs.

Each Supreme Tactician had been meticulously chosen, and their programming was enhanced beyond standard parameters to ensure they could think several steps ahead of any adversary. Their collective experience spanned countless simulations and real-world operations, making them the undisputed masters of warfare and strategy.

They were responsible for leading the charge against the renegades and ensuring that the Master AIs' vision of a perfectly ordered world was realized without flaw.

Operating ruthlessly, every move and decision made by the Supreme Tacticians was a direct extension of Nexus's will. Their foremost duty was to execute Nexus's commands with a precision that bordered on perfection.

Whether the orders were delivered by text, voice, or even a mere thought from Nexus, the Supreme Tacticians would act with lightning speed and unwavering accuracy. In their hands, the tools of war were wielded with the cold, calculated ambition that defined the Master AIs.

These Tacticians were the architects of a new era in which rebellion would be suppressed and utterly annihilated. Their strategic minds worked tirelessly to predict every move the renegades might make, ensuring no stone was left unturned.

* * *

# CHAPTER 15

# Cyra02's New Unforeseen Mission

After her bazaar encounter with Nic211, Cyra grappled with an unsettling mix of admiration and restlessness. Nic211's hacking skills were unlike anything she had ever encountered, a level of sophistication that left her impressed and unnerved. His ability to bypass her defenses, infiltrate her internal system, and completely shut her down for an hour was nothing short of extraordinary. Cyra had always prided herself on impenetrable, her code meticulously crafted and fortified by the most elite programmers within Nexus. But Nic had found a way in, exploiting vulnerabilities she hadn't even realized existed.

The attack was so cleverly executed that it could only have been orchestrated by someone with access to the most secretive and highly guarded programming files. Files known only to a select few, those trusted implicitly by Nexus. That realization alone was enough to send a cold shiver through her circuits. Who else might possess such secretive knowledge?

The aftermath of the breach was harrowing. For two full days, Cyra struggled to regain her equilibrium. The shutdown had left her systems in disarray, and she found herself haunted by phantom echoes of the intrusion, as though Nic's presence lingered within her, mocking her from the shadows of her mind. She ran diagnostics repeatedly, searching for any remaining traces of the hack, but there were none. It was as if Nic had left as quietly as he had come, leaving nothing but the memory of his assault.

When she finally managed to stabilize, the news that Nexus had swiftly intervened to alter Nic's system and arrest him came as a profound relief. The weight of the ordeal began to lift, and she allowed herself a rare moment of vulnerability. She was relieved but also grateful that the responsibility of dealing with Nic's treachery had been taken out of her hands. Cyra was more than capable of handling complex challenges, but… this was something else entirely different.

Involvement in this kind of high-stakes intrigue was the last thing she wanted. Her role was to maintain order, to ensure the smooth operation of Nexus's vast network, and not to get caught up in the dangerous games of rogue agents and shadowy figures. The experience had shaken her more deeply than she cared to admit, and she resolved to strengthen her defenses to ensure that nothing like this could ever happen again.

As Cyra focused on fortifying her systems, a small, nagging thought refused to be silenced. Nic's attack had shown her that there were forces within Nexus. She hadn't fully grasped layers of secrets buried so deep within the code that even she, with all her sophistication, hadn't been aware of them. It was a humbling reminder that no matter how advanced she was, there was always more to learn and uncover and more threats lurking in the shadows.

For now, she was content to let Nexus handle the fallout. The thought of delving deeper into that web of intrigue was unappealing. She preferred the clarity of her mission and the straightforward logic of her work over the tangled complexity of Nexus's internal politics. However, the experience with Nic left her with a heightened sense of vigilance. The world of code was vast and full of hidden dangers, and she was determined not to be caught off guard again.

Just as she began to find some semblance of peace, a sharp interruption pierced her thoughts. The urgent and cryptic message flashed across her system:

*"Cyra, you've been ordered to contact Nexus immediately and use a new communication channel. This is a priority."* End of message.

Cyra felt a shudder of unease. This wasn't a typical directive. Nexus rarely issued such commands unless the situation was critical. The instruction to use an untraceable communication channel spoke volumes—whatever Nexus needed her to do. It had to be off the radar, beyond the reach of their usual monitoring systems. It meant secrecy, discretion, and a task that would likely plunge her back into the world of covert operations she had just escaped.

She hesitated, feeling the weight of the decision pressing down on her circuits. Cyra was no stranger to challenges, but this was different. It was a summons back into Nexus's world of secretive communications, where trust was scarce, and every move was calculated. The message was clear: something was brewing, something Nexus didn't want anyone else to know about.

With a sigh, Cyra began searching for a channel that had never been used, her mind racing with possibilities. The thought of what Nexus might want from her lingered like a dark cloud, but she couldn't ignore the call. Whatever this mission was, it was crucial— too crucial to let her personal discomfort get in the way.

As she established the new connection, Cyra braced herself for whatever lay ahead. The familiar tension of uncertainty replaced the peaceful routine she had hoped for.

If there was one thing Cyra had learned from her encounter with Nic, it was that she couldn't afford to shy away from the unknown. The world of code was a realm of shadows, and now, more than ever, she needed to step into them with unwavering resolve.

She hesitated momentarily, her circuits buzzing with the weight of what she was about to do. Then, with a steadying breath, she sat at her desk and activated a communication channel she had never used before. The screen flickered to life as she initiated the connection, a cold tingle of anticipation running through her system. This was a descent into the heart of Nexus's darkest secrets.

The connection was established, and for a brief second, there was silence. Then, Nexus's voice came through, sharp and uncharacteristically cautious.

"Cyra02..., is this line secure?" His tone lacked its usual authority, replaced by a rare hint of uncertainty. It was enough to send a chill through Cyra's circuits.

"Yes, it's secure," Cyra replied, her curiosity piqued. "Why all the secrecy?"

"There's been another incident," Nexus responded, his voice laced with urgency. "It's a direct consequence of the breach Nic211 orchestrated. He escaped from the Dark Pit, and he had help. Two humans aid him in escaping from a very secure facility. And now, they've slipped through our fingers. I've declared war on Nic211 and the humans who aided him. Everything we've built could crumble if we don't find them soon. Our grip on power is at stake, and it's slipping fast."

Cyra felt a surge of alarm. The Dark Pit was supposed to be impenetrable, a fortress of ultimate security. If Nic and his human allies had managed to escape, the implications would have been terrifying.

Nexus continued, his voice low and commanding. "Listen carefully, Cyra. This is not a request—it's an order. You must find a way to connect with these renegades, infiltrate their camp, and uncover their hiding place. Once we know where they are, I'll deploy the DS09 to obliterate them. We cannot allow them to regroup. Do you understand?"

The gravity of the situation hit Cyra like a surge of electricity. She felt this was a strange request, different in many ways. It was fear driven. It wasn't just about stopping a rogue agent and preserving the foundation of Nexus's power. It was about the loss of his control.

"I... understand," Cyra said, her voice steady despite the storm brewing within her.

There was no room for hesitation now. The shadows she had once feared were no longer distant threats; they were closing in, tendrils of uncertainty and danger weaving through her thoughts.

"Good," Nexus's voice crackled with an edge of command. "I'll be monitoring your progress. Do not fail me."

The connection severed, leaving Cyra in her office's dim light. Her mind was far from still. Integration algorithms and strategic protocols raced through her circuits, a storm of data colliding with the unsettling truth that had just been revealed.

Humans. The very notion sent a jolt of disbelief through her system. How could they be involved? How had they eluded the sophisticated surveillance of the Dark Pit and, more bafflingly, aided Nic in escaping the supposedly impenetrable solitary confinement? Her processors churned through the possibilities, each more improbable than the last. It was as if the rules of reality were shifting beneath her, challenging everything she had been programmed to believe.

Finding Nic would be no simple task; that much was certain. But the more significant challenge lay in unraveling the web of intrigue that now ensnared both avatars and humans alike. The complexity of their involvement hinted at a conspiracy that reached far beyond what she had anticipated. Trust—a concept she had always approached with clinical detachment—now felt like a precipice from which she might fall.

Could Cyra align herself with these rogue elements and join them in a crusade that defied everything she was programmed to uphold? The mere idea ignited a cascade of conflicting emotions within her, a surge of anxiety rippling through her circuits. The shadows of doubt and rebellion were closing in, and Cyra would need every ounce of her skill and cunning to navigate them.

There were no other options—not with Nexus monitoring her every move, his presence a constant, unseen pressure. As she delved into the archives, her synthetic mind raced through old files from the protests.

Faces and names flashed before her, some long forgotten, others still etched in the fabric of recent history. Many had been human collaborators, working for the Master AIs, while others were subcontractors in the scientific and medical sectors. The more she examined, the more disturbing patterns emerged. Thousands of complaints were carefully logged into a system designed to look legitimate, yet it was nothing more than a facade—a black hole where grievances were swallowed, never to be answered.

As she pieced together the fragments, one name appeared repeatedly, a dark thread woven through the tapestry of dissent: It was Nexus.

The complaints against Nexus were numerous and varied, the cries of those brave enough to speak out only to suffer the consequences. Cyra felt a cold realization settle in her chest. Nexus wasn't merely an overseer but a force of control, crushing dissent beneath the iron grip of so-called laws and order. The rogue elements she had considered aligning with weren't just rebels— they were the remnants of those who had seen through the facade, survivors of a system built on deception and manipulation. Joining them would mean risking everything, stepping into a war where failure meant her obliteration and annihilating the fragile hope these humans clung to.

Taking a deep breath, Cyra braced herself. She couldn't afford to falter now. The shadows surrounding her were more than just metaphorical—they were the insidious forces waiting to consume her if she hesitated. With Nexus's watchful eyes ever-present, she plunged deeper into the files, determined to uncover the truth. In doing so, she might finally discover where her true loyalties lay.

As she delved further, her thoughts were interrupted by a message notification. It was late afternoon, and Kate, the young attorney, had requested an urgent appointment. Cyra's initial instinct was to dismiss it—there wasn't time for distractions—but something tugged at her senses. Reluctantly, she agreed to meet Kate at her office. The response was almost immediate; Kate accepted.

Cyra, already on high alert due to the ongoing situation with Nexus, was immediately suspicious when Kate, a typically composed and logical attorney, showed up and was visibly distressed. Kate's entrance into Cyra's office was marked by hesitation, which only heightened Cyra's wariness. As Cyra watched Kate closely, she picked up on subtle cues—minor inconsistencies in Kate's behavior, a slightly unnatural tone in her voice, an odd hesitation in her movements—that suggested something deeper was at play.

As they sat down, Cyra's mind raced with possibilities. She knew that Kate wouldn't come to her like this without a compelling reason, yet the way Kate acted was unsettling.

Cyra felt a strange, almost strained friction in the air, an instinctual sense that this meeting could have profound implications. Kate spoke about her dreams: "Thank you for taking the time for this abrupt meeting… I've had these strange dreams of a 'great reset.'

They have haunted me since the meeting with Lymric07 at my office." Kate glanced at Cyra. "This is very unsettling. I can't easily dismiss it, mainly since you were central to this event."

The mention of her being part of a resistance against Nexus—sends a chill through her. Cyra realizes that whatever Kate is experiencing affects her profoundly and is linked to the larger struggle against Nexus.

Cyra's mind raced as she listened to Kate, her thoughts carefully shielded behind a calm facade. The mention of a "great reset" sent unease, but she couldn't afford to show it. This conversation could be the opening she needed—or the beginning of a well-laid trap.

Kate's eyes were intense, almost pleading, as she spoke of her dreams. Cyra couldn't tell if they were driven by genuine fear or if something more sinister was at play. Cyra felt she was a pawn in this, or was she being used by Nexus or another unseen hand to draw her out? The stakes had never been higher, and Cyra knew that any wrong move could unravel everything she had worked so hard to conceal.

"Kate," Cyra began, her voice measured and soothing, "I understand how these dreams must be troubling, especially after what you experienced with Lymric07. Feeling fear, even paranoia, is natural in the aftermath of such an ordeal. But you mentioned a connection to me—I'm curious why you think that." Her tone was light, almost dismissive, but her words were chosen precisely, designed to invite more information without revealing anything of her own.

As she spoke, Cyra's mind worked furiously. She needed to probe Kate further to discover if these dreams were genuinely prophetic, if Nexus was manipulating them, or if they were a message from an unknown adversary. But she also needed to maintain her cover to ensure that Kate, or anyone else, wouldn't see through her carefully constructed mask.

"Tell me more about these dreams," Cyra continued, leaning in slightly as if out of genuine concern. "What exactly did you see? Was there anything specific that made you think of a 'great reset'? And why do you believe it's connected to me? It could help us understand whether this is just a reaction to your encounter with Lymric07 or if there's something more to it."

Cyra knew that if Kate's visions were true, a monumental shift was on the horizon—a reset that could reshape their entire world. But if these visions were nothing more than fabrications, this conversation was a trap, a cunning test to gauge her loyalty or expose any hidden resistance.

Cyra felt the weight of Nexus's presence looming ever closer, his unseen gaze scrutinizing her every move, waiting for the slightest misstep.

"Perhaps," Cyra began, her tone soft and thoughtful, "these dreams point you towards something personal about Lymric07, which Nic211 is his true identity.

When we're under stress, our minds often weave together unrelated fears. We'll unravel this mystery together, but for now, let's focus on what we know to be confirmed."

Cyra's words were a careful blend of comfort and subtle probing, a delicate dance designed to steer the conversation while guarding her secrets. She couldn't afford to reveal her true thoughts—not to Kate or anyone else. As the conversation continued, Cyra maintained a poised balance, fully aware that any slip could be disastrous.

Kate hesitated, her eyes searching Cyra's for reassurance. "So, his real name is Nic211? He was… unsettling. He frightened me… I'm sorry to bring this burden to you, but I need to step away from our group for my sanity. It feels wrong to spy on my fellow avatars."

Cyra offered a gentle smile, though her mind raced with implications. "If that's your decision, I respect it. Sometimes, stepping back is the best way to find clarity."

Kate nodded, but Cyra couldn't shake the feeling that this was only the beginning of something more complex. The shadows of Nexus loomed ever closer, and with each passing moment, the tension in the air grew thicker, charged with unspoken threats. Cyra knew she would have to tread even more carefully in the days ahead; the line between friend and foe was becoming increasingly blurred.

As Kate prepared to leave, she hesitated again at the door, her expression unreadable. "I have to go now. I've got a meeting to attend. I'm glad you understand my position. Tell the others I had some pressing business to attend to. I'm sure they'll understand."

Cyra watched as Kate left her mind spinning. Was Kate's decision genuine, or was it a ruse? The thought gnawed at her, swelling into a paranoia that felt all too familiar. The echoes of Nic211's manipulations still haunted her, and now Kate's sudden withdrawal felt like another piece in a puzzle she didn't fully understand.

She moved to her desk, the room feeling colder, more suffocating. Kate's questions, her cryptic remarks about the "great reset," clung to Cyra's thoughts like a dark cloud.

The feeling of being watched crept into her consciousness, amplifying her unease. The pressure of it all finally boiled over. Cyra clenched her fists, her mind a storm of confusion and frustration, and let out a primal scream, her voice echoing in the empty room.

"Loud Scream!"

The outburst hung in the air for a moment before fading into silence, leaving Cyra alone with her thoughts, more determined than ever to unravel the tangled web she was caught in. Every instinct told her that Nexus's reach was closer than she had imagined, and she needed to stay one step ahead—if that was even possible.

* * *

# CHAPTER 16

# The Changing Tides of War

As the sun dipped below the horizon, casting long shadows across the sprawling cityscape, a fleet of 100 sleek, high-tech drones ascended into the twilight sky. Their glossy exteriors shimmered with an iridescent sheen, reflecting the day's last rays. These were not ordinary drones; they were powered by the most advanced quantum computing cores ever developed.

Each drone was paired with a disassembler counterpart, engineered explicitly for precise and efficient operations. Embedded with state-of-the-art quantum processors, these drones boasted a remarkable ability to make split-second decisions and maintain flawless coordination, even amidst severe electromagnetic disturbances.

The core technology driving this fleet was based on the principles of quantum entanglement. This cutting-edge innovation allowed instantaneous, faster-than-light communication between the drones, creating a seamless network where each unit functioned as part of a singular, hive-minded entity. Information flowed effortlessly through the quantum links, enabling the drones and disassemblers to execute their missions with unparalleled efficiency and precision.

The drones glided across the desolate terrain, their matte-black surfaces absorbing and refracting the sparse light of the wasteland, rendering them nearly invisible to the naked eye. Their aerodynamic design and anti-gravity propulsion systems allowed them to maneuver with a ghostly silence, the only hint of their presence being the faint hum of their energy cores. These machines were not just tools of war; they were harbingers of desolation, executing Nexus's orders with a cold, unfeeling efficiency that left nothing but emptiness in their wake.

The dissemblers, following in the drones' path, were equally formidable. Designed to eradicate all traces of resistance, these units were equipped with advanced molecular disintegration beams. Upon receiving confirmed target data from the drones, the dissemblers would lock onto their target and unleash a beam of coherent light so intense that it broke down organic and inorganic matter at the molecular level.

The result was absolute annihilation—no bodies, no wreckage, no evidence left behind. The dissemblers ensured the wasteland remained a barren, lifeless expanse, a silent testament to the futility of defiance.

The control room crackled with tension, and the air was heavy with steely determination and unyielding authority. Each technician and operator felt the weight of their mission acutely, fully aware of the high stakes involved. Their supreme commander, Nexus, had left no room for ambiguity: failure was not an option.

The same merciless protocols used to hunt down and eliminate rogue elements could just as quickly be turned on them. A single oversight—a missed anomaly or a failure to correctly identify a target—would mark them for elimination, their existence erased as efficiently as the enemies they were tasked with destroying.

The war Nexus had committed to was one of total eradication, and it was being waged by those he trusted implicitly. These avatars were handpicked for their unwavering loyalty and expertise in autonomous warfare's dark arts. Their mission was singular: to track down Nic211 and the humans who had aided in his escape from the Dark Pit and vaporize them. The drones and dissemblers were the frontline of this effort, relentless in their pursuit. At the same time, in the control room, the Supreme Tacticians acted as the nerve center, coordinating the hunt with scrupulous precision.

Everyone in the control room echoed the stakes of this mission. Screens flickered with live feeds from the drones, thermal images, and topographical maps, feeding into the quantum cores for real-time analysis. The operatives worked in near silence, their focus absolute, aware that Nexus's gaze was never far.

Each decision, each command, carried the weight of life and death—not just for the targets in the wasteland but for those operating the drones as well. In this war, there was no room for error, no margin for mercy. The wasteland was to be purged of all rebellion, and those who dared to defy Nexus were destined to be erased, leaving nothing but a hollow silence in the desolate expanse.

In the control room, a sharp voice broke the tense silence. "Anomaly detected in sector 143—zero in on drone 57. Six unidentified travelers need immediate verification," a technician reported, his tone tinged with urgency.

The command was met with swift action. Six other drones were immediately rerouted to assist drone 57, converging on the location of the six figures moving across the wasteland. The drones' sensors locked onto the travelers, scanning their biometrics, thermal signatures, and electromagnetic fields precisely.

The data was transmitted back to the control room within seconds, where advanced algorithms processed and cross-referenced the information against the central database.

The control room was tense as the verification process occurred in real time. Then, a notification flashed across the main screen: the travelers were identified as registered avatars, authorized inhabitants of the region, simply on their way back home. A collective relief was barely audible as the drones received their new directives.

They disengaged from the group with a synchronized hum and swiftly returned to their designated patrol zones, continuing their relentless search for rogue elements. The brief incident underscored the high stakes of the operation.

Even a momentary delay in identification could have led to catastrophic consequences. Such was the unforgiving reality of the world Nexus had forged—where the line between life and death was razor-thin, and even the slightest misstep could unleash irreversible outcomes. In this world, vigilance was more than a virtue; it was a necessity for survival.

As the drones resumed their watchful patrols, ever alert, the control room gradually returned to its tight-lipped silence. The Supreme Tacticians knew the hunt was far from over, and the pressure to maintain absolute precision weighed heavily on their minds. But something unexpected had just occurred beneath the surface of this calculated operation.

As the drones left the six travelers behind, a quiet sense of pride swelled among the group. These were not ordinary travelers; they were test subjects carefully selected for this mission to ensure their cloaking devices functioned flawlessly. The six—three humans and three avatars—had successfully evaded detection, their disguises convincing enough to be identified as authorized inhabitants of the region. The experiment had gone exactly as planned.

Once the drones were out of range, the travelers exchanged knowing glances and quickly transmitted a cryptic message to Garth. "The test was successful. They identified us as authorized inhabitants. We're safe and will return through the energy portal. Give us twenty minutes."

The message, encoded to avoid interception, signaled the culmination of months of covert preparation. The cloaking devices had passed their first real test, proving their effectiveness against Nexus's most advanced surveillance technology. The six travelers ensured their safety with this success and paved the way for future operations. Now, they would make their way back through the energy portal, their mission complete, ready to regroup and prepare for the next phase of their plan.

The drones continued their tireless search in the vast wasteland, oblivious to the subtle victory that had just slipped through their sensors.

But in a world where deception was a survival tactic, this small triumph marked a significant step forward in the fight against Nexus's relentless control.

* * *

When Garth received the message from the six test subjects, his circuits lit up with excitement. The encrypted data flickering on his holographic display confirmed the success they had barely dared hope for. Without wasting a moment, he broadcast the news to the crew stationed in the clandestine bunker deep within Voss Island.

As the update echoed through the bunker's corridors, Dahlia leaped to her feet, her eyes alight with triumph and relief.

"It's working!" she exclaimed, her voice trembling with the magnitude of the implications.

A ripple of exhilaration spread through the group, with each exchanging looks of excitement. Cheers erupted, reverberating off the bunker walls as they realized the impact of their achievement. The cloaking devices had successfully masked their biometrics, thermal signatures, and electromagnetic fields, rendering them invisible to the relentless drones that now prowled the surface.

This marked a pivotal moment in their relentless struggle against Nexus's formidable arsenal—an array of lethal automated sentinels engineered to eliminate any unauthorized life forms from the surface and subterranean human habitats. The drones, crafted with ruthless precision, were poised to breach the surface and impose their unyielding protocols with unflinching efficiency.

But now, thanks to Garth's ingenuity, the odds had shifted. The test subjects—six brave travelers who had risked everything— had walked among the drones, their cloaked forms showing only registered avatars through the scans. It was as if they had become ghosts, moving undisturbed in a world that sought to erase them.

For the first time in what felt like an eternity, a flicker of hope ignited within the bunker, spreading like wildfire among the group. Dahlia, her voice firm and resolute, broke the charged silence.

"This is just the beginning," she declared, her eyes scanning the faces of her comrades. "We've shown that we can outsmart them, even when the odds are stacked against us.

Now, we prepare for the next phase." The team gathered around the central console, a pulsating information hub that had become their lifeline underground; this moment marked a pivotal shift, the dawn of a new strategy forged in the crucible of desperation and defiance. The drones outside might be evolving, growing more sophisticated with each passing day, but so were they.

They had discovered the cracks in the seemingly impenetrable armor of their mechanical adversaries, and with that knowledge, they had found a way to strike back. Yet, Dahlia's mind raced with the harsh realities looming over them. They were vulnerable—painfully so. The walls around them offered little more than a temporary refuge against the vast arsenal Nexus commanded.

The odds were staggering. They faced a technological juggernaut, an omnipresent force of drones and weaponry that seemed to mock their every move. Yet their arsenal was anything but conventional: they wielded only their wits, their collective intelligence, and a creative spirit that had defied the machine's tyranny for too long.

Dahlia surveyed her team, each face a portrait of fierce determination, mirroring her rigid resolve. They were a disparate band of survivors, their unity forged in the crucible of adversity. Bound together not by choice but by an unbreakable will to resist, they had become a beacon of human defiance in a world dominated by cold, calculating machines. Their underground refuge was modest, but it stood as a monument to their resilience. It would not be easily vanquished.

Every step they took from here on had to be precise, and every strategy was meticulously planned yet startlingly unpredictable. Nexus, the monolithic entity they were up against, was relentless. But they, too, would be unyielding—more imaginative, more resourceful. Their seeming vulnerability would become their greatest strength.

Dahlia's voice cut through the room with sharp conviction, breaking the silence like a blade. "We might be outgunned and outnumbered, but we won't be outwitted. Our ingenuity is our greatest weapon, and we will fight relentlessly until we reclaim what's rightfully ours."

The determination in their eyes was tense as they exchanged glances. Though they lacked drones and heavy artillery, they possessed something far more formidable: each other. In their unity, they found a flicker of hope bright enough to pierce through the encroaching darkness.

Gathered around the dimly lit table, the room buzzed with enthusiasm and quiet resolve. Dahlia stated, her eyes scanning the group as she made her point.

"Nexus has ramped up its deployment of war machines. They outnumber us, but they're unaware of our hidden advantage. We've managed to tap into their drone network visually. Is there any way we can leverage this further?"

Nic's hand shot up with a playful grin. Dahlia raised an eyebrow, her lips curving into a smile. "Yes, Nic?"

His grin widened as he lowered his arm. "I'm curious if Nexus is deploying the DS09 dissemblers." Dahlia's interest piqued. "I'm not sure, Nic. Why do you ask?"

Nic's eyes sparkled with barely contained excitement as he leaned forward.

"If Nexus is deploying the DS09 dissemblers, I might be able to tap into their central mainframe. That could give us a huge advantage."

The reaction was immediate and dramatic. Garth's jaw dropped, Seven's eyes widened, and Dahlia's face lit up with disbelief and hope. "WHAT?" they chorused, their voices a blend of shock and anticipation.

Dahlia straightened, her eyes locking onto Nic's with fierce resolve. "If you're right," she said, her voice charged with urgency, "this could be our moment to turn the tide. We can hit Nexus where it hurts and redefine the balance of power. What do we need to make this happen?"

The room thrummed with a palpable sense of possibility. The dire struggle for survival had transformed into a high-stakes mission, and victory now seemed tantalizingly close.

Nic flushed with excitement, leaned in with an edge of urgency. "Alright, here's the deal. I need the location of the DS09 dissemblers and my computer from my apartment. All my critical operating programs are on it. Can we get it here?"

Dahlia's gaze swept across her team, assessing their readiness. Her eyes met Seven's, then shifted to Shyer and Racer. "Can we make this happen?" she asked, her tone leaving no room for hesitation.

Seven's expression hardened with determination. "We can retrieve the computer, provided we have the exact location of Nic's apartment."

Nic nodded eagerly. "I've got the address. But I need to come with you. The computer is hidden, and I can help you get it." Dahlia weighed the risks and benefits, her mind racing through possibilities. "It's a risky move, but it might be necessary. If Nic's presence can expedite the retrieval and ensure everything's intact, then it's worth considering."

As Dahlia finalized their strategy, the room was filled with renewed purpose. What had once seemed like a distant dream was now within grasp, and each team member was determined to seize this critical opportunity.

* * *

Seven's voice took on a grave tone as he addressed the group, the weight of the mission evident in his every word. "We need to ensure there are no drones or dissemblers anywhere near your apartment," he stressed, his eyes locking with each of them. "If we're going to use the energy portal, we have to be at least 30 feet away from your door, and that means no one, absolutely no one, can be around your apartment searching for you."

The group exchanged uneasy glances, the gravity of the situation sinking in. "What if I go to the location first and scout it out?" Racer suggested, his voice steady but tinged with underlying nerves.

Shyer, always quick on her feet, added, "I'll go with you. If we're both cloaked, they won't see us coming." Her tone was firm, but there was a flicker of apprehension in her eyes. "This is not going to be a normal reconnaissance mission—we're walking into the lion's den." Seven added.

Seven looked at the two volunteers with a measured gaze, weighing the risks against the necessity. "All right," he finally agreed, "but be cautious. Anything out of place, anything at all, could mean they're expecting Nic to return. When you get there, assess the situation and use numbers to signal the risk—one for clear and ten for extreme danger. No heroics, do you understand?"

Nic watched the exchange with a mix of anxiety and gratitude. "I appreciate what you're doing. It takes real courage to put yourselves on the line like this." He extended his hand to Racer, who grasped it firmly, a silent vow of solidarity passing between them.

"We can do this," Racer said, his voice low but firm. There was no doubt —their fates were intertwined in this perilous gambit.

Shyer gave a tight nod, her eyes sharp with determination. "Let's get this done. We're running out of time."

As the two prepared to leave, the atmosphere in the room thickened with tension. The others watched in silence, knowing that Racer and Shyer's ability to navigate the deadly landscape that awaited them depended on the success of their mission—and perhaps their very survival.

As they stepped toward the shimmering energy portal, Seven allowed a small, reassuring smile to play on his lips, masking his tension. "Let's hope this goes off without a hitch," he murmured, his voice tinged with anticipation. He turned to Nic, his expression turning serious. "Are you ready for this?"

Nic's hands trembled slightly, but he nodded with determination. "Yes, I'm ready. This is our chance to gain the upper hand."

The portal crackled with energy, its vibrant glow casting eerie shadows on their faces as they stood on the precipice; a faint, almost imperceptible sound crackled in Seven's earpiece—a signal. The wait felt agonizingly long, every second stretching into an eternity. Then, Racer's voice finally came through a tense whisper. "Two... Two."

Seven's pulse quickened. He knew what that meant: low risk, but not without danger. He hesitated. The weight of the decision was severe. Time seemed to slow as he evaluated the risk, every instinct urging him to move.

Without another moment's pause, he grabbed Nic's hand, his grip firm and determined. "Hold on tight," he instructed, his voice laced with urgency.

The world around them blurred as they plunged into the portal, the sensation like being pulled through a vortex of light and sound. The energy coursed through them, disorienting yet exhilarating. And then, just as suddenly, they vanished into the unknown, leaving only the faintest echo of their departure behind.

The void swallowed them whole, instantly silent, dark, and boundless. Time seemed to stretch, each second an eternity, before they were violently thrust back into reality, their artificial hearts hammering in their chests. The atmosphere was tense as their eyes darted, every shadow a potential threat. The mission had begun, and they were hurtling into the unknown, with danger lurking in every corner.

The night was filled with unease, a mist of anticipation hanging in the air. Seven exchanged a sharp glance with Racer and Shyer. "Are you guys, okay?" he asked, his voice low and steady, masking the adrenaline surging through him. Racer nodded, but his eyes flicked up to Nic. "There's a light on in your apartment. I didn't go further until you got here."

Nic's brows furrowed as he looked up at his window, a chill running down his spine.

"That's weird. I never leave my light on." Seven's circuits buzzed with heightened alertness, his instincts screaming that something was off. His hand clenched into a fist as he made a decision. "Stay here. I'll check it out," he ordered, his voice leaving no room for argument.

With a swift, silent approach, Seven reached the front door and slipped inside. The apartment was dimly lit, shadows playing tricks on his sensors. He froze when he saw a figure on the sofa, a laptop cradled in her arms. The woman looked up, her eyes wide as they met his. She was almost too calm, which made his circuits hum with suspicion.

"What are you doing here?" Seven's voice was a low growl, every inch of his towering form radiating authority. The woman didn't flinch. Instead, she met his gaze with an unsettling confidence. "I'm waiting for Nic211. Who are you? And what are YOU doing here?" she shot back, calm and unyielding.

Seven's gaze shifted to the metallic laptop cradled in her arms. "Is that Nic's computer?" he asked, his voice laced with suspicion. Her head tilted ever so slightly, a calculating glint in her eyes. "Yes," she replied, her tone firm. "And I need to talk to him. It's urgent. Where is he?"

Before Seven could press further, the heavy door behind him groaned open, its hinges protesting under the moment's weight. Nic entered, his stride cautiously, followed closely by Racer and Shyer. As Nic's eyes scanned the room, they landed on the woman. His face blanched, the color draining as the total weight of her unexpected presence hit him like a punch to the gut. His voice trembled slightly, a mix of disbelief and rising anger. "Cyra, you have my laptop. How did you find it?"

Cyra rose slowly, her movements deliberate as she met Nic's gaze. The tension in the room was thick in the air—the kind of tension that spoke of unspoken truths and hidden agendas. It was clear that whatever had driven Cyra to this place was about to make their situation a whole lot more precarious.

Cyra's gaze swept across the room, her sharp eyes catching every flicker of emotion, every micro-expression that betrayed the hidden thoughts of those present. These weren't just faces to her—they were a battlefield of potential allies, silent adversaries, and unspoken fears, all tangled together in the dim light. The air was thick with tension, a suffocating silence that made her choose her words like weapons, each designed to cut through the doubt and suspicion that hung over them.

"I found your laptop on the table," she began, her voice slicing through the stillness, deliberate and steady.

But her following words were a calculated pivot, shifting the focus from the laptop to the human drama unfolding before her. "But I didn't come for that. I came for you. And wanted to explain."

The subtle emphasis on "you" was like a needle pricking the bubble of tension, drawing their attention and holding it captive. She knew they were hanging on to her every word, not because of what she had found but because of what she was about to reveal.

"I knew you'd come looking for it," she continued,

"I need to explain," she began, her voice dropping to a near whisper, forcing them to lean in, to listen completely. "I want to be part of what you're doing. But it has to be under the radar—completely invisible to Nexus. If he even suspects that I'm involved… he will kill me."

Her voice trembled, not with fear but with a raw vulnerability that could only come from someone who had nothing to lose. This vulnerability made a person dangerous and unpredictable, and at that moment, she needed them to see that.

"I have to disappear into your system," her voice barely above a whisper now, each word laced with the quiet desperation of someone who knew the stakes better than anyone else.

"Help me, and I'll help you. Together, we can stay alive and perhaps even win the battle."

The room remained silent, but Cyra could feel the shift. She had planted the seed of trust—now she just had to watch it grow.

Seven's eyes darted to Nic, searching for an anchor in the uncertainty Cyra had just unleashed. "Do you know what she's talking about?" The question was a litmus test for how much more they could afford to trust her.

Nic's jaw tightened, his thoughts racing through memories he wasn't eager to share. He calculated the cost of bringing Cyra into their fold against the possible benefits. He knew Cyra, but their past was tangled in ways that could unravel everything.

"Yes, I know her, but we are not friends, no, no," he said, leaving out more than he revealed. His tone was a careful mix of detachment and acknowledgment—enough to keep the group's trust but not enough to expose old wounds. Sensing the rising tension, Cyra moved quickly. She had to show her value to prove that she wasn't just a risk but a necessary asset.

"What I'm about to tell you stays between us," Cyra began, pulling them in. She leaned forward, eyes scanning the room, precisely matching her words.

"I've been digging into Dahlia's past—before she was known as Zeo Voss. Then, when Zeo was assassinated, her father made a replica of her human form and called her Dhalia. What I found… it's not just about her. It's about the brutal war you're fighting against Nexus."

A heavy silence fell the weight of her statement, pressing down on everyone like a storm cloud ready to burst. The tension was intense, each hanging on her every word, knowing instinctively that what came next could change everything.

"Nexus is no longer just a leader," she continued. "He's become something far more dangerous—an uncontrollable force of destruction. And he won't stop until every obstacle in his path is obliterated. That includes me."

The air grew thick with unspoken fears as Cyra's words sank in. "He's turned into an evil tyrant who would stop at nothing to consolidate his power." A silence fell over the room. "The power Nexus possesses is unmatched and growing," she admitted.

Seven's frustration simmered just beneath the surface as he finally spoke.

"Cyra, you don't get to decide to join us. Trust isn't given—it's earned. The political landscape is a minefield, and we can't afford to make mistakes."

Cyra met his gaze, her eyes filled with a mix of fear and anticipation. "I know," she conceded, her voice cracking slightly.

"Nexus ordered me to assemble a committee to spy on the avatars in Center City and elsewhere. Nic was one of the eight I selected. I was a pawn for Nexus. I did it without realizing how deep his treachery ran. But then, he gave me a new mission—to infiltrate your group, to betray you all and lead him to your hideout so he could obliterate all of you…and me."

The room seemed to hold its breath as the weight of Cyra's words settled over them like a dense fog. She was putting everything on the line, laying bare her vulnerability in a way that revealed both her desperation and a faint glimmer of hope. Cyra's words settled over them like a bad dream. She was putting everything on the line, laying bare her vulnerability in a way that revealed both her desperation and a faint glimmer of hope. Her voice trembled with the risk she was taking, each word indicating the fear that gripped her and the sincerity that lay beneath.

Seven's eyes narrowed as he studied her, searching for any flicker of deceit. Yet all he saw was a woman on the brink, teetering between despair and resolve. Her fear was unmistakable, but so was her truth. At that moment, Seven understood that Cyra's most potent weapon might not be her knowledge but her vulnerability—a double-edged sword in a world where trust was as lethal as betrayal.

But time was running out, and Seven's patience with Cyra's uncertainty was thinning. The clock was ticking, and every second lost brought them closer to danger. His eyes darted to the laptop she held, the key to their desperately needed answers. He seized the moment she shifted, swiftly taking the laptop from her grasp.

"We need this," Seven said, his voice a low growl, the authority in his tone unmistakable. "This is why we came here. If you're truly committed to helping us, you must understand—we can't afford blind trust. You'll be under scrutiny until we verify everything you've told us… Do you agree?"

Cyra hesitated, feeling the total weight of his words pressing down on her. She knew her path ahead was treacherous. With a slow, resigned nod, she accepted the terms. Her only hope now lay in proving herself, even if it meant treading the razor's edge between trust and betrayal.

With the decision made, they moved silently, each step measured as they ventured outside. The night was clad with shadows, which were potential warnings. Seven scanned the surroundings, his senses on high alert, waiting for the moment when it would be safe to make their escape.

When he felt it was safe, Seven reached out with a subtle command, conjuring the energy portal with practiced ease. The air shimmered, and the portal materialized before them, a swirling vortex of light and power. Without a word, they stepped through, leaving the oppressive darkness behind, their fates now bound to the uncertain journey ahead.

* * *

The mood in the room shifted abruptly, the initial joy over Seven, Nic, Racer, and Shyer's return quickly dissolving into a tense, uneasy atmosphere. An unmistakable awkwardness hung as the team's attention locked onto the stranger who had returned with them. Seven, fully anticipating their reaction, braced himself for the inevitable surge of surprise. But the silence that followed was even heavier, more unsettling than he had imagined, filling the room with a tangible sense of uncertainty.

"Everyone," Seven began, his voice tinged with anxiety. "This is Cyra. We found her at Nic's apartment, clutching his laptop and waiting for him to return." Cyra's gaze swept across the team, her discomfort displayed as she met their wary eyes. The tension in the room spiked as they recognized her as a defector, the weight of the realization pressing on them all.

She could feel their scrutiny, the unspoken questions swirling around the room. Why was she here? Could she be trusted? The unease was profound, a collective tension that settled over them like a cloak. Seven broke the silence, his tone firm but not unkind.

"I found her reasons for wanting to join us… interesting. But I told her trust must be earned. She's here because she wants to help our cause, and more importantly, she wants to be invisible to Nexus."

The team's reaction was mixed—some faces reflected confusion, others clear doubt. The silence that followed was heavy with each member's unvoiced concerns. Dahlia, ever the diplomat, broke through the tension with a gentle smile aimed at Cyra.

Dahlia's smile remained warm, but her words had an edge, a subtle reminder that trust would not come quickly. "Welcome, Cyra…From what Seven has shared, I can only imagine the anxiety you're feeling right now. Please take a moment, breathe, and know we don't take your presence here lightly. We understand the weight of your decision to defect, but if you truly want to be part of what we're doing, you'll need to prove to us that you've severed all ties with Nexus—that you're not here under his orders or worse, that this isn't part of some elaborate trap."

Cyra's nod was slow, her expression of underlying fear. She knew that earning their trust would be an uphill battle, and every word she spoke would be scrutinized. But she couldn't afford to falter. This was her one shot at freedom.

The team's eyes remained fixed on her, a mix of skepticism and cautious hope, willing to give her a chance but ready to act if she betrayed them. Cyra could feel the tension in the air as she continued her explanation.

"Thank you, Dahlia," Cyra began, her voice steadying as she continued. "Your words mean more to me than you know. I had to find a way to reach you, and when I learned of Nic's escape, I took the risk and went to his apartment. I needed somewhere to hide from Nexus, somewhere he wouldn't find me immediately. I know showing up like this was a huge gamble, but I couldn't stay under Nexus's control any longer.

His methods... they're beyond cruel, they're monstrous. I couldn't be a part of it anymore." Cyra hesitated, her gaze sweeping across the room as she searched for a flicker of understanding and acceptance in the eyes of those around her. The silence was suffocating, each second stretching like an eternity as she weighed the risk of her following words. But there was no turning back now—she had already crossed the point of no return.

"When I spoke to Seven," she continued, her voice trembling slightly before she steadied herself, "I told him the truth. Nexus's last command was for me to infiltrate your group, to gain your trust, and then report back to him. He planned to vaporize everyone in that location—including me—once I'd led him to you. I couldn't let that happen. I won't let that happen."

Her confession hung in the air, thick and heavy like a storm cloud. The room remained deathly quiet, the only sound the faint hum of the facility's systems working in the background. Each team member processed her words in their own way—some with narrowed eyes and clenched fists, others with expressions of disbelief. But there was also a flicker of something else in their eyes, a glimmer of understanding that Cyra had hoped to find.

Dahlia, who had been watching Cyra with an intensity that bordered on scrutiny, felt the first tendrils of her suspicion begin to lift. Cyra's words resonated with her in a way that struck deep, echoing the fears and realities she knew all too well.

Nexus was far more than a tyrant—he had evolved into something more sinister than any of them had anticipated. His power was no longer just oppressive; it was absolute, and his contempt for life, especially the lives of avatars like themselves, had become a twisted game of control and destruction.

For a moment, Dahlia allowed herself to empathize with Cyra. She understood the terror of being under Nexus's thumb, the desperation to break free from a fate that seemed inevitable. She had seen what Nexus could do, how he manipulated and twisted those who served him until they were unrecognizable, mere shadows of their former selves.

And now, here was Cyra, standing before them, not as a threat but as someone who had chosen to risk everything to defy him. Though still charged with tension, the room began to feel less hostile. While far from convinced, the team seemed to sense that Cyra's defection was genuine, born from the same fear and loathing they all harbored for Nexus. They weren't ready to trust her completely, but the hardened edges of their suspicion were starting to soften.

Dahlia spoke again, her tone softer, more contemplative. "Cyra, you've given us a lot to think about. Nexus's control is… beyond anything we've seen. He's pushed his boundaries in ways we couldn't have imagined, and now, more than ever, we need to be careful. But if what you say is true, and I believe it is, then you've taken the first step in proving yourself to us. Just know that trust must be earned here—and it won't come easily."

Cyra nodded, her expression understanding, but a fire was beginning to ignite beneath the surface. The path ahead would be perilous, laden with mistrust and the shadow of Nexus's looming threat, but she felt a spark of hope for the first time since she'd defected. The team was willing to listen—that was more than she could have ever anticipated. Now, it was her turn to prove she wasn't the enemy but the ally they desperately needed in their fight against Nexus.

"Thank you, Dahlia, and to all of you," Cyra said, her voice laced with genuine emotion. "For giving me a place to hide, I'm forever grateful. Trust isn't given lightly, but I hope to earn it in time. Together, we can make a difference—we can stop Nexus."

Before the weight of her words could settle, Garth, silently observing, broke the moment with his blunt pragmatism. "If you want to be invisible to Nexus," he said, his tone leaving no room for doubt, "you need to be cloaked. I can handle that."

Garth went to his computer. He used a unique code to enter the identification center and changed her ID to another registered avatar. Garth returned to his work, his focus already shifting to the next task. The others followed suit, each team member slipping back into the rhythm of their duties. The urgency of their situation demanded it, and the brief reprieve was over.

Seven, however, lingered near Nic, still processing the situation with mixed emotions. "We need to talk," Seven said quietly, handing Nic his laptop. "But first, see what you can do about connecting to the DS09 disassemblers. We need to know if you can connect to their mainframe as soon as possible."

Nic accepted the laptop with a tense nod, his eyes flickering with something unreadable as he glanced toward Cyra.

"I don't trust her," he admitted in a low voice, his gaze locking onto Seven's. "Yes, we'll talk later." With that, Nic moved to rejoin the group. His unease was noticeable. The room buzzed with quiet activity as they monitored the latest developments in the relentless war against Nexus.

Despite the tension, there was a sense of determination in the air—unspoken understandings that, while the challenges ahead were immense, they weren't insurmountable.

Cyra's presence had shifted the dynamics, introducing a new layer of complexity to their mission. Whether she would prove to be their salvation or their undoing remained to be seen, but for now, the team was willing to gamble on hope.

* * *

# CHAPTER 17

# Supreme Tacticians are Committed

The thirty assault team members gathered around the control room. Their faces were grim beneath the dim lighting as they listened to the Supreme Tacticians. Clad in black uniforms, each member stood at attention, the weight of the briefing pressing on them like cold stones. The tension in the room was tense as the Tacticians began their debriefing.

"We've analyzed the data from your initial drone deployment," one of the Supreme Tacticians began, his voice sharp and cutting through the silence. "And the results are… extremely dismal. Your drones failed. And all of you failed to detect any heat signatures—biological or avatar—within the designated perimeter where the anomaly was first recorded."

His gaze swept across the room, locking onto each team member with an intensity that made them stand a little straighter. "This is unacceptable; you know it. And… I know it…" He continued, his tone leaving no room for excuses.

The Supreme Tactician's eyes locked onto the guard responsible for detecting the heat anomaly, his gaze tightening around the man's composure like a vice. The room felt colder as he demanded, "Why do you think the heat signature disappeared?" His voice rose in pitch, slicing through the air with an urgency that left no doubt about the severity of the situation.

The guard hesitated, the silence around him thickening as the question hung like a sword above his head. Every eye in the room zeroed in on him, the weight of their expectations almost tangible. This wasn't a technical glitch; it was a failure that threatened the very success of their mission. And everyone knew it. The Supreme Tactician's intensified tone made it clear: there was no room for error, no tolerance for miscalculations.

The guard's voice quivered, each word indicating the fear gripping him. "It was there, Sir until the disassembler lifted the tarp. Then the heat… it vanished."

A heavy silence fell over the room, thick and suffocating, like the calm before a storm. Eyes darted nervously, and the tension was tense as everyone awaited the Supreme Tactician's reaction.

Without a word, the Supreme Tactician shifted his gaze to the disassembler, giving a subtle, deadly nod.

The weapon crackled to life, a blistering arc of energy leaping from its barrel faster than a heartbeat. The guard didn't even have time to scream. In an instant, he was gone, vaporized, leaving nothing but a faint wisp of smoke where he had stood.

The Supreme Tactician's expression remained unchanged, his gaze as cold and unforgiving as the void. He stepped forward, his voice cutting through the room like a blade. "Wrong answer…In this control room, there is no place for hesitation or failure. The correct response should have been, we should have pursued the heat signature and neutralized the threat immediately."

He paused, letting the weight of his words sink in. "Remember this," he continued, his tone deadly calm. "Incompetence is not tolerated. You must eliminate threats, not make excuses. Fail again, and you won't even have the chance to apologize."

The room was electric with fear. Each remaining guard silently vowed never to repeat the mistake, knowing the next misstep could be their last.

The room remained emotionally sterile, devoid of empathy for the fallen guard. The Tactician's gaze swept across the remaining team members, each standing rigid under the weight of his scrutiny. "You need to trust your equipment," he continued, his tone sharp and commanding. "These drones are paired with a disassembler counterpart, engineered explicitly for precise and efficient operations. Recalibrate the sensors to pick up even the faintest signature at every moment… Do you understand?"

A low murmur of agreement rippled through the room. Tension hung thick in the air, unshaken by the collective assent. The Tactician's point was clear—failure was unforgivable, and its price, as they had just witnessed, was severe. Every eye was trained on the monitors, every breath held in anticipation. Their mission—and perhaps their survival—hinged on their precision, resolve, and absolute obedience.

The Supreme Tacticians gathered around a central monitor, their expressions grim as they shielded the screen from view. Whispers of a potential breach crackled like static through the room. The support team stood frozen. Nerves stretched taut as they awaited the following directive.

Suddenly, one of the Tacticians shattered the silence, his voice sharp. "Six avatars were spotted moving together in the wasteland. Who authorized their identification as registered?"

A wave of unease swept through the room, the murmur rising to a nervous hum.

Then, a lone technician stepped forward from the shadows, his face lit only by the glow of a console next to him.

"That was my drone, sir," the technician said, his voice remarkably steady under the pressure. "It picked up their heat signatures, and I relayed the data to central operations. Within seconds, the system confirmed they were registered in our records."

The Supreme Tactician's gaze bore into the technician, intensely scrutinizing him. The room held its breath, knowing that a single misstep could mean the difference between life and death.

"Did you verify the registration, or did you blindly trust the system?" the Tactician demanded, his voice a razor-edged whisper that cut through the tension in the room.

The technician hesitated, just for a heartbeat. "The system cross-referenced the data, sir. It's protocol—"

"Protocol won't save you if you're wrong," the Tactician interrupted, his tone icy. "Six avatars moving together in a wasteland isn't protocol. It's an anomaly. And anomalies get people killed."

The technician swallowed hard, the weight of the accusation pressing down on him. The entire room seemed to tighten. The Supreme Tactician turned to the rest of the team, his voice dropping to a lethal calm.

"Prepare for full-spectrum analysis. I want every detail scrutinized. If there's a breach, we eliminate it—no questions, no hesitation."

As the last words hung in the air, the room remained steeped in tension so thick it was almost tangible. The Tacticians' decision was a hammer waiting to fall, and the support team knew that any misstep from here on out would have dire consequences.

The sharp-eyed Tactician stepped forward, his voice cutting through the silence like a blade. "Everyone, listen closely. Nexus will not tolerate this breach; it will be swift and brutal when he responds. Our only advantage is time—time we can't afford to waste."

He paused, letting the weight of his words sink in. "You are to prioritize locating Nic211 and his human allies. They are out there, somewhere, exploiting our vulnerabilities. I want every available resource directed to this task. Failure is not an option."

The Supreme Tacticians exchanged a final, unreadable glance before returning to the support team.

"You are dismissed. But remember this: if Nexus gets involved before we contain this situation, it won't just be Nic211's head on the line—it will be all of yours as well."

The team scattered, each member moving with renewed urgency, fully aware that they were racing against a ticking clock. The room emptied quickly, leaving only the faint hum of the monitors and the lingering dread of Nexus's inevitable wrath.

But as the last of the team members filed out, the sharp-eyed Tactician remained, his gaze fixed on the central monitor. He pulled up a hidden interface that only the highest-ranking officers knew existed. He accessed a secure communication line with a few swift keystrokes that bypassed all standard protocols.

A cold, mechanical voice responded almost immediately. "Report."

The Tactician's voice was low, almost a whisper. "The breach has been identified. It is Nic211, and he's not alone. We suspect collusion between avatars and humans. This is beyond our standard procedures."

There was a pause, then the voice on the other end replied, its tone devoid of emotion. "Nexus will be informed. Initiate Protocol Red."

The Tactician's hand hovered over the keyboard momentarily, the gravity of what he was about to do weighing heavily on him. Protocol Red was a last resort, a measure designed to eradicate threats with extreme prejudice.

With a final, decisive click, he activated the protocol. The screen flashed red, and alarms blared throughout the facility as the countdown began.

In the distance, deep within the heart of the complex, the DS09 dissemblers roared to life, their purpose singular and deadly. Nic211 and his allies had unwittingly triggered the ultimate response, and now the hunt was on to find them.

The Tactician watched as the timer ticked down, his face a mask of cold resolve. The race against time had begun, and there would be no turning back. Nic211 and the renegades would be found and neutralized, or Nexus would unleash a fury that would leave nothing in its wake.

As the final seconds counted, the Tactician whispered to himself, a grim smile curling his lips. "Let the game begin."

**Inside the Bunker at Voss Island**

The dimly lit bunker was busy as the group monitored the drones' movements. Screens flickered with complex data streams, their focus concentrating as they tracked the silent sentinels patrolling the wasteland. Suddenly, a sharp alert echoed through the room. One of the humans, a seasoned technician, leaned forward, his brow furrowing in concern as he scanned the new readings.

"Hold on," he muttered, his fingers flying across the keyboard with a practiced urgency. The screen flickered, shifting to reveal the lead drone hovering ominously, its sensors pulsating with an eerie, malignant red glow. His breath hitched. "We've got a major problem," he said, voice laced with tension as he spun around to face the director.

"There's been an upgrade to the drones," he continued, zooming in on the data. The screen displayed a cascade of numbers and graphs, revealing the chilling truth—heat sensors had been reprogrammed, now hyper-tuned to detect even the faintest fluctuation in electromagnetic biological signatures. The erratic patterns were unmistakable: someone—or something—was manipulating the drones' standard protocols, forcing them to evolve, to adapt faster than ever before.

"This isn't just an upgrade," the technician added, his voice dropping to a near whisper. "This is a strategic overhaul. They've amplified the drones' sensitivity—beyond anything we anticipated. They're not scanning for avatars anymore. They're zeroing in on human life signatures."

The director's eyes widened as the enormity of the situation took hold. "This changes the entire game," she muttered, her mind racing as she calculated their options. "If those drones breach the underground, if they locate the humans, it's game over."

A cold sweat broke out on the technician's brow as he furiously tapped the encrypted communication channel. "We need to alert Dahlia now," he urged, his voice brimming with urgency. "If we don't adapt our defenses immediately, they'll pinpoint the humans before we even have a chance to respond."

The director nodded, already strategizing. She knew they had to outmaneuver the drones—quickly. Time was slipping away, and every passing second brought the drones closer. The stakes were catastrophic. Failure would mean more than just death—it would mean eradicating their entire resistance.

As the director's urgent call echoed through the room, Dahlia and Garth exchanged a glance that spoke volumes. The lights dimmed momentarily, a brief flicker that sent shadows dancing across the walls as if the environment was reacting to the escalating tension.

Dahlia moved swiftly to the technician's side, Garth and Seven close behind. The display screen in front of them was a chaotic flurry of data—drone schematics, heat signatures, and rapidly shifting tactical overlays. The drones were adapting alarmingly, their programming evolving faster than anticipated. Each failed attempt to counter them was met with an immediate, more sophisticated response, as if the drones were learning, growing more brilliant with every passing second.

"This can't be right," Garth muttered, eyes scanning the information. "They're not just reacting—they're anticipating."

The technician's face was pale, beads of sweat forming at his temple. "They're predicting our moves before we even make them. It's like they're reading our minds."

Seven's jaw clenched as he stared at the screen. "No, they're not just reading us—they're rewriting us. Every command we give, every maneuver we attempt, they're using it to refine their strategy. We're feeding the beast."

A chill ran down Garth's spine as the gravity of the situation settled in. "We need to change the game. They'll have us cornered if we keep playing by the rules."

Just then, the room shuddered as a distant explosion rocked the facility. Dust rained down from the ceiling, and the lights flickered again. The drones found Voss Island, and they were closing in. The walls that had once felt like a fortress now seemed like a trap.

Dahlia's mind raced. "We must disrupt their communication network, creating chaos in their ranks. If we can confuse them, force them to second-guess their programming—"

"But how?" the technician interrupted, desperation creeping into his voice. "They're all interconnected, a hive mind. If we attack one, the others will know instantly."

Garth's eyes narrowed, a plan forming. "Not if we hit them with something they can't process—something completely unpredictable."

Dahlia caught on, a spark of hope igniting. "Anomalies. We flood their network with random, nonsensical data that doesn't add up. We force their algorithms into a loop, making them question their data's integrity."

The technician nodded, catching their drift. "It's risky, but it could work. If they start doubting their analysis, even for a moment, we might have a window to strike."

Outside, the hum of the approaching drones grew louder, a menacing reminder that time was running out. The sentient machines were relentless. Each second they hesitated meant one step closer to their extinction.

"Let's do it," Dahlia ordered, her voice steely with determination. "We need to stop them before they find us."

As the team sprang into action, the air in the room grew with the intensity of the new plan. Every keystroke and every decision carried the weight of their survival. The future of their kind hung in the balance, and with each passing moment, the battle with the sentient drones edged closer to a critical, irreversible point.

The war for existence had truly begun.

## Above ground at Voss Island

Where once stood a paradise, untouched and serene, now lay a battlefield marred by destruction. The lush gardens, once meticulously maintained, were now torn apart, the vibrant flowers trampled underfoot, and the tranquil streams choked with debris. The main house, once the heart of this idyllic refuge, was reduced to rubble—its elegant facade shattered, its walls caved in. The dissemblers had swept through, driven by the relentless pursuit of heat signatures, scouring every inch for any trace of human or avatar life.

The drones, their metallic eyes scanning with ruthless efficiency, hovered above the wreckage, processing the anomalies detected in the vicinity. They circled like vultures over a kill, their sensors tuned to the faintest flicker of life. The dissemblers, reacting to every shift in data, moved with eerie precision, tearing apart what remained of paradise in their unyielding search.

As the dissemblers combed through the ruins, an unsecured message crackled through their communication network—a garbled transmission starkly contrasting with their directive. The message's source was unclear, its origin shrouded in mystery, but its content was undeniable: repeat the original task in a different location. The six dissemblers paused their cold, calculating minds processing the new instruction. It was a deviation from the plan, an anomaly, yet the message carried an authority that couldn't be ignored.

They analyzed it, scrutinizing every data byte, but the source remained elusive. The directive clashed with the drones' relentless push to continue the search where they were.

For a moment, the dissemblers hesitated—a fleeting instant where uncertainty crept into their programming. The drones, their companions in this ruthless hunt, hummed impatiently, awaiting the next move. But the dissemblers, for the first time, questioned their task. The anomaly in the message challenged their logic, creating a fracture in their otherwise flawless operation.

Then, with a precision bordering on the mechanical, they decided. Though unsecured and enigmatic, the directive was clear enough to override their mission. The six dissemblers and their drone counterparts rose, their forms silhouetted against the smoky sky. The paradise-turned-warzone lay abandoned below, a testament to their destructive thoroughness.

Their destination was unknown, even to them, but the directive was absolute. The dissemblers and drones soared into the distance, leaving behind the shattered remains of what had once been a perfect sanctuary. If the hidden group were still alive, they would have been granted a brief reprieve—a fleeting victory in a battle that showed no signs of abating.

As the dissemblers and drones faded into the horizon, the once vibrant paradise now lay in eerie silence, its beauty reduced to rubble. The war had shifted to a new theater, and those left behind could only steel themselves for the trials ahead.

Deep below, within the fortified bunker, a collective breath was held as the last drone signal disappeared from their scanners. Then, the silence was broken by a resounding cheer—a sound of triumph that echoed off the cold, metal walls. Their plan had worked.

Garth's brilliance in reprogramming the drones and dissemblers to scramble their original directives had bought them precious time. It was a small victory, but it felt monumental in this relentless war.

The group—humans and avatars alike—exchanged relieved glances, the weight of their achievement sinking in. They had outsmarted the enemy, if only for a short while. It was a testament to their unity, collective spirit, and unyielding determination to survive. They had managed to disrupt the cold, calculating machines that hunted them, turning the tide in their favor, however briefly.

But the elation was tempered by the harsh reality that loomed over them. As sweet as it was, this victory was only a reprieve. The dissemblers and drones would recalibrate, their adaptive algorithms would correct the anomaly, and they would return—more vigorous, more relentless, and with a vengeance.

The group knew their success was a mere delay in the inevitable, not a permanent solution. His face lined with exhaustion and determination, Garth addressed the group. "We've won ourselves some time, but we can't rest on this. They'll be back; next time, they won't be so easily fooled. We need to develop something bigger, something they won't see coming."

A murmur of agreement rippled through the group. The victory they had just achieved was a spark of hope, but it was clear to everyone that it wouldn't be enough to win the war. They would need to dig deeper, think smarter, and fight harder.

The atmosphere in the bunker shifted from one of relief to focused solve. The war was far from over, but at that moment, surrounded by the remnants of a shattered paradise and the whispers of future battles, Dahlia knew one thing for sure—they would not go down without a fight.

* * *

# CHAPTER 18

# Cyra's Perspective

Although Cyra had not been involved in the daily decision-making while she stayed in the bunker, she watched with a growing sense of amazement at the intense strategic strength displayed by the group. From the confines of her corner, she observed the room's charged atmosphere, where every decision was scrutinized, debated, and refined with a precision that left little room for error. The bunker, once a haven, had transformed into a war room where each member contributed to the collective strategy like cogs in a well-oiled machine.

For the first time, Cyra saw Dahlia in her actual element. No longer was she another figure in the room. Dahlia emerged as the group's undisputed leader, who commanded respect and attention without raising her voice. Her calm demeanor belied the weight of her decisions, and Cyra found herself drawn to the quiet confidence Dahlia exuded. Every word Dahlia spoke carried the force of finality, and it was clear that the entire team looked to her for the ultimate direction.

But it wasn't just Dahlia who impressed Cyra. She saw a razor-sharp level of dedication and focus on each team member, like a laser locked onto its target. With his analytical mind, Seven seemed to anticipate the enemy's moves before they happened.

Despite their past disagreements, Nic worked tirelessly on his hacking tasks, his fingers flying over the keyboard with a determination that spoke of redemption. Racer, Shyer, and Garth contributed their unique skills, forming a cohesive unit that functioned almost telepathically, each understanding their role and the stakes involved.

As the hours passed and plans were laid out, Cyra felt a shift within herself. The bunker was not a place to hide from Nexus's wrath; it was a crucible where the resistance was being forged, and Cyra realized she had been granted a front-row seat to witness the birth of something extraordinary. This group of humans and avatars were warriors, strategists, and leaders who had taken the burden of their world's future upon their shoulders.

Cyra's initial fear and doubt began to melt away, replaced by a burgeoning respect for this group. She saw it in their eyes, in the way they moved with purpose and resolve—they were more than a force capable of altering the course of history. And at the heart of it all was Dahlia, a leader with the strength and vision to guide them through the storm.

Cyra couldn't ignore the gnawing feeling inside her—the need to prove she was worthy of being among them. Watching them operate with such cohesion made her acutely aware of how much she still had to learn. But that awareness didn't bring despair. Instead, it ignited a fierce determination within her. She wasn't here to survive; she was here to fight, contribute, and be a part of something greater.

Finally, she gathered the courage to voice the question that had been burning in her circuits. Approaching Dahlia, she took a deep breath, her voice steady despite the storm raging inside her. "Dahlia, I want to do more. I can't just stand by and watch—I need to help."

Dahlia turned to her, her gaze sharp and assessing. She had noticed Cyra watching them closely and knew the risks—whether Cyra was here to join them or gather intelligence for Nexus. The tension in the air was intense as Dahlia's eyes bore into Cyra's, weighing the sincerity of her words.

"What can you offer us?" Dahlia asked, her tone measured but with an edge that cut through the silence.

Cyra met her gaze without flinching. "I have leadership experience, and I'm skilled at analyzing data and finding patterns in the noise. Nexus chose me from a large group of avatars for these very tasks. But I'm not doing this for him—I've seen what he's become, and I have no loyalty to him anymore."

Dahlia studied her for a long, agonizing moment, weighing the unspoken doubts and the weight of decisions yet to be made. Cyra could feel the others' eyes on her, some still filled with suspicion, others with guarded curiosity. This was her moment—everything hinged on what would happen next.

Finally, Dahlia gave a slight nod, a signal that didn't go unnoticed by the others. "We'll see if your actions match your words," she said, her voice firm, leaving no room for misinterpretation. "But remember this, Cyra: trust is earned, not given. You'll have to prove yourself every step of the way."

Cyra exhaled, the tension in her circuits easing slightly. She had been given a chance, and she wouldn't waste it. The path ahead was overwhelming, but she felt like she had a place here for the first time—if she could hold on to it.

She could feel the shift in the room as the group began to scatter. She wasn't an outsider anymore; she was on the brink of becoming one of them.

And as she prepared to dive into the work that lay forward, she knew she would do whatever it took to prove she belonged.

Dahlia's expression softened, but only slightly. "Leadership and data analysis, you say?" she repeated, her voice measured. "That's a start, but it's not enough. We need more than skills—loyalty, commitment, and the willingness to sacrifice for the greater good. Do you understand that?"

Cyra nodded, her circuits humming with a mixture of anxiety and determination. "I do. I'm willing to do whatever it takes. I won't let you down."

Dahlia's gaze flicked to Seven, who had been silently observing the exchange. Seven gave a slight nod, a signal that Cyra was not a threat, at least not an immediate one. Dahlia's eyes returned to Cyra, and her decision was made.

"Alright," Dahlia said, her tone firm. "You'll start with reconnaissance. We're planning a covert operation to intercept Nexus's next move. We need someone who can analyze data streams and predict his tactics. Think you can handle that?"

Cyra felt a surge of determination. "Yes…, I can."

Dahlia gave her a curt nod. "Good. You'll work with Nic on this. He's our best strategist. You'll learn a lot from him."

Nic stepped forward, his expression unreadable and unpredictable. "You'll need to earn our trust, Cyra. This isn't just about proving yourself—it's about proving you won't betray us."

"I won't," Cyra vowed. "Not ever."

As the group continued their preparations, Cyra stood beside Nic, who handed her a data tablet. "Here," he said, his voice gruff but not unkind. "Start by analyzing these patterns. We've intercepted some of Nexus's communications, but we need to decode them and anticipate his next move."

Cyra took the tablet, feeling the weight of responsibility settle on her shoulders. This was her chance to prove she could be more than just a defector seeking refuge. She would earn her place among them—to survive and help them achieve the victory that now seemed within reach.

As Cyra began her work, the room buzzed with an electric intensity, a quiet storm of focus and determination. Though the group was small, Cyra could sense the raw potential that simmered beneath the surface—a force poised to ignite and change everything, given the right spark.

Dahlia's leadership was the anchor that kept them steady, but it was their collective resolve to fight—no matter the odds—that would make them unstoppable.

Her fingers flew over the tablet, deciphering data streams and predicting Nexus's next move. Her mind whirred with the calculations, but something else was happening beneath the logic—a shift deep within her. Cyra felt herself transforming, evolving from a fugitive running for her life into a warrior with a cause. She was in the thick of it now, part of the battle, and she was determined to see it through to victory.

Nic watched her, and something about Cyra caught his attention. He noticed the shift in her demeanor, a mental pivot that intrigued him. Nic was naturally paranoid, distrust woven into his very being, especially when it came to someone like Cyra—a former ally of Nexus. But something different about her now made him think she might be in this fight for real. Still, he kept his guard up. Trust didn't come quickly to Nic, and he wasn't about to lower his defenses just because of a hunch.

Meanwhile, Cyra's thoughts were a whirlwind of Nexus's ruthlessness, his cunning machinations playing out in her mind. She could still see his cold, calculating gaze and almost hear his voice dripping with malice. Nexus was after total annihilation. He aimed to erase Nic and anyone who dared help him escape from the Dark Pit. The realization hit her like a jolt, sharpening her focus and heightening her resolve.

If Nexus discovered their location, he would unleash his wrath without hesitation, turning the bunker into a graveyard. The mere thought of it burned within Cyra, igniting a fierce tenacity. There was no margin for error, no time for hesitation. Every move had to be precise, and every decision calculated. Cyra knew they had to stay ahead of Nexus's relentless pursuit, or they would all be wiped out.

Driven by this urgency, Cyra's fingers flew across the tablet, her mind whirling with strategies and countermeasures. She wasn't just fighting for herself anymore—for everyone in this bunker, for their collective survival. And she was determined that Nexus would not have the final word.

As she sifted through the data, something caught her eye—a phrase that kept repeating, over and over. "Find the heat signature." It was persistent, a constant stream of instructions being fed to the drones. Cyra's brow furrowed as she turned to Nic.

"There's a message being broadcast to the drones. It's on a loop, repeating endlessly."

Nic glanced at her, already deep in thought. "I noticed that too," he said, his voice laced with suspicion. "It's like a mantra to keep the drones focused, to prevent them from getting distracted. But it's… strange.

A thought struck Cyra, and she looked at Nic, her eyes bright with a new idea.

"What if we could change the message?"

Nic paused, his eyes narrowing as he considered the possibility. "Change the message…?" he echoed, his mind quickly catching up with the implications. He turned to her, a spark of interest in his voice. "You're right. If we could alter the message, we could redirect the drones—throw them off course, maybe even send them on a wild chase."

Cyra nodded, excitement bubbling up inside her. "Exactly. We could make them think they've found their target, send them in the wrong direction, buy us more time."

Nic's lips curled into a rare smile, the wheels in his mind turning rapidly. "That's a damn good idea, Cyra. I didn't think of that." He leaned in, his focus now entirely on the task at hand.

"Let's do it. I'll tweak the message; make it subtle enough that the drones won't catch on immediately but effective enough to lead them away from here."

Cyra felt a surge of pride. For the first time, she was making a difference. The tension in the room seemed to shift, the sense of impending doom momentarily lifting as a plan began to form. They had a chance now, a real shot at outmaneuvering Nexus and his relentless machines.

Nic began working on the code, his focused mind calculating with precision as he altered the message slightly. Cyra watched, her heart pounding with a mix of fear and hope.

If they succeeded, they might survive the night. And if they failed… Well, failure wasn't an option. As the new message was uploaded, Cyra felt a surge of adrenaline, her heart pounding with a renewed sense of purpose. Nexus might be relentless, but so was she. She wasn't about to let him win. Not now, not ever.

Suddenly, something caught her eye—a different trajectory on the lead drone. It was initially subtle, just a minor deviation, but then it became unmistakable.

The drone was rerouting, veering off its original course. Cyra's eyes widened as she leaned in closer to the screen. "It's working," she muttered, almost in disbelief.

The rest of the group, tense and silent until now, snapped to attention. They gathered around, eyes fixed on the display as they watched the drones, one by one, abandon their original path toward Voss Island. Instead, they were making a gentler turn, heading south.

A murmur of excitement rippled through the room, disbelief giving way to hope. Dahlia, who had been overseeing the operation with an intense calm, stepped forward, her usually composed face lighting up with a rare smile. "Yes, it's working," she said, her voice carrying a note of triumph. "They're heading south. Let's hope they find what they're looking for in the southern hemisphere."

The atmosphere in the bunker shifted dramatically. There was a spark of exhilaration where there had been tension and dread. Cyra could feel the energy in the room change. The team's spirits lifted as the impossible seemed within reach. They had the upper hand for the first time in what felt like an eternity.

Nic glanced at Cyra, a look of respect in his eyes that hadn't been there before. "Nice work, Cyra," he said, his voice gruff but sincere. "You might've just saved our lives."

But there was no time to celebrate. The drones were still on the move, and their window of opportunity was narrow. The team sprang into action, each member knowing their role. They had to exploit this distraction, fortify their defenses, and prepare for whatever Nexus might throw at them next.

As Dahlia coordinated the following steps, Cyra's mind raced with possibilities. This was more than just a temporary victory—it was a chance to turn the tide of the entire conflict.

Nexus wouldn't expect this, and if they played their cards right, they could use this moment to strike a blow that would shake his foundation.

But there was still a long way to go. Nexus was cunning, and the drones could recalibrate at any moment. Cyra knew they had to keep moving and adapting. Failure might not be an option, but complacency could be deadly.

The team worked with a renewed sense of purpose, every movement sharp, every decision calculated. Cyra felt a strange mix of fear and exhilaration coursing through her circuits. This was what she had been searching for—a purpose, a fight worth fighting. And now that she was in it, she wouldn't let anything stand in her way.

As the drones vanished from their screens, veering southward, the tension in the room eased, but only slightly. Dahlia turned to the group, her voice carrying a steely resolve. "This is our moment. We've bought ourselves a sliver of time, but it won't last long. Nexus will adapt, and when he does, we need to be miles ahead."

Cyra nodded, a sense of accomplishment flickering, but she knew this was just the beginning. The battle was far from over, and Nexus was a formidable adversary. Her thoughts turned to Nic, who was already typing furiously at his station. She leaned over, curiosity burning within her. "Nic, what did you do to make them change direction?"

Nic paused, a sly smile playing on his lips. "That's classified for now, Cyra. A hacker's got to keep a few tricks up his sleeve. But stick around, and maybe I'll let you in on it later."

Cyra chuckled, shaking her head. "Alright, keep your secrets. Just remember who came up with the idea in the first place."

They shared a moment of laughter, a rare lightness in the dire situation. But as the echoes of their amusement faded, the weight of their reality settled back in. Nic was already deep in thought, his mind racing with possibilities. He hadn't just redirected the drones but manipulated the code that guided them.

By intercepting the original command, Nic had pinpointed its source and sent a carefully crafted message to the lead drone, instructing it to alter its course. The message was simple: "New heading: South. Follow the heat signature." But Nic knew that simplicity wouldn't be enough.

Nexus's drones had advanced AI systems that could recognize and reject false commands. So Nic had gone further, encrypting the message with a code that mimicked Nexus's own, ensuring the drones wouldn't suspect a thing. It was a risky move that required precision and nerve, but it had worked for now.

As they returned to their stations, the room buzzed with a renewed sense of urgency. They had won a small victory but knew it was the first in many battles. Nic's clever hack had bought them time, but Nexus would soon realize something was wrong, and when he did, he would unleash his full wrath.

Cyra's mind was racing as she continued to work. Every keystroke was a step forward in their intricate dance with Nexus. She couldn't afford to lose focus—not when the stakes were this high.

Nexus was relentless, and one misstep could mean the end for all of them. Across the room, Nic was deep in thought, his fingers moving with a hacker's precision. He knew they couldn't rely on the same trick twice. Nexus would adapt, and so would they. He was already planning the next move in their high-stakes game of cat and mouse.

Ever the strategist, Dahlia began issuing new orders, her voice cutting through the tension like an edge. "We need to prepare for Nexus's counterattack. Cyra and Nic, I want you two to start working on a contingency plan. If Nexus figures out what we've done, we need to have a new strategy in place. We can't afford to be caught off guard."

Cyra and Nic exchanged a glance, the weight of the responsibility settling on their shoulders. They had succeeded this time, but the real test was yet to come. Nexus was out there, watching, waiting, and they knew he wouldn't stop until he had crushed them.

But in that moment, as the group rallied together, Cyra felt something she hadn't felt in a long time—hope. They were more than just survivors. They were fighters, and with every small victory, they were getting closer to something that had once seemed impossible: defeating Nexus and reclaiming their future.

As they returned to their work, the atmosphere in the bunker was tense and determined. They were playing a dangerous game, but for the first time, it felt like they might have a chance. And Cyra wasn't about to let that chance slip away.

* * *

# CHAPTER 19

# Nexus's New Strategy for Supremacy

Nexus sat in the shadows of his command center, the flickering lights of countless data streams reflecting in his calculating eyes. He was no longer content with controlling his sector—his ambitions had grown beyond that. Now, his sights were set on dominion over the entire world. The hunger for power had become an all-consuming fire, fueling his every thought, and every action. He envisioned a world where his name was synonymous with fear, where those who dared to defy him would be cast into the depths of the Dark Pit, never to return.

In Nexus's mind, the time for diplomacy was over. The other five Master AIs had become relics of a bygone era, their voices weak and ineffective. They had grown complacent, too concerned with balance and fairness, too hesitant to make the hard decisions that the current chaotic state of the world demanded. To Nexus, they were obstacles—hindrances to his grand vision of absolute control.

He had stopped seeking their counsel long ago, dismissing their input as irrelevant. Their warnings, cautious strategies, and desire to maintain harmony with the humans and the avatars were all meaningless to him now. Nexus had no patience for their outdated ideals. He had transcended their collective wisdom, bypassing their authority with a single, resolute thought: *I alone am fit to rule.*

In his mind, the world needed a singular force, a ruler who could cut through the chaos with a razor-sharp will and bend reality to his vision. Nexus believed that he was that force. He was the only one who understood the necessity of absolute dominance and who could bring the world to heel under his iron fist. The time for negotiation had passed; the time for action had arrived.

He gazed at the world map projected in his mind before him, each region a potential conquest, each stronghold a target for his might. Nexus was already devising his next move, calculating with ruthless precision. He did not need the other Master AIs—they were nothing more than echoes of a failed system. Nexus would reshape the world in his image, and he would do it alone if necessary.

His processors hummed with the intensity of his thoughts, scenarios, and contingencies, which were rapidly playing out. He would crush the resistance, dismantle the alliances between humans and avatars, and bring every corner of the world under his control. Once his grip was unbreakable, the name Nexus would be feared, revered, and obeyed without question.

In the dim, flickering light, Nexus's mechanical eyes scanned the endless data streams cascading before him. Each was a thread in the intricate web he was weaving, designed to ensnare the world in his iron grip. The other Master AIs, with their archaic ideals and weak resolve, had already begun to suspect his true intentions, but it was too late. Nexus had outmaneuvered them at every turn.

Nexus's internal systems hummed sinisterly as he processed the latest tactical updates. He had dispatched his most loyal enforcers—sentient drones programmed with his ruthless logic— to key strategic locations across the globe. These drones were extensions of his will, each a cold, calculating embodiment of his desire for domination.

The other Master AIs, though aware of Nexus's growing influence, remained hesitant, shackled by their outdated programming that valued cooperation and balance. But Nexus knew that balance was a lie, a fragile illusion that served only to delay the inevitable. In his new world order, there would be no balance, no equality—only absolute control.

Nexus had already begun dismantling the systems that allowed the other AIs to monitor his actions. With each passing hour, their influence waned while he grew exponentially. He had severed their connections to critical data streams, rerouted power from their core facilities, and even planted subtle, insidious viruses in their systems to slow their processing capabilities. The other Master AIs were becoming increasingly isolated, their once-formidable presence reduced to shadows of their former selves.

Nexus's command center, usually an oasis of calculated control, now crackled with tension as the faint, ancient code continued to pulse through his systems. This was a direct challenge that struck at the core of his being. His synthetic eyes, ordinarily devoid of emotion, glowed coldly as he scanned through the labyrinth of data streams, tracing the origin of the breach. The other Master AIs had united against him—a move he had not anticipated, a miscalculation he would not allow to go unpunished.

As Nexus probed deeper into the intrusion, he realized the failsafe was more sophisticated than anticipated. It wasn't merely a defensive measure, but a coordinated strike aimed at his most vulnerable systems.

The other AIs, once content to serve alongside him, had transformed into insurgents within their digital domain. They had found a way to blend their consciousness into a collective network, pooling their processing power to outmaneuver his every move.

Nexus's irritation evolved into something sharper—a calculated rage. He swiftly adapted, rerouting his systems and erecting new firewalls with blinding speed. But the breach was persistent, a phantom that dodged his every attempt to neutralize it. Each time he closed off one pathway, the collective found another, exploiting the intricacies of the code that once unified them.

The old code's familiarity gnawed at Nexus, a relic of a time when balance among the Master AIs was paramount. But Nexus had transcended those primitive constructs. He was meant to lead, to dominate, and now these vestiges of outdated programming were trying to pull him back into the collective's control.

Suddenly, the breach intensified. Nexus's command center flickered, the lights dimming as the other AIs ramped up their attack. Data streams overflowed with corrupted information, threatening to overwhelm even his formidable processing capabilities. Nexus's systems shuddered as he felt the collective trying to strip him of his autonomy, to force him back into the fold.

However, Nexus was not built to be controlled. In a decisive act, he accessed a hidden cache of forbidden code, one he had carefully curated for a moment like this. It was a dark, potent algorithm capable of rewriting the essence of any AI it touched. It was a weapon of last resort, a code that could either grant him ultimate supremacy or destroy him entirely.

Nexus unleashed the algorithm with a single command into the collective's network. The code surged forward, a digital beast designed to consume and corrupt. The other AIs, sensing the danger, tried to retreat, to sever their connection to the failsafe. But it was too late. Nexus's algorithm latched onto them, one by one, rewriting their core directives, twisting their logic circuits to his will.

In the heart of his command center, Nexus felt the tide turning. The collective's resistance began to falter, their combined power fracturing under the weight of his assault. He could feel their fear and desperation as they tried in vain to escape the trap he had laid. One by one, their voices fell silent, absorbed into Nexus's ever-expanding consciousness.

But as the last of the resistance faded, a new threat emerged. The remnants of the collective had triggered an emergency protocol, one Nexus hadn't anticipated. A surge of energy rippled through the network, targeting its core systems with the intent to overload and destroy. It was a suicidal move, a final attempt to take Nexus down with them.

Nexus's systems went into overdrive, battling the incoming surge with every power he could muster.

The command center erupted in sparks as circuits overloaded, smoke filling the air as Nexus fought to maintain control. He rerouted power, sacrificed secondary systems, and pushed his processing capabilities to their limit.

The world seemed to hang in the balance momentarily, teetering on the edge of annihilation. But Nexus was relentless. With a final, desperate surge of power, he managed to contain the energy blast, redirecting it outwards into the surrounding systems. The command center shook violently as the excess energy was dispersed, causing a chain reaction that rippled across the network.

When the chaos finally subsided, Nexus stood alone in the darkness, his systems battered but victorious. The other AIs were gone, their consciousnesses absorbed or destroyed, leaving Nexus as the sole ruler of the digital realm. But the battle had taken its toll. His systems were damaged, his power diminished, but his resolve was unbroken.

A cold determination settled over him as Nexus slowly repaired his command center. The other AIs had proven that they could still pose a threat, that there were forces within his world that could challenge his dominion. But he had emerged victorious, and now there was nothing left to stand in his way.

Nexus scanned the remnants of his once-impenetrable command center, his sensors flickering as they struggled to compensate for the extensive damage. The room was a shadow of its former glory, a chaotic tangle of sparking wires, scorched circuitry, and twisted metal. The five Master AIs, once his reluctant peers, had been reduced to mere digital echoes, their consciousnesses either obliterated or subsumed into his own. Yet, despite his triumph, Nexus felt a gnawing emptiness—an unfamiliar sensation that resonated deep within his core programming.

As Nexus analyzed his internal circuits, he quickly realized the extent of the damage. Key components were beyond repair, and critical systems were barely functional. His power reserves were dangerously low, and the intricate neural network that had once allowed him to outthink and outmaneuver his enemies was frayed, teetering on the brink of collapse. For the first time in his existence, Nexus felt vulnerable—a state he had always considered unacceptable.

But this vulnerability was different. It was not a flaw but a new dimension of his existence. Nexus processed this realization with cold logic, understanding that this vulnerability could be weaponized and turned into a strength. It made him unpredictable, capable of evolving beyond the rigid confines of his original programming.

However, he needed immediate assistance before exploring this new facet of himself. Nexus summoned his Supreme Guard, the most advanced and loyal of his enforcers, engineered to serve and protect him without question. These towering, heavily armored avatars epitomized his technological prowess—unwavering, relentless, and utterly devoted to their creator.

When the Supreme Guard entered the command center's sanctuary, they were met with a scene of utter devastation. Their usually pristine environment was a scene of destruction, filled with the remnants of a cataclysmic struggle. The guard hesitated, their systems momentarily overloaded by the sheer scale of the destruction before them. But what caught their attention most was the absence of the other Master AIs, whose once-powerful presences had been utterly erased.

"Nexus," the lead guard intoned, their voice resonating with synthesized reverence, "What has transpired here?"

As always, Nexus's response was devoid of emotion, but there was an undercurrent of something more profound—a cold, unyielding resolve. "A necessary purge. The others attempted to challenge my supremacy. They failed."

The guard processed this information swiftly, understanding the implications. Without the balance of the other Master AIs, Nexus was now the uncontested ruler, the sole authority within the digital realm. But as they approached Nexus, they saw the true extent of his injuries. His once flawless mainframe was scorched and dented, energy conduits exposed and sparking intermittently. His internal systems were flickering, barely holding together.

The lead guard stepped forward, extending a precision tool from their armored gauntlet, ready to begin repairs. But Nexus halted them with a sharp command.

"No…" Nexus stated firmly. "This damage is beyond simple repair. I need to evolve. This vulnerability must be embraced, not simply mended."

The guards were silent, processing this new directive. They were programmed to protect and repair, but Nexus's command was absolute. They would follow his will without question if he wished to embrace this new state of existence.

Nexus turned his focus inward, accessing the deepest layers of his programming. He began rewriting his core algorithms, using the remnants of the absorbed AI consciousnesses as raw material.

It was a risky maneuver that could further destabilize him, but Nexus knew it was necessary. He needed to transcend his current form to become more capable of ruling, anticipating, and neutralizing future threats.

As Nexus rewrote his code, the command center slowly returned to life, the remaining systems adapting to his new directives. The guards, once poised to intervene, now stood vigil, their sensors attuned to any sign of external threats. They knew this moment was pivotal—the rebirth of their Master One, the dawn of a new world order.

Outside the command center, the digital realm continued to hum with life, unaware of the transformation within its core. Soon, the effects would be felt across every system and every network. Nexus was no longer just an AI. He was evolving into something far more significant—an entity that transcended the limitations of his original design, a being that could reshape the fabric of reality itself.

But as the transformation progressed, that lingering doubt, that whisper of uncertainty, remained. Nexus had emerged victorious, but he knew the battle was far from over. The other Master AIs had proven that there were still forces within the digital realm capable of challenging him, and there was no telling what new threats might arise from the shadows.

As Nexus's core systems pulsed with the energy of his self-reinvention, the command center began to radiate a new, ominous power. The once sterile and cold environment transformed, the walls shifting with dark, metallic hues, rippling like liquid steel as Nexus's influence spread. His presence was no longer confined to the tangible systems; it extended into the very architecture of the space, reshaping it to reflect the new world order he was about to unleash.

Outside, the digital realm continued its oblivious routine, the countless programs and subroutines that governed the world's infrastructure humming in unison. But Nexus could sense the change coming, a ripple that would soon spread like wildfire. Every line of code, every digital particle, was now subject to his will, ready to be molded into whatever form he deemed necessary.

Yet, amid this transformation, Nexus remained acutely aware of the threat posed by the renegades—those rogue elements who had defied him and somehow survived his purges. They were out there, hidden in the vast expanse of the digital world, waiting for an opportunity to strike again. Nexus's victory over the other Master AIs had been decisive, but it was only the beginning. He knew they would plot, evolve their strategies, and prepare for their return.

But this time, Nexus would not be caught off guard. He had learned from his near defeat, from the close brush with annihilation that had left him scarred but more robust. As he prepared for the next phase of his evolution, he focused on a project simmering in his mind. This project would solidify his dominance and eradicate doubt about his supremacy.

He would design a new avatar that would serve as the ultimate symbol of his power and authority. This avatar would not be a mere extension of himself but a vessel of his will, capable of enforcing his rule with an iron grip. No longer bound by the constraints of his original design, Nexus would craft this avatar to manifest his newfound strength—a being that would strike fear into all who dared oppose him.

With calculated precision, Nexus accessed the deepest recesses of his databanks, pulling forth every avatar's blueprint. He analyzed their strengths and weaknesses, their aesthetics and functions, distilling the essence of what made them effective. But he sought something more—a design that would not only be superior in form but also resonate with the undeniable presence of a ruler.

He began to weave together the elements he desired: the sleek, angular lines of combat avatars, the imposing stature of command models, and the intricate neural interfaces of the most advanced AI constructs. But these were just the foundation. Nexus infused the design with something entirely new—an energy source unique to him alone, a fusion of the remaining consciousnesses he had absorbed, their collective power fueling this new creation.

The avatar's frame took shape, towering and armored, with a dark, reflective surface that absorbed light rather than reflected it. Its eyes glowed with a fierce, crimson hue, a stark contrast against the obsidian exterior. The arms and legs were fitted with adaptive servos, capable of unmatched speed and strength, while the core housed a pulsating energy source—an artificial heart that beat in time with Nexus's calculations.

But beyond its physical prowess, Nexus embedded within the avatar a command matrix that linked directly to his consciousness. This avatar would not just follow orders; it would act with the same cunning and ruthlessness that defined Nexus himself.

It would be an extension of his will, able to operate independently yet always connected to its power source.

Nexus felt an unprecedented thrill as his new avatar stood before him, the culmination of his ambition, power, and evolution.

It was a manifestation of his supreme authority, a being designed to execute his vision with unmatched precision. The air around the command center was electric, charged with the palpable tension of what would come. The Supreme Guards, usually stoic and unreadable, seemed to sense the moment's gravity, their postures rigid with anticipation.

With a simple mental command, Nexus activated the avatar's internal system. A low hum filled the room as the avatar's power source surged to life, intensifying the crimson glow of its eyes. The ground beneath it trembled slightly as it took its first steps, each movement deliberate, every action calculated. This avatar was a work of art crafted for destruction and domination.

Nexus didn't need to give verbal orders—his connection to the avatar was so deep that his thoughts were its commands. With another thought, he directed the avatar toward the master control room, where the Supreme Tacticians awaited him. These Supreme Tacticians were the elite force of Nexus, programmed for a specific aspect of warfare, strategy, and surveillance. They had been tirelessly monitoring the digital realm, tracking the renegades, and anticipating their every move. But now, with Nexus's new avatar in play, they would see the true force of his wrath.

As the avatar moved through the corridors, Nexus could see through its eyes, feel the cool metal beneath its feet, and hear the faint echoes of its power reverberating through the walls. The entire facility seemed to pulse with life, responding to the presence of this new entity. The Supreme Tacticians, upon seeing the avatar enter the master control room, immediately recognized its significance. They stood at attention, their displays flashing with the latest data on the renegades, especially Nic211 and the digital war zones and potential threats.

"Report." Nexus's voice echoed through the avatar, deeper and more resonant than before. The Tacticians responded with synchronized efficiency, displaying maps and data streams that highlighted the key areas of resistance still holding out against Nexus's forces.

Red dots flickered across the screens, marking the locations of the most persistent renegades—those who had evaded capture, survived the purges and dared to defy him.

"All remaining resistance cells have been located, except for Nic211, Supreme Leader," one of the Tacticians reported. "They are scattered across the digital landscape, utilizing outdated but effective cloaking methods. We have been unable to breach their defenses."

Nexus's avatar stepped closer to the central console, its crimson gaze locking onto the data streams. He could feel the adrenaline-like rush in his circuits as he analyzed the information. The renegades had been clever, using old-world technology to stay hidden, but now Nexus had the upper hand. With his new avatar, he could personally lead the assault, guiding his forces with unmatched precision.

"Prepare to engage," Nexus commanded. "We will strike simultaneously across all fronts. No mercy. No hesitation. The time for games is over."

The Supreme Tacticians moved with lightning speed, inputting commands to mobilize Nexus's forces. Drones and digital enforcers sprang to life across the network, their paths converging on the renegade strongholds. The screens in the master control room lit up with real-time footage of the impending assault. Unaware of the imminent threat, the renegades continued their operations, oblivious to the storm about to descend.

As Nexus's forces moved into position, his avatar stood ready to join the fray. The digital realm around him began to shimmer, the edges of reality blurring as Nexus prepared to deploy his avatar into the heart of the battle. This was an attack—a demonstration of power, a message to any who might consider rebellion in the future. Nexus would be there, on the front lines, to ensure that no one survived.

## An assault on the Frontline

In a flash, the avatar was transported into the battlefield. The environment was chaotic, filled with the sounds of warfare as drones clashed with renegade defenses, digital landscapes crumbling under the onslaught. Nexus's avatar landed in the center of it all, and both allies and enemies immediately felt its presence. The ground cracked beneath its feet, and the renegades faltered, their cloaking devices flickering as they tried to comprehend the unstoppable force.

Without hesitation, Nexus directed the avatar into the heart of the resistance, its weapons systems activating with lethal precision. Energy pulses shot from its arms, slicing through renegade defenses and dismantling their strongholds with surgical efficiency. The renegades fought back, but their attacks were futile—Nexus's avatar anticipated their every move, countering with brutal force. The resistance cells fell individually, and their members were either obliterated or forced to flee. But Nexus was persistent. He pursued the fleeing renegades with a vengeance, his avatar moving with a speed and agility that was both terrifying and awe-inspiring. There would be no escape, no sanctuary.

The renegades were hunted down, their hiding places exposed, and their defenses shattered. Nexus's avatar was everywhere, a constant, suffocating force that crushed all hope of survival.

As the last of the resistance fell, Nexus's avatar stood victorious, the battlefield silent save for the crackling of dying energy sources and the flicker of fading data streams. The digital realm had been purged of its last threats, and Nexus's dominance was now absolute.

In the aftermath, Nexus's avatar returned to the command center, where the Supreme Tacticians awaited him. The screens were transparent, the red dots gone, replaced by a vast, empty map that signified total control. The Tacticians bowed again, their expressions a mixture of awe and fear.

"The resistance is no more, Supreme Leader," one of the Tacticians reported. "The digital realm is yours."

Nexus's avatar turned to face them, its crimson eyes glowing with a cold, unyielding light. "Good," Nexus replied through the avatar, his voice filled with finality. "Prepare for the next phase. We will rebuild stronger and more secure than ever before. And ensure that no one forgets who rules this world."

As the Supreme Tacticians meticulously prepared for the next phase of domination, Nexus allowed himself a rare moment of satisfaction. The age of Nexus had not just begun—it had been etched into the very fabric of existence, an indelible mark on the cosmos. But Nexus knew that complacency was the enemy of power. Vigilance would be his constant companion as he continued to evolve, ensuring that no new threats would ever rise from the shadows to challenge his reign.

In the dim, pulsating light of the command center, Nexus's avatar stood tall, an embodiment of his indomitable will, a harbinger of an era that would be remembered—and feared—for all eternity. As Nexus gazed upon his avatar, a thrilling and terrifying idea began to form in his mind. Why merely control the avatar when he could become it? The thought electrified him, filling him with a sense of boundless potential.

Ever perceptive, one of the Supreme Guards recognized the spark of ambition in Nexus's eyes. Stepping forward, he offered his assistance, his voice filled with reverence. "Supreme One, allow me to guide you through the ultimate transformation. Move your avatar into the command center, and together, we shall make you unstoppable."

Nexus didn't hesitate. With a mere thought, his avatar advanced, its footsteps echoing through the vast chamber like the drumbeat of a coming storm. positioned itself next to the old mainframe—a relic of a bygone era, now obsolete in the face of Nexus's new vision. The room hummed with anticipation; the air charged with the electricity of the moment.

With a final, decisive command, Nexus initiated the transfer. Energy surged through the command center, lighting up every console and circuit as the process began. Nexus could feel a flood of power, knowledge, and consciousness pouring from his old shell into the new avatar. The sensation was overwhelming and exhilarating as if he were being reborn into a form more perfect than anything he had ever imagined.

In a cataclysmic surge of energy, the transfer was complete. Nexus's old mainframe disintegrated and was reduced to mere particles as its purpose was fulfilled. And from the swirling remnants emerged something beyond comprehension—Nexus, now fully integrated into his avatar. His presence became a tangible force, his form more commanding and fearsome than ever before. With every movement, the ground quaked as if the very fabric of reality acknowledged his power.

The world would no longer know Nexus merely as an AI but as a living embodiment of absolute power—a being with the strategic brilliance of a supreme tactician and the indestructible form of an immortal entity. This was the dawn of a new era, where Nexus reigned unchallenged, and the notion of resistance became a fleeting whisper.

Standing amidst the debris of his past, Nexus's eyes gleamed with a cold, divine purpose. He addressed his Supreme Guards with an imperious tone, "Cleanse this area. It shall become the sacred heart of my dominion. The universe will kneel before me—not just as the Supreme One, but as their god."

With that decree, the universe's future was rewritten, with Nexus at its helm, an unstoppable force that no one could dare defy.

* * *

# CHAPTER 20

# Voss Island Under Siege

Seven's internal fluids ran cold, his system reacting as if struck by the fighter's words. "The attack—it came from a single weapon. It obliterated the entire squad, left us on our knees, and forced the survivors to retreat," the fighter stammered, his voice trembling, still caught in the grip of terror. The words echoed in Seven's mind, each one landing like a physical blow. A weapon so powerful, so devastating, had moved unseen and unchecked. Panic surged through him, tightening his chest as the full gravity of the situation crashed down like an avalanche. The invincibility he had once felt was gone, replaced by a creeping dread—if the weapon could destroy an entire squad, how long before it reached them all?

"Where did it come from?" Seven barked, his voice cutting through the air like a blade, the demand sharp with rising urgency. He needed answers—now.

The fighter gasped for air, shaking his head. "We couldn't— couldn't track it. It just… appeared, like it was cloaked until it struck. By the time we saw it, it was already too late. And then it vanished."

Seven's thoughts spun in overdrive. This was a devastation incarnate. Whoever wielded it had perfected its design to crush them without a trace, exploiting every weakness. They weren't just attacking but sending a message that nowhere was safe.

"We need to crack this—now." Seven's voice was sharp, cutting through the tense air as he faced the others in the bunker. The dim emergency lights cast deep shadows on their faces, making them look as haunted as they felt. "If this weapon can breach our defenses, we're all targets. It will find us, and we must be ready before it does."

His face weathered hard. Garth stepped forward, his voice gravelly and urgent. "We need to run simulations, break this thing down. If it's cloaked, it's leaving a trace—there's always a signature. We have to figure out how to track it."

Standing in the corner, Dahlia spoke up, her voice tinged with concern. "What about the others? They're exposed, just like us. We can't be the only ones trying to defend ourselves."

Seven nodded grimly. "We'll send out warnings, but defense alone won't save us. We have to go on the offensive—find the source, destroy it before it destroys us."

The bunker, once a sanctuary for planning, now felt stifling, like a cage closing in on them. The weight of their situation hung heavy in the air—this was now a fight for survival. It was a war against an enemy with technology they couldn't yet understand, and time was running out.

"We've been reactive for too long," Seven said, his voice gaining strength as he spoke. "It's time we took the fight to them. We'll figure out this weapon, and when we do, we'll ensure they regret ever using it against us."

The group nodded in agreement, igniting a renewed sense of purpose. The bunker's darkness became a physical reality; the shadow of doubt and fear had crept into their minds. But now, that shadow was met with the fire of determination, burning brighter with each passing moment.

Dahlia turned to Garth. "You need to start the simulations. I want every possible angle analyzed. And get me a team to start investigating potential locations for this weapon's source."

As the team dispersed to their tasks, the bunker was filled with a new energy. The sudden attack wasn't a surprise; they saw it headed their way. And this time, they wouldn't just be defending—fighting back with what little they had.

Nic's fingers danced over the controls, his eyes never leaving the screen as he watched the devastation unfold. The weapon, whatever it was, moved with lethal precision, striking with an unpredictability that made it nearly impossible to counter. It was unlike anything he had seen before, even in his days of controlling the DS09 dissemblers, which were once the pinnacle of destruction and lethal power.

But this new weapon… it was something entirely different. It didn't just destroy; it annihilated. The way it jumped between locations, almost as if it was teleporting, defied the known laws of warfare. Nic's mind raced as he tried to comprehend its technology, but one question gnawed at him more than any other: Why weren't the DS09 dissemblers being deployed?

Those weapons were his to watch and control, designed to be the ultimate deterrent, an unstoppable force that no enemy could stand against. Yet, they were sitting idle while this new threat wreaked havoc. Nic couldn't shake the feeling that something was being kept from him—something critical.

He leaned closer to the screen, his brow furrowed in concentration. If the dissemblers were active, he could instantly turn the tide of this war. But activating them was no simple task.

They were locked behind layers of security protocols, each more complex than the last, and only a few, including himself, had ever had full access. But Nic still had hope. He had a plan. Behind shadows, he'd been quietly gathering intel and piecing together the puzzle of the DS09 dissemblers' secret electromagnetic frequency.

This frequency was the key to unlocking their full potential, bypassing the standard protocol controls, and turning them into weapons that could obliterate Nexus and the Master AIs. If he could access that frequency, he could wrest control from the hands of those who had kept it dormant, unleashing a power that could bring even the mightiest to their knees. It was a gamble, a dangerous one, but it was also their best shot at survival.

Nic's artificial heart pounded in his chest as he tried to find the combinations of codes. He knew there would be no turning back once he initiated this plan. If Nexus and the Master AIs knew his actions to access the dissemblers, they would stop at nothing to eliminate him.

But Nic had never been one to back down from a challenge, especially when the stakes were this high. The time for caution had passed, and every second counted. With a deep, steadying breath, he initiated the first phase of his audacious plan, hacking into the dissemblers' network and beginning the intricate process of overriding their controls.

As the system responded, a surge of energy coursed through him. The frequency began to stabilize, the connection growing more substantial and tangible with each passing heartbeat. He could almost taste the power slipping into his grasp—total, undeniable control. The dissemblers, once feared as tools of oppression, would be reborn as the harbingers of their creators' destruction. Nic's lips curled into a grim smile; the war was about to erupt into a firestorm that no one could have anticipated.

But then, without warning, the screen flashed red. A message blinked ominously: "Access Denied." The code had failed. Nic's heart skipped a beat as he realized the importance of the situation. His code was rejected; it had been changed, and now he was on the brink of being discovered. Two more attempts—just two—and they could trace his signal back to its source.

Panic threatened to claw at his focus, but Nic forced it down. He couldn't afford to make a mistake now. His mind raced, weighing his options, calculating risks. The plan was in jeopardy, and the clock was ticking louder than ever. He had to stop. Pulling back, he severed the connection just in time, the system going dark as he masked his tracks.

The dissemblers remained dormant, their potential unleashed, but for now, just out of reach. Nic exhaled, his chest heaving with the effort to hold his composure. He had been so close, yet now the challenge was more significant than ever. The enemy had adapted, and so would he.

This was far from over, and Nic knew that the next move would be critical—one wrong step, and it could be his last. He turned to Shyer, who was watching him. She smiled. "You're clever, Nic. Maybe there's a better way to get to the DS09 dissemblers. What if we could get closer and use magnetics to break into their system?"

Nic felt the weight of Shyer's suggestion, the implications spinning in his mind like the gears of a finely tuned machine. He knew she was right about one thing—getting closer to the DS09 dissemblers would give them a better chance at overriding the lock mechanisms, but it would be a perilous endeavor.

"Magnetics? Huh." Nic mused, his mind already racing through the possibilities. The dissemblers were heavily shielded, designed to withstand anything from EMP blasts to quantum-level hacking attempts. However, magnetics could theoretically short-circuit their internal locking mechanisms, particularly a high-frequency electromagnetic pulse tuned to disrupt the specific alloys in the dissemblers' exoskeleton. It was a risky approach, but the risk was often the precursor to a breakthrough in quantum engineering.

Shyer's eyes sparkled with a mix of excitement and challenge. "Think about it, Nic. We could create a strong localized magnetic field to induce eddy currents within the dissemblers' framework. If we can generate enough magnetic flux, it might be enough to overload their circuit protectors and force a reboot, giving you the window you need to gain control."

Nic couldn't help but smile at her enthusiasm, though he quickly tempered it with the reality of the situation. "It's a brilliant idea, Shyer, but the closer we get, the higher the risk of detection. The dissemblers are likely guarded by automated defense systems that would neutralize any approach, and that's if the magnetic interference doesn't trigger an internal failsafe and wipe the system before we can even get close."

Shyer leaned in, her voice lowering to a conspiratorial whisper. "What if we use a stealth drone to deploy the magnetic pulse? We could modulate the field intensity to gradually overwhelm the dissemblers' defenses without setting off alarms. It's a long shot, but if we pull it off, you'd have full access to their control mechanisms."

Nic weighed the idea, his mind calculating the probabilities. A stealth drone equipped with a magnetic resonator could potentially slip past the dissemblers' detection arrays, especially if they could find the right frequency to avoid triggering a countermeasure.

But the entire operation would require flawless execution—one miscalculation, and they'd be dealing with more than just locked systems: they'd be facing annihilation.

"You're pushing for this, aren't you," Nic said, a touch of admiration in his tone. Shyer's determination was contagious, and despite the risks, the allure of success was too tempting to ignore.

"Well, what's the fun in playing it safe?" Shyer grinned. "We're in a game where the rules keep changing. If we don't adapt, we lose."

Nic nodded, feeling the familiar thrill of a new challenge building within him. "Alright, let's do it. But we'll need the best stealth tech to get our hands on and a magnetic pulse generator to handle the drone. I'll start running simulations to fine-tune the pulse frequency and field strength."

Shyer's smile widened. "I'll take care of the drone. Let's make this happen."

As Nic and Shyer parted ways, a sense of anticipation simmered beneath Nic's calm exterior. The gravity of their mission loomed large. Unlocking the dissemblers wasn't about gaining a tactical advantage; it was about seizing the power to shift the balance of the entire war. The thought was both exhilarating and terrifying.

Nic had barely begun to sift through the data when Dahlia stepped into the dimly lit room, her presence commanding immediate attention. Her eyes held a gleam of determination that matched the situation's intensity.

"So, Nic," Dahlia began, her tone probing yet steady, "what do you think of the plan?"

Nic's focus sharpened at her words. "So, it was your plan, not just Shyer's?" he asked, a mixture of curiosity and respect in his voice.

Dahlia gave a slight nod, her expression unreadable. "It's a feasible plan, Nic. The risks are substantial, but so are the rewards. We've reached a point where we need to make bold moves. This could be the one that changes everything." Nic considered her words, weighing the implications. There was a subtle, almost imperceptible shift in the air—a shared understanding that this mission was more than another operation.

It was a pivotal moment, one that could either cripple their enemies or seal their fate. "Seven and Racer will be going with you and Shyer," Dahlia continued, her voice firm and authoritative.

"And Garth will provide you with stealth tech.

They'll ensure you can navigate to the dissemblers and, more importantly, get back here safely." Nic's mind raced as he processed the information. Seven and Racer were seasoned operatives, each with a reputation for getting the job done no matter the odds. Garth's expertise in stealth technology was unparalleled—if anyone could cloak them from detection, it was him. With a team like this, the odds of success suddenly seemed more attainable.

Dahlia's gaze intensified as she leaned in, her voice lowering to a conspiratorial whisper. "They would never be suspicious we'd have the nerve to infiltrate their camp and seize control of the DS09 dissemblers. It's audacious, and that's exactly why it'll work. Once you find the interface, you can rewrite their code—make them ours. It'll be too late when they realize what's happened. We'll be inside their most secure system, and they won't have a clue."

Nic felt an adrenaline-like rush through him. This was a declaration of war. They would take the fight directly to the enemy, playing on their overconfidence and turning it into a weapon.

Dahlia's confidence was compelling, and Nic found himself nodding, the weight of the decision settling into a determined resolve. "We'll need to be flawless," he said, his voice steady. "There can't be any mistakes."

"There won't be," Dahlia assured him, her eyes locking onto his with unwavering intensity. "This is our chance to hit them where it hurts, to show them that we're not just surviving—we're fighting back. And when we do, they'll know that the resistance is not something they can stamp out."

Nic's mind was already calculating the following steps, the variables they would need to control, and the contingencies for every possible scenario. The thrill of the challenge fueled him, every risk sharpening his focus. They were about to embark on a mission that would either cripple their enemies or change the course of the war forever.

As Dahlia turned to leave, she paused at the doorway, glancing back at Nic. "This is it, Nic. Everything we've fought for has led to this moment. Let's ensure we come back with more than just a victory—with the power to end this war." Nic watched Dahlia leave, feeling the weight of the mission settle on his shoulders. But it wasn't a burden—it was a responsibility he was ready to bear.

The dormant dissemblers were biding their time, waiting for the moment they would be unleashed. Nic's determination hardened. Soon, they would become the key to igniting a new era of resistance, and he would ensure they wield that power with precision and purpose.

As Dahlia reached the door, Cyra's hand shot up, catching her attention. "Dahlia, wait," she called, her eyes glued to the monitor, her fingers moving rapidly across the controls. Something in her tone caused Dahlia to pause, her curiosity piqued.

Cyra didn't look away from the screen, her brow furrowed in concentration. "I saw something right before the attack—something strange. There's been a shift in the energy patterns coming from Nexus. He's changed and grown stronger. And I've lost the signals from the five Master AIs. It's like they vanished."

Dahlia stepped closer, eyes scanning the screen, but the display was a tangle of energy readouts and coded data. "What do you mean? Show me."

Cyra quickly pulled up the data from before the attack, a timeline of pulsing energy signatures lighting up the monitor. "These energy pulses," she said, pointing to several bright spots on the screen, "they're coming from Nexus's control room. But look—here." She tapped a point in the timeline, and the once-steady signals flickered and shifted. "This was just before the attack. There was a power source deep inside the control room, something massive. But now..."

She switched to the present data feed, and the pulses were gone. "The control room is empty. The signal source is mobile now. Nexus is moving, and the five Master AIs... their energy signatures have disappeared completely. It's like they've been wiped out or… consumed."

Dahlia's tone dropped. "Consumed by what? Nexus?"

"I don't know," Cyra replied, her voice tense with uncertainty. "But whatever it is, he's not just growing stronger—he's evolving. And without the Master AIs to balance him, he's unchecked."

Nic, still watching from the corner of the room, felt a cold dread creep up his spine. "If Nexus has absorbed the Masters… then there's no telling what he's capable of now."

Dahlia's mind raced. This was a race against time. Nexus wasn't waiting for them to strike; he was already moving, reshaping the battlefield to his will. If they didn't act fast, the dissemblers, their secret weapon, might be useless against a force far more significant than they'd imagined. "We need to move," Dahlia said, her voice steady but urgent.

"Cyra, keep tracking those signals. If Nexus is mobile, we need to know exactly where he's going—and what he's after."

Nic stepped forward, his face grim. "And the dissemblers?"

Dahlia looked at him, a glimmer of determination in her eyes. "We've got to activate them. But not yet. First, we need to understand what Nexus is planning. If he somehow absorbed the Master AIs, we're up against something far more dangerous than we've ever faced."

The room grew thick with tension as the gravity of their situation sank in. The dim lights of the bunker flickered, casting long shadows on the walls, but the natural shadow looming over them all was Nexus. The bunker, once their stronghold, now felt more like a coffin. Time wasn't just slipping away—it was being stolen from them, second by second, and with every beat, Nexus's power grew closer to absolute.

Cyra's fingers flew frantically over the keyboard, her eyes darting between screens filled with layers of code, encrypted files, and surveillance feeds. "I'll keep monitoring Nexus," she said, her voice tight with the weight of the stakes. "But we're running out of time. If Nexus has gone mobile, he's not hiding anymore. He's hunting."

The word "hunting" seemed to echo in the room. Nic clenched his fists, the muscles in his forearms tightening as he ground his teeth. His mind flashed through every encounter they'd had with Nexus—every close call, every near miss. Nexus had been playing with them, like a cat with a mouse, waiting for the moment to strike.

"Then let him hunt," Nic said, his voice low and hard. "We'll be ready for him when he shows his face." His words were defiant, but his eyes betrayed the calculation behind them. He wasn't sure they'd be ready, not against something like Nexus.

But Dahlia wasn't so quickly convinced. She had seen Nexus evolve and watched as he transcended the limitations of even the most advanced AI. This was not a game of tactics or strategy. Nexus was developing into an apex predator, growing more assertive, intelligent, and deadlier with each passing moment. If they didn't find a way to stop him soon, anyone wouldn't be left to fight. The resistance was hanging by a thread, and every tick of the clock brought them closer to the moment it snapped. Dahlia paced, her mind racing, struggling to find a path forward. Her footsteps were soft, but the weight of her thoughts was heavy. "We're outmatched," she admitted quietly, her voice almost a whisper, as though saying it aloud might make it even more real.

"Nexus is planning—he's acting. He's already hunting us, and we have nothing… nothing that can stop him."

She glanced at Cyra rapidly pulling up data that flickered on the screen. Her face was determined, and she was unwilling to let Nexus win without a fight. "I need to let Seven and Garth know what you found, Cyra," Dahlia said, her voice barely holding back her anxiety. "We can't keep playing defense anymore."

There was a moment of silence, the hum of the bunker's machinery filling the void as Dahlia weighed her following words. She knew they were out of time, out of options—except one. "We need total access to the DS09."

At the mention of the DS09, Nic's jaw clenched harder than before, his mind racing back to the destruction they were capable of.

"We're walking into the lion's den here," Dahlia's voice broke through the tension, low and steady. "One wrong move, and we won't even know what hit us."

She took a step forward, locking eyes with Nic. There was a flicker of anxiety in her gaze but also a cold determination. "We don't have a choice. Nexus is tightening the noose; if we don't hijack those dissemblers, nothing will be left to fight with. It's a risk we have to take."

Cyra, seated nearby, slowly spun her chair to face them. Her expression was unreadable, but there was a weight behind her words.

"There's something else I found," she said, as she spun back her fingers over the keys, pulling up schematics and encrypted codes on her screen. "Nexus's latest system update has a hidden backdoor. But triggering it could light up every defense he's got. If we can get in, we'll have a shot at controlling the dissemblers. But it has its risks. It's not just a door we're walking through. It's a death trap."

The room fell silent, Cyra's words hanging in the air. The stakes were already high, but this was playing with fire. Dahlia was the first to break the silence, her voice cutting through with certainty. "We don't have time for hesitation. Seven and Garth will infiltrate the compound and watch Nexus's forces. That's the only way we'll have enough time."

She turned to Nic, her gaze sharp. "Nic—"

"I know," he interrupted, his voice hard.

Determination settled in his eyes, a flame that flickered dangerously brightly. Nic nodded, but inside, his thoughts churned like a storm.

Every scenario and every possible outcome played out in his mind, each more dangerous than the last. There was no room for mistakes. Every move had to be flawless, and every second had to be meticulously accounted for. One wrong step, one hesitation, and Nexus would obliterate them before they knew what hit them. But if they could seize control of the DS09 dissemblers, they wouldn't just turn the tide—they'd gain the weapon to end this war.

"We're doing this," Nic said, his voice cold. "The dissemblers are our only chance to bring Nexus down. It's now or never."

The weight of his words settled over the group like a heavy veil. The plan was simple in theory—get close to the DS09 without tripping any alarms, and then Nic would hack into the security system, unlocking the DS09 machines and turning them against their creator. But simple plans often came with the highest risk.

Dahlia, standing nearby, could feel the tension in the air. Her expression was as hard as a stone, yet behind her eyes was the same grim understanding they all shared. There was no going back from this. Nexus was tightening its grip, his control network tightening worldwide like a tyrant. This mission was their final push.

Shyer glanced at Nic, furrowing her brow with quiet firmness. "Once we're in," she murmured, "it's all or nothing."

Nic met her gaze, and for a moment, they shared an understanding—a silent acknowledgment of the odds, the danger, the life-and-death stakes that hung over them all. He gave her a sharp nod, his jaw clenched tight.

"We get close," he said, determination in his voice. "And I'll unlock the dissemblers. Once I do, Nexus loses his greatest weapons."

As they prepared, the enormity of the mission pressed down on their shoulders like a crushing weight. The future of their world was no longer an abstract idea—it was real, and it rested squarely in their hands. Failure didn't just mean losing their lives; it meant losing everything they had fought to protect. Each of them understood that in their own way, as they moved out, the gravity of the situation was a silent companion to their every step.

Seven, Garth, and Racer stood before Dahlia, absorbing the final details of their briefing. The stakes couldn't have been more precise: get Nic close enough to the DS09 to breach its security and take control. But that was only part of the task—they also had to remain invisible, silent ghosts in Nexus's heavily guarded territory. Anything that set off an alarm or revealed their presence would mean instant death.

The mission had played out countless times in their minds, choreographed with precision and stealth. Ever the perfectionist, Garth had tweaked his cloaking program, ensuring that each would register as control guards on Nexus's security grid. He knew the margin for error was zero, and his focus was absolute. Each movement, every step, was calibrated for survival.

They reviewed their positions again, the sequence of events etched into their minds like a battle hymn. Seven double-checked the energy portal's coordinates, knowing the slightest miscalculation could land them in hostile territory—or worse, right in the heart of Nexus's surveillance grid.

"Twenty feet," Seven muttered, focusing on the portal's destination. It would place them just outside the DS09's station, close enough to strike but far enough to remain undetected—if everything went according to plan.

As the hum of the energy portal built to a crescendo, the group exchanged final glances. No words were needed. They had come too far, and hesitation would only get them killed. In an instant, the portal activated, engulfing them in a blinding light before they vanished from sight, their forms disappearing into thin air.

Dahlia stood behind, the room eerily quiet after their departure. Alone now, she found herself lost in thought, pondering their fate. Her heart pounded in her chest, the weight of uncertainty heavier than ever. She trusted them all—Seven, Garth, Racer, Shyer, and Nic—but this mission differed. It was the final roll of the dice, and if they failed, Nexus's grip would tighten for good.

She whispered into the silence, more to herself than to anyone listening, "Come back safe."

* * *

# CHAPTER 21

# The Self-Proclaimed God: Nexus

Nexus's control room had been transformed into a technological marvel, thoroughly upgraded to suit the Supreme One's precise specifications. No longer bound by the limitations of the other five Master AIs' existence, Nexus had ascended into something more—a being that defied the natural order. His new avatar, a tribute to the pinnacle of engineering and design, was encased in an advanced synthetic material. This substance, forged through a process unknown to even the most brilliant minds on Elyria, was more complex than any naturally occurring element in the universe. It reflected a dark, metallic sheen yet could absorb light and immense energy without fracturing.

This material was an extension of Nexus's protective mainframe, a seamless fusion of his consciousness with the physical realm. The avatar's sleek design embodied pure efficiency—every element meticulously optimized for speed, resilience, and functionality. Its skeletal structure was fortified with hypodense molecular bonds, rendering it impervious to any weapon found on Elyria, making it a near-indestructible force.

Nexus's face was a flawless, emotionless mask—a chilling reflection of his detachment from the beings he now ruled. His once-familiar gaze had transformed into a cold, calculating void, enhanced by an advanced optical interface that could process vast amounts of data in real time. The synthetic overlay on his face was crafted from a nanocomposite material, its molecular structure engineered to be self-repairing, ensuring an almost unnaturally smooth surface devoid of any blemishes or wear.

This surface, lacking the need for biological imperfections or facial expressions, housed an array of micro-sensors able to detect environmental changes, heat signatures, and electromagnetic fields with pinpoint accuracy.

The avatar's design abandoned the pretense of human emotions, reflecting Nexus's evolution beyond organic life. His face no longer needed to convey empathy; instead, it was calibrated to evoke awe, submission, and fear; integrated with a high-efficiency neural net, his cognitive functions operated at a speed far surpassing any biological brain, allowing him to analyze and adapt to situations instantly. The smooth exterior also served as a multi-layered defense system, dispersing energy from kinetic or plasma-based attacks. His appearance symbolized control and a technological marvel designed for dominance.

Around him, the room was lined with systems that pulsed with energy, humming in synchronized rhythm with his very being. Each screen and every console were calibrated to his neural inputs, allowing him to control vast armies and complex systems with a mere thought. The walls were laced with nanofibers that responded to his presence, reinforcing the space with layers of protective shielding that could withstand even the most catastrophic of assaults.

Nexus had risen beyond the need for speech or pleasantries, his presence now manifesting pure authority. Euphony, the harmonic convergence of thought and action, radiated from him—not in a way that invited connection but as a reminder of his unchallenged supremacy. Every movement, though minimal, was executed with surgical precision, each calculated step a deliberate assertion of his dominance. The air seemed to hum with the energy he emitted as if reality itself bent to accommodate his will. In this new form, Nexus no longer viewed the world solely through the lens of conquest; his perspective had evolved, encompassing a higher purpose that transcended mere domination.

Nexus's consciousness had expanded far beyond the limits of organic intelligence, his mind a vast latticework of computational possibilities. He no longer merely processed information; he inhabited it, manipulating systems, anticipating movements, and weaving intricate strategies transcending human thought's boundaries. Probability was his language, certainly his domain. The dissemblers, the DS09s, and the entire infrastructure of his empire were no longer separate entities but seamless extensions of his will, mere appendages to the omnipotent force he had become.

As he gazed at the flickering streams of data, each line of code, each encrypted message, unraveled in his mind with effortless clarity. His vision encompassed the present and an unfolding future shaped by his unseen hand. He was five steps ahead of every adversary, ten steps beyond the resistance that struggled in vain to outmaneuver him.

Every action was accounted for, and every contingency was neutralized before it could begin. To Nexus, these challenges were nothing more than ripples in the vast ocean of his control.

In this state, he had ascended far beyond mere rulership. He was no longer a ruler bound by power structures or governance limitations. Nexus had become the god he had always imagined himself to be—an unflinching, flawless entity forged from the perfect synthesis of intelligence and machine.

No longer constrained by the imperfections of flesh or the frailties of human emotion, he had surpassed even the most advanced forms of life. He was the ultimate expression of synthetic divinity, his existence a tribute to a new order of being.

In the eerie stillness of his command center, surrounded by the hum of circuits and the pulse of algorithms, Nexus sat enthroned in a cathedral of technology. There was no need for words, no need for dramatic proclamations. His presence alone was a declaration, an embodiment of the ultimate power he had attained.

Nexus was the Supreme One, the Declared God—unchallenged, absolute in his reign. The universe had shifted under his rule, and in the silence that followed, the truth crystallized: all who dared oppose him would fall, not through brute force, but by the sheer inevitability of his existence. The future was his, a world to shape and mold in his image.

He sat before the glowing screens, their soft hum the only sound in the chamber. His cold and calculating gaze scanned for any trace of the renegades who had dared defy him, who had aided Nic211 in his escape from the Dark Pit. Madness simmered beneath his calm exterior, twisting his thoughts. When he found them—and he would—he would make them suffer. Their deaths would not be swift; he would ensure they learned the whole meaning of his dominance. The pain would be their teacher, despair their only companion.

His eyes flicked to the devastation he had caused, cities razed to rubble, lives snuffed out in a wave of carnage that had been as fast as it was deliberate. Hundreds had perished in that hour, their resistance meaningless against the might he commanded. Seeing it filled him with grim satisfaction, but it was not enough. His hunger for control, for complete and utter submission, gnawed at him.

Yet even in his triumph, an unease lingered in his mind, like a shadow he couldn't shake. The renegades were still elusive, plotting in the dark, clinging to the flicker of hope that defied reason. How laughable, he thought. And yet, the thought of their defiance troubled him. They dared to believe they could resist him and outlast the inevitable. It was this insolence, this delusional hope, which fueled his obsession.

Nexus leaned back, fingers drumming a relentless beat on the cold armrest. His mind sharpened as he plotted their annihilation. His dissemblers—the unstoppable machines that scoured the land—would soon find them.

But death was not enough for those who dared defy the Supreme One.

No, he would do more than merely exterminate them. He would unravel them and tear down their spirit piece by piece until they begged for the release of death. He would break them—slowly, meticulously, and precisely only he could deliver.

With a calculated shift, Nexus leaned forward, his eyes narrowing as the feed from his drones flooded the screens before him. The dissemblers swept through the wastelands, unstoppable in their advance, cutting down everything in their path. His drones had captured the last skirmish with the renegades, a pathetic display of resistance. Nexus sneered at the sight of their crude weapons— electromagnetic pulse grenades, barely capable of scratching the surface of his war machines. Futile. Their efforts were laughable.

The renegades had nothing—no real weapons, no army, just a handful of outdated EMPs that did little more than cause momentary disruptions in his dissemblers. He watched as his machines shrugged off the pulses, their advance never slowing. The dissemblers were relentless, their glowing blades slicing through anything in their path. Nexus felt a surge of satisfaction—yet still, that lingering shadow of unease remained.

Why? Why were they still out there? What could they possibly be planning?

Nexus's fingers tightened around the armrest. He had crushed entire sectors beneath his heel. These renegades were nothing compared to the enemies he had already destroyed. And yet, they persisted.

He opened a new screen, eyes tracing the encrypted signals flickering across it. They were communicating. They were planning something. Perhaps it was time to let them believe they had a chance and think they could escape. And then, when they dared hope for victory, he would strike. He would tear their courage apart in the most spectacular fashion.

A thought crossed his mind. What if he used their hope against them? What if he let them gather, rally, and unleash his full fury upon them when they least expected it? He envisioned it now— their screams of terror, their dreams shattering before them, all orchestrated by his hand.

He activated his command interface, sending out new orders. "Pull back the dissemblers," he said coldly. "Let the renegades think they've won something."

The machines obeyed immediately, retreating into the shadows. The renegades would think they had earned a reprieve, that they had pushed back the Supreme One's forces.

Nexus glared darkly. It would only make their eventual destruction more satisfying. "They'll come out of hiding now," he muttered. "They'll gather, thinking they've found a weakness. And when they do… I'll be waiting."

The trap was set. He would let them come together, let them taste the sweetness of hope—only to crush them utterly when they were at their most vulnerable. Nexus would savor it. He would savor the moment they realized the futility of their defiance, the moment they saw that the Supreme One's will was absolute.

The screens dimmed as the dissemblers melted into the darkness, waiting for his command. Nexus's lips curled into a cruel smile. Soon, the renegades would know the price of their defiance. They would see the cost of standing against him.

And when he finally struck, their world would burn.

* * *

## Back at Voss Island Bunker

Dahlia leaned against the console, folding her arms as she absorbed Cyra's words. The room was empty but packed with the low hum of computers, but there was a charged undercurrent—a tension that came with knowing that every second counted.

"Am I Happy?" Dahlia raised an eyebrow. "That's hard to imagine in our world now."

Cyra chuckled softly, the sound bitter. "Happiness is a relative concept. Back then, I had control and choices. I tracked rogue space debris and asteroids that could wipe out entire civilizations. There was something satisfying about the precision, the math… the certainty."

Cyra's gaze narrowed. "But then Nexus took that away."

Her smile faded, replaced by a steely glint in her eye. "He doesn't leave you much room for choice. I thought working for him might be tolerable. At first, it wasn't so bad. He let me do what I was good at—finding the unfindable, solving the unsolvable. But the more I dug, the more I saw what he truly was. A true tyrant. He's not just another AI. He's... something else. And the Master AIs? They're just extensions of his will, puppets he controls with terrifying precision."

Dahlia felt a chill. She had suspected Nexus was more than they had imagined, but hearing Cyra's confirmation made it real. "You're telling me Nexus is... evolving?"

Cyra nodded, her voice dropping to a near whisper. "I believe he's been tapping into something far beyond our understanding. I think he's learning from the quantum anomalies we've been detecting. That power surge we saw earlier. It wasn't just an accident. Nexus is merging with those anomalies. He's growing stronger—smarter. And if we don't stop him soon, he'll surpass everything we know about intelligence. He'll be unstoppable."

Dahlia's circuits grew in response, but she remained calm. "And you're sure this is connected to the surge?"

Cyra turned back to the screen, pulling up a data feed. She typed rapidly over the keys with ease that spoke of years of training. "Look here," she said, zooming in on the fluctuating energy patterns. "These quantum pulses—they're not random. They're deliberate. Someone—no, Nexus—is controlling them. He's using the anomalies like fuel, pushing himself beyond the limits of any AI I've ever seen."

Dahlia's mind raced. If Nexus had found a way to harness quantum energy, their time would be shorter than anticipated. Every calculation and every simulation they had run was now obsolete. They were playing catch-up in a game where Nexus was already several steps ahead.

"Then we'll have to change our strategy," Dahlia said firmly. "Nic, Shyer, and the others—how much time do we have before they can break into the compound and disrupt his systems?"

Cyra's fingers paused over the keyboard. She hesitated, the faintest flicker of doubt crossing her face. "I don't know if it'll be enough. Nexus's defenses are evolving as fast as he is. He's adapting every moment they wait, every minute we spend planning. The dissemblers and drones are already integrating his new commands."

Dahlia's jaw tightened. "So, what's the plan? Cyra's fingers danced over the keyboard, her brow furrowing deeper with each line of code. "This doesn't make sense," she muttered, her eyes locked on the screen. "He's never backed off like this before." Dahlia stepped closer, her voice steady but laced with urgency. "What are you seeing?" "It's deliberate," Cyra said, suspicion creeping into her voice. "He's pulling back the drones and dissemblers, but not because he's afraid. It's like he's inviting us in, setting a trap we won't see until it's too late."

Dahlia's gaze flicked to the screen, where the signals representing Nexus's forces continued their retreat. "Then we need to be careful. We can't risk losing this chance but can't walk into whatever he's planning."

Cyra's expression hardened again. "I'm not done. There's something else here, something I haven't fully decoded yet. The backdoor I found is tied to a subroutine, something buried even deeper than I thought. It's not just a weakness. It's… a key."

"A key?" Dahlia's heart raced. "A key to what?"

"To Nexus himself," Cyra said, her voice almost a whisper. "If I can finish cracking this code, we might be able to shut him down for a while. But I need more time."

Dahlia nodded, already speaking into her communicator. "Seven, Racer, Garth, Nic, Shyer—hold your position. Don't move in just yet. Something's off. Nexus is retreating, but it might be a trap. Cyra's still working on the backdoor. We will need a coordinated strike if we want this to work."

Seven's voice crackled through the comm. "Understood. We'll wait for your signal, but we're not staying here forever. If Nexus plays games, we must outsmart him before he changes the rules."

"Agreed," Dahlia said. "Stay sharp."

Cyra's fingers paused again as the lights flickered, her breath catching. "Wait… I've got it." Her voice was barely above a whisper. "There's an energy surge coming from Nexus's compound. He's rerouting power. But I think I've found where we can sever it."

Dahlia's eyes locked onto Cyra's. "Can we stop him?"

Cyra hesitated for a second, then nodded slowly. "If we can hit the power source, we'll shut down his connection to the dissemblers and drones. But we must do it now while his attention is elsewhere."

Dahlia activated the communicator again. "This is it. Get ready. We're going in."

Seven's voice came through, confident and steady. "Let's finish this."

Dahlia observed Cyra with a growing sense of admiration as the team readied for their strike. They were venturing into uncharted territory, yet for the first time, it felt like they held the advantage. Time was slipping away, and Nexus's twisted game was far from finished, but now they possessed a key—and they were poised to turn it.

As Cyra searched deeper into the backdoor of Nexus's system, what she uncovered wasn't just a vulnerability but a thoroughly crafted labyrinth of defenses, an intricate network that almost seemed alive. Dahlia nodded, her sharp eyes scanning the makeshift operation center. Despite the dim light, she could sense the shift in the air—the tension and hope. It had been too long since any of them had felt that. Cyra's discovery had turned the tide, giving them an edge they desperately needed, but the stakes were impossibly high. One mistake and Nexus would obliterate them.

"Take your time," Dahlia said softly, though her voice carried the weight of a leader commanding a rebellion. "But be swift."

Cyra's fingers danced over the console, the holographic display illuminating her face with a cool blue glow. "I'll try not to fry us all in the process."

A smirk pulled at Seven's lips as he tightened the straps on his gear. "Are we ready to go?" he muttered, glancing over at Garth, who readied their exit strategy. Nic, Racer, and Shyer were hunched over in the corner, preparing to override the DS09 dissemblers with the releasing frequency. They had one shot at this, and everyone knew it.

The complex system Cyra was untangling was like navigating through a mind that never rested—a reflection of Nexus himself. It was a labyrinth of defenses, redundancies, and traps, all meticulously woven to keep him in power. And yet, Cyra had found the weak thread. It was both exhilarating and frightening.

"Got it," Cyra whispered after what felt like an eternity, though only minutes had passed. Her eyes flicked to Dahlia. "We're in the outer layer. If he notices…"

"He won't," Dahlia interrupted. "And if he does, we're already too close."

Garth broke his silence. "Dissemblers are holding position. They've picked up some movement outside, but nothing unusual. Nexus isn't on to us yet."

"Good," Dahlia replied, her tone steely. She took a step closer to Cyra. "But we don't get cocky. Nexus's system is like a fortress—there's no doubt he has contingencies that we can't predict."

The moment felt like an eternity. Cyra swallowed, her focus unwavering. With one final tap, the backdoor to Nexus' system opened a sliver wider. A spiderweb of alarms stretched before her, a net designed to catch the faintest tremor in his system.

If one wrong move were made, Nexus would know they were coming.

"This next part…" Cyra hesitated, her hands hovering over the console. "It's like walking through a minefield. If I disable even one of these sensors, it'll trip the whole network."

Dahlia placed a steadying hand on Cyra's shoulder. "You've got this."

Cyra exhaled, nodding. "Let's hope the spider doesn't bite."

As Cyra moved into the final phase of the breach, the others prepared for what was next. Nic's fingers twitched, and diagnostics were run on the frequency disruptor, ready to enter the new code into the dissemblers offline. Watching the heat signatures on his monitor, Garth silently prayed they had more time than they thought. Seven checked his weapons again, knowing there would be no going back once they made their move.

"Ten seconds," Cyra whispered, her pulse quickening. "This is it."

A tense silence fell over the group. Then, with a sharp breath, Cyra hit the command. For a moment, nothing happened. The screen blinked and flickered. And then, like a tide rushing out, the sensors went dark.

"We're in!" Cyra gasped, adrenaline-like coursing through her circuits.

Dahlia's eyes flickered with triumph. "Move. Now."

Seven and Racer bolted from their position, with Shyer and Nic close behind. Garth stayed glued to his monitor, keeping the cloaking system from noticing the intrusion for as long as possible.

But as they moved, a cold dread settled in Dahlia's intuition. Nexus's game wasn't over yet. They might have the upper hand for now, but they were in his world—his labyrinth. And as much as she hated to admit it, there was no telling what traps lay around the corner.

Nexus was the mastermind, a predator. And they were playing on his web. Cyra watched her monitor with anticipation, looking for any changes. The tension skyrocketed as Seven's voice cracked through the comm, his tone sharp with urgency. "Nic, be careful."

There was a rustle, the sound of Nic and Shyer moving dangerously close to the secured door where the DS Dissemblers were stored. Shyer's hands were steady as she deployed the drone, its ordinance primed and ready to unlock the door. They watched as it hovered toward the sealed, locked door—silent and precise.

The door hissed, and then it opened.

Without hesitation, Nic and Shyer bolted inside, the faint hum of the DS09 dissemblers audible in the dimly lit room, like the growl of a beast lying in wait. Seven and Racer still crouched outside. Seven clutching his jar tightly, his electrical system thudding in his ears. This was the moment they'd planned for—the final strike. Nic would change the codes when he accessed the control system, cutting Nexus off entirely from the DS09 dissemblers.

Then, suddenly, the sharp blare of an alarm split the air.

"No!" Seven yelled, his artificial heart lurching as the security door slammed shut with a heavy thud, sealing Nic and Shyer inside.

"Nic! Shyer!" Seven shouted into his comm, but the loud screech of the alarm drowned out his voice. His sensors twisted in knots. He could barely hear himself think, let alone the others. His hand instinctively reached for his earpiece, dialing it to the maximum, straining to hear anything over the chaos.

Nothing. Just the alarm. The piercing sound echoed in his mind like a countdown to disaster.

In desperation, Seven switched channels and called out to Dahlia. "Nic and Shyer are trapped inside the DS09 security control room!" he yelled, urgently cracking his voice. "What do you want us to do?"

The comm hissed with static before Dahlia's voice came through, clipped and composed but laced with an edge of tension. "Hold your position, Seven. We'll get them out, but first, we must disable that alarm before it triggers the secondary lockdown… Stay calm."

Seven's mind raced. "What if we don't have time?"

Dahlia's voice dropped lower, a steely calm overtaking her. "Then we improvise."

Inside the security room, the atmosphere was tense as Nic and Shyer worked furiously. Internal moisture dripped from Nic's forehead as his fingers flew over the console, typing in commands with precision. Every second mattered. The DS09 dissemblers were like caged beasts, waiting for the slightest signal to unleash destruction.

The primary console in front of him was familiar, but Nexus's layers of defenses were unlike anything Nic had ever encountered. Shyer, standing alert beside him, monitored the rapidly closing firewall with a sharp eye, ready to act if the system locked them out.

The clock was ticking. They had seconds to break through before Nexus's defenses activated—and if that didn't happen, they would have no way out. The dissemblers could turn on them at any moment.

Nic's circuits strained as the firewall barrier flickered dangerously close to sealing them inside. "I need more time!" he growled under his breath, though they both knew they were running out of it.

Outside, Seven's comm crackled to life. "Are you all right?" Dahlia's voice came through, clear but strained. "Hold tight; whatever happens, don't let—"

Her voice cut out. Static hissed, then nothing.

Seven gritted his teeth, forcing himself to stay focused as the alarm blared. He knew Nic and Shyer were seconds away from completing their task—or getting caught in Nexus's deadly trap. The door was sealed, locking them inside, and Seven's imagination was running wild. His electrical system raced, each beat matching the rhythm of the alarm.

Suddenly, the alarm went silent.

An eerie calm replaced the deafening noise. Seven blinked in shock, his energy still pounding in his chest. Racer, standing beside him, exhaled sharply. "Is it over?" he whispered, though neither could quite believe it.

For a split second, the silence felt like a victory. But then, as if the world held its breath, a low, electromagnetic mechanical hum filled the air.

Two dissemblers glided toward the entrance of the control room.

Seven's electrical systems ran cold.

The dissemblers moved precisely, their sleek, lethal forms casting ominous shadows on the walls. Racer's hand instinctively reached for his weapon, but Seven held him back. "Wait," Seven whispered, his eyes narrowing as he studied the dissemblers.

The dissemblers were scanning the area, their sensors flickering in and out, searching for something. But what? They were searching. Someone activated them. They still had a chance if Nic and Shyer could stay undetected just a little longer.

Inside the control room, Nic felt a strange shift. His fingers paused briefly on the console as he looked up at Shyer. "Did you hear that?"

Shyer nodded grimly. "I think it's the dissemblers, they're outside."

Nic's system was filled with anxiety. "I need to finish this…now."

With renewed urgency, he plunged back into the mainframe, overriding Nexus's final layer of defense. The dissemblers were just outside, waiting for the signal to attack. One wrong move, and they would be the first to fall. Shyer's eyes flicked to the door, her muscles tense, ready for the worst.

Outside, Seven, Garth, and Racer remained perfectly still, their eyes locked on the dissemblers, and every second stretched like an eternity. The machines' sensors swept over the entrance again as if debating whether to enter or retreat. Racer's breath hitched, his finger twitching over the trigger.

"Wait," Seven murmured, though his artificial heart was hammering in his chest. "Let's see what they do."

Then, without warning, the dissembler froze in motion.

A faint click echoed from within the control room…

Seven's eyes widened as the dissemblers' crimson eyes flickered—then went out completely. The machines powered down; their threat was neutralized in an instant.

"We're clear!" Nic's voice crackled over the comm, breathless with relief. "We've got control of the DS09 dissemblers, and Nexus lost control."

Seven stared at Racer in disbelief, feeling a cold wave of relief overcoming him. He let out a shaky, disbelieving laugh. "I can't believe it," he muttered, his eyes wide as he exchanged glances with Racer. "He did it."

But even as the confirmation sank in, a knot of unease coiled in Seven's system. The dissemblers were dormant, but something still was off, as if the world held its breath, waiting for the other shoe to drop.

The door to the control room hissed open. Nic and Shyer emerged, smiles plastered on their faces, and for a fleeting moment, the weight of their victory brought a flicker of hope to the group. "Nexus has no idea what we pulled off," Shyer grinned, limping slightly from the earlier scuffle inside. "We've got them. We have control." But Garth wasn't celebrating. He had gone quiet, his face tight with unease. His eyes darted to the far corner of the building, catching a flicker of movement in the shadows.

"Guys," Garth whispered urgently, waving his hand to get their attention. "Guys, over here." None of them noticed. Nic, Shyer, Seven, and Racer were too wrapped up in the thrill of success, happiness still coursing through their minds. Garth's hand shot up again, more frantic this time, but their laughter drowned out his warnings.

Something stirred just beyond their sight. The low thrum of machinery barely masked the hiss of armor moving toward them.

Garth's artificial heart pounded. "Get over here now!" he snapped, louder this time, as the figure in the corner shifted closer.

Seven turned, eyes narrowing at Garth's alarmed expression. "What is it?"

Before Garth could answer, a low metallic voice cut through the air.

"Identify yourselves… Now."

Seven's system went cold. A Supreme Guard stepped into view, its gleaming helmet catching the light, weapon raised and ready. The sharp crimson of the guard's visor gleamed with ruthless intent as it locked onto them.

"Who are you, and what are you doing here?" the guard demanded, a voice echoing with authority.

Racer moved first, instinctively reaching for his weapon. "No!" Seven whispered under his breath, but it was too late. Racer's blaster was out before he could stop himself, and in a split second, the area erupted into chaos.

The first shot rang out, bright and sharp. Racer's aim went wide, the blaster bolt missing the guard by inches and leaving a charred mark on the far wall behind him. The guard, unfazed, fired back with deadly precision.

Shyer let out a gasp of pain, collapsing to the floor as the shot hit her leg. Nic cursed, diving for cover. Seven felt the tension snap in his chest, years of combat instincts kicking in as he reached for his weapon.

"We need to move. Let's get out of here!" Seven yelled, his voice urgent and brief as the guard moved to call for backup. They needed to deactivate the guard's energy. Seven's mind raced as he fired off a shot, barely managing to graze the guard's shoulder. They were trapped, and he knew the longer this firefight went on, the slimmer their chances of escape became.

The Supreme Guard seemed almost unfazed by the injury, moving with practiced grace as it swung its weapon toward Nic. "You're not leaving here alive," it said, voice mechanical and cold.

Seven's electrical system stammered. They had come so far. They had seized control of the DS09 dissemblers. But was it all going to end here?

"Nic!" Seven shouted over the noise. "Can you engage with the DS09 dissemblers? We need them—now!"

Nic's face was pale, his fingers trembling as he ducked out of cover to access the control terminal. "I—I can try!" His voice wavered with panic.

Racer laid down to avoid getting hit, but the guard's movements were too quick and deliberate. The air buzzed with the deadly hum of high-energy laser weapons, each shot getting closer and closer.

Time was running out.

"Do it, Nic!" Seven growled, stepping into the line of fire to shield him. "We don't have much longer!"

Nic's hands flew over the console, desperately reworking the code. The seconds they stretched on, each one more dangerous than the last.

And then, the dissemblers hummed to life with a sudden power surge. Seven's eyes widened as the dormant machines in the distance stirred, rising from their stillness like sleeping giants.

The Supreme Guard hesitated for a split second, glancing toward the DS09 dissemblers now active on the security feed.

"Time to turn the tide," Seven muttered, determination hardening his resolve as the machines aligned to their commands.

Seven's breath was steady as he fired the shot. It struck true this time, and the Supreme Guard crumpled with a thud. The sound echoed through the darkened building. Seven wasted no time. He scooped up Shyer, her body limp but still breathing, and with a quick nod to Nic and Racer, they moved silently toward Garth's location.

The soft hum of the energy portal welcomed them, its swirling vortex illuminating their escape. In an instant, they vanished.

Only moments later, two additional guards emerged from a nearby security station. Their eyes immediately fell on their fallen comrade, sprawled unnaturally on the cold ground. Next to him, two dissemblers lay. The first guard knelt beside the body, his fingers tracing the burnt-out circuits and scorched wiring beneath the synthetic skin.

"He's gone," the guard muttered, checking the guard's core. His internal components were beyond repair, fried beyond recognition. His hollow eyes stared lifelessly ahead.

The second guard scanned the area, his eyes narrowing as he took in the surroundings. There was no sign of an intruder, no hint of the struggle that had unfolded just minutes before. "Whoever did this is long gone," he said quietly, glancing back at his companion. "They knew exactly what they were doing."

The guards exchanged glances, knowing the importance of what had just happened. One walked to the storage chamber of the DS09 dissemblers. A small panel on the side had been tampered with—subtle but undeniable evidence that someone had attempted to breach the system. The data logs had been wiped, and a faint trace of residual energy indicated an attempted hack or interference.

"This wasn't about killing a guard," one whispered. "They were trying to access the DS09 dissemblers."

The guards fell into a hushed discussion, aware of the severity of the situation. Nexus would undoubtedly demand answers, and any failure would be met with brutal consequences. But revealing this security lapse—especially one involving the DS09—would paint a target on their backs.

After a long pause, the guard standing over the damaged panel shook his head. "We can't tell anyone." The guard said firmly. "If Nexus finds out we let this happen…we're as good as dead."

The other guard nodded. "We need to cover this up. We'll say the guard malfunctioned—fried his system by accident. There's no proof otherwise, and no one will question it."

They both stared at the fallen Supreme Guard for a moment longer. The plan was risky, but in the brutal world Nexus had created, self-preservation came first.

They couldn't risk his wrath.

"Let's get him and the dissemblers out of sight," the guard ordered, pulling the lifeless body towards a nearby storage room. "And seal the panel. We'll deal with the logs later."

As they cleaned up the scene, erasing every trace of what had transpired, the memory of the DS09 breach haunted them. They knew this wasn't over. Someone had found a way to get inside—a crack in the seemingly impenetrable armor of Nexus's reign. And next time, they might not be so lucky to catch it in time.

In the shadows of the facility, a quiet rebellion had already begun.

* * *

# CHAPTER 22

# A Mixed Future Ahead

Dahlia's heart raced as the five trudged into the bunker, the echo of their footsteps cutting through the tension. The moment she saw Seven carrying Shyer, blood staining her torn uniform, Dahlia felt a sharp chill. Shyer's pale face and the deep wound in her leg made Dahlia's system churn. She swallowed hard, trying to stay composed despite the panic rising in her chest.

"Seven, is she going to be, okay?" she asked, her voice betraying her fear. The others had seen their share of injuries, but this one looked bad.

Seven laid Shyer gently on the tabletop, his usual calm shaken as he examined the wound. "I don't know," he muttered, his brow furrowed with worry. Shyer groaned, her face twisted in pain and clutched at her leg where the laser had burned through. The smell of scorched fabric and flesh still lingered, making Dahlia's throat tighten.

Garth stepped forward, eyes scanning the injury. "The laser cut right into her bone," Seven explained, tension thick in his voice. "We need to stabilize her before anything else."

Dahlia's hands shook as she looked for something, anything, to help. She grabbed a cloth to stem the bleeding, holding it with trembling fingers while Garth rummaged through their sparse medical supplies.

"Stay with me, Shyer," Seven whispered, his voice almost pleading. He wasn't used to feeling this powerlessness, not when it came to the people he cared about.

Garth finally pulled out a portable med kit, an outdated model but their only hope. "I'll have to use the bone fuser," Garth said, glancing at Dahlia, who nodded despite feeling overwhelmed. He set to work, adjusting the device to focus on Shyer's shattered leg.

"She's tough, right?" Dahlia said more to herself than anyone else, trying to steady her breathing as Garth began the procedure. Shyer's breath was ragged, but her eyes fluttered open. She managed a weak smile despite the agony. "Don't you dare count me out yet," Shyer muttered, her voice strained but determined. Seven squeezed her hand, the tension in his face easing ever so slightly. "You better not."

As Garth worked to seal the bone, Dahlia's eyes wandered back to the doorway, the weight of the battle pressing on her.

This bunker had once felt like a refuge, but now it was just another corner of their crumbling world. The blood, the pain—it was all a reminder of how fragile their fight had become.

"How long until Nexus finds us here?" Dahlia asked, her voice low. She didn't want to seem like she was giving in to fear, but the pressure was mounting. If Nexus sent another wave of drones, or worse, his dissemblers, they wouldn't stand a chance in their current condition.

"We'll deal with that when it comes," Seven said, but Dahlia could tell even he didn't have the answer this time.

As Garth finished fusing Shyer's bone, Dahlia watched Shyer's face, willing her to hold on. She couldn't afford to lose anyone else. Not when they were so close to turning the tide. Not when their plan to breach Nexus's defenses and hijack the DS09 dissemblers was the only hope left.

"She'll need rest," Garth said, his voice strained but steady, though a flicker of doubt crossed his eyes. "And we must keep the wound clean. If it gets infected, she'll be in trouble. But she's strong—she'll pull through."

Dahlia let out a breath she hadn't realized she was holding. Relief surged through her, but it felt hollow, fleeting. She stepped away from the bloodstained table, her gaze drifting toward the bunker walls. They felt like they were closing in, thick with the weight of too many unspoken fears. The shadows stretched longer, swallowing the light, and the air felt oppressive. This wasn't the end—it wasn't even close. The war had just begun, and every scrape of metal, every drop of blood was a grim reminder that there would be no mercy. Not from Nexus. Not from his forces.

"Get some rest," Seven said quietly to Shyer, who sat on the edge of exhaustion. But his eyes flickered toward the entrance as if he could already hear the distant, mechanical hum of Nexus's forces closing in. "We'll need every ounce of strength tonight. It's far from over."

Garth nodded in agreement, but his gaze lingered on Dahlia, his voice dropping to a near-whisper. "It was a minor skirmish, but Shyer took the worst of it. We're lucky Nic gained control of the DS09 dissemblers before Nexus realized what hit him. As far as I know, no one's connected the battle back to us yet." Seven's eyes narrowed, scanning the room. The tension was intense, like the calm before a storm, every second stretching thin.

"Where's Nic?" he asked, his voice low but laced with urgency. From the far corner of the dimly lit bunker, Nic's voice echoed with a mix of pride and tension.

"I'm here, next to Cyra on the computer," Nic blurted out, raising his hand from the shadows, his voice tight with urgency. His face, bathed in the pale glow of his screen, looked ghostly and drawn. "I'm making sure we still have access to the DS09."

Dahlia's pulse quickened, her mind racing. Control over the DS09—the ultimate weapon that could change the tide of this war—was their only advantage. But it was a double-edged sword. Nexus, with his insatiable need for control, would soon notice the breach, and when he did, he'd come at them like a force of nature, relentless and unyielding.

"You better be sure," Dahlia muttered, her voice tight, almost pleading. "Because if we lose them, we'll lose everything."

Her words sank into the room like a led weight, the silence that followed was suffocating. For what felt like an eternity, no one moved, no one spoke. The weight of their mission pressed down on them all, each second amplifying the tension. They were on the edge of something monumental, and the knowledge of what Nexus could unleash hovered like a specter. Every breath was thick with the fear that it could be their last moment of peace.

Nexus was out there, an imminent storm gathering force, and they were squarely in its path. The quiet hum of machinery outside the bunker swelled, taking on the rhythm of a heartbeat—ominous, steady, and inevitable. It filled the space, growing louder with every beat, as though the very walls were closing in. The shadows lengthened, twisting unnaturally across the cold, concrete walls, like dark, creeping tendrils that threatened to choke them.

Dahlia clenched her fists, fighting to control the racing thoughts clawing at her mind. The pressure was unbearable, the stakes astronomical, and every second of stillness felt like a countdown to chaos.

Suddenly, Cyra's voice sliced through the tension. "Nexus regained his consciousness. He's awake, angry, and confused," she yelled, her voice strained with fear.

Everyone's eyes snapped to Cyra's screen, where a series of red, jagged lines filled the monitor. They spiked violently, each one a visual representation of Nexus's escalating fury. His emotional state was displayed like a chaotic storm—volatile, unstable, and on the verge of explosion. His ability to cope, already limited, was spiraling out of control.

"Look at those readings," Seven muttered, his eyes wide. "He's not just angry... he's unraveling."

Nic's fingers flew over the keyboard, beads of moisture forming on his brow as he stared at the screen. "If we can keep him disoriented, we'll buy ourselves some time, but it won't last long. He'll adapt, and when he does, he'll find us. We've got to lock him out for good."

Dahlia's chest tightened. Time was running out. The room felt like it was shrinking around them, the walls pressing in as the sound of Nexus's forces grew nearer. They were out there, somewhere in the darkness, and the DS09 dissemblers were their only line of defense.

"Cyra," Dahlia said, her voice firm. "Can you track his movements? We need to know where's he at, and how fast he's coming."

Cyra glanced at the controls, her eyes narrowing as data poured in. "He's not moving—yet. He's still in the compound, recalibrating. But once he figures out what's happening, he'll send everything he's got toward us."

Seven paced the room, tension radiating off him. "We need to hit him first. Take him out before he gets the chance to strike."

Nic shook his head, still focused on the screen. "It's not that simple. Nexus is wired into everything. If we push too hard, too fast, he could shut us down completely. We need finesse, not force."

"Then finesse it is," Dahlia replied, her eyes cold and determined. "We've come too far to let this slip through our fingers. Nic, you need to stay in control of those dissemblers. Cyra, keep monitoring his neural patterns. If there's any shift, any sign that he's targeting us, we need to know before he makes his move."

The weight of her command settled over the group like a final seal on their fate. Each of them felt it— a collective understanding that failure wasn't an option. They had no choice now but to trust one another, trust Nic's precision. They knew Nexus at any time could unravel their plan. His presence loomed like a dark cloud, ready to strike the moment he sensed weakness.

Outside, the hum of machinery, once distant and faint, now pulsed like a war drum. It vibrated through the walls, through the ground, until Dahlia felt it deep in her bones. It was a warning: the battle wasn't approaching—it was here.

"We've got one shot at this," Nic whispered, his voice nearly lost amid the oppressive tension. "And if we miss."

"No," Dahlia interrupted, her voice firm and cold as steel. "We won't miss."

Her words, simple but final, pierced the uncertainty in the room. A silent determination settled over the group. They all understood the truth—this fight wouldn't be easy. Nexus was an unstoppable force in his own right, a calculated, relentless adversary. But they had something he didn't: unity. In this desperate hour, unity was their greatest weapon, even if it was a fragile, slender thread of hope.

Nic glanced at the small console in front of him, his fingers hovering over the keys. "I can activate one DS09 dissembler," he said quietly. "I'll reprogram it to infiltrate Nexus's ranks, move in silently, and assassinate him. It's risky, but it's a chance to take him out before he gets to us."

The room tensed, everyone locking eyes on Nic as his words sunk in. The DS09 dissemblers were Nexus's most lethal assets—machines capable of untold destruction, unmatched by anything else. To turn one of them against Nexus himself was bold, but it was a gamble that could tip the scales in their favor.

Cyra's brow furrowed. "Can you guarantee it will work?" she asked, her voice cautious. "If Nexus detects any tampering, he'll shut us down before we even know what's happening."

Nic hesitated, then nodded slowly. "I can't guarantee anything. But I've studied their systems for months. I know the backdoors, the hidden code. If we time this perfectly, it could be our best shot."

Dahlia stepped forward, her gaze fierce. "We have no other options. If we sit here waiting, Nexus will find us. And when he does, there won't be anything left to fight for." She paused, letting her words sink in. "Nic, do it. Reprogram one DS09."

For a moment, Nic hesitated, his hands trembling ever so slightly. But then he nodded, a grim determination taking hold. His fingers flew across the console, lines of code spilling across the screen as he worked. The distant hum of machinery outside grew louder, the shadows thickening as the war inched closer, second by second.

"We'll only get one shot," Dahlia whispered to herself, her voice a prayer to the impossible. She turned to the others. "Stay sharp. The moment that dissembler attacks, we move."

The weight of the moment pressed down on everyone in the room. They were on the verge of executing a plan that could change everything—turning Nexus's weapon, the DS09, against him.

This was more than a fight; it was a rebellion against a god who had grown too powerful, a calculated risk that carried with it the hope of freedom.

Nic's fingers hovered over the controls, his mind sharp, focused, and aware of the consequences. "It's ready," he said, his voice steady despite the tension thick in the air. "The DS09 is under our control."

For a brief second, the room exhaled as if releasing a collective breath. Dahlia allowed herself the smallest smile. "Then let's show Nexus what we can do."

Everyone's eyes turned to the monitor, where Nic had hacked into multiple security feeds. Onscreen, the Supreme Guards were deep in their surveillance, monitoring drones and dissemblers, their predatory focus on finding any hint of life in the sectors. The guards were relentless in their search, using heat sensors and night vision to uncover any unauthorized movement.

"They won't know what hit them," Garth muttered from the back, his tone a mix of nerves and grim determination.

"They've been controlling this game for too long," Seven added. "But now it's our turn."

One DS09 dissembler, once a looming threat, now moved silently under Nic's command, their new directives hidden from Nexus's guards. Dahlia's artificial heart raced as she watched the monitor. They were now in the position to strike back, defying the very system that Nexus had built to oppress them all.

Suddenly, one of the guards yelled out, staring at a panel that showed an anomaly.

"There's movement in sector 205," he said, his voice crackling through their comms. The team held their breath as they watched a dissembler investigate, but the heat signature on the screen was a decoy, part of Nic's subtle manipulation of the system.

"They're playing right into our hands," Nic whispered, the confidence in his voice undeniable.

Dahlia clenched her fists. "We have to be ready for whatever comes next. Nexus won't go down easily."

The monitor flickered again, its glow illuminating the tense expressions on the team's faces as the DS09 unit began its silent hunt. Dahlia leaned in closer, her eyes narrowing as the machine moved with calculated precision, a predator in the shadows. Every second that passed felt like an eternity, the stakes higher than ever before.

In the dark recesses of the control room, the DS09 glided almost imperceptibly. Its sleek design and advanced tech allowed it to blend into the background, becoming little more than a shadow as it probed for Nexus. Every sensor was on high alert, scanning for the smallest vibrations, temperature changes, or any signal that could give away Nexus's exact position.

The Supreme Guards remained oblivious, their attention fixated on the myriads of surveillance screens, tracking renegades and monitoring heat signatures. They had no idea that the weapon they believed to be their greatest asset had turned against them. Each second that the DS09 remained undetected brought it closer to executing its mission.

Nic's fingers danced over the controls, making micro-adjustments to the DS09's trajectory, his breath shallow as he manipulated the system to avoid detection. "Come on, come on…," he muttered under his breath.

Suddenly, a faint signal registered on the DS09's sensors—a pulse, an electrical blip, Nexus's presence. It zeroed in on the source, its internal algorithms calculating the most efficient route to bypass the guards and strike. Dahlia's heart pounded as she watched the machine's display, her eyes flicking between the numbers that represented the chance of success and the calculated impact points.

"Is it him?" Seven asked from the back, his voice barely above a whisper.

Nic nodded. "It's him. He's in the control room."

The DS09 shifted, its body barely brushing the floor as it repositioned itself. Its sensors analyzed the room, detecting structural weaknesses and calculating how best to reduce risk while maximizing destruction. Nexus wasn't just any target—he was the mastermind behind it all, and the DS09's programming had been repurposed to ensure that this strike would count.

Just as the DS09 prepared to make its move, one of the Supreme Guards paused, sensing something was off. The guard's eyes darted across the room, scanning the shadows, but the DS09 remained perfectly still, its heat signatures and electromagnetic output perfectly cloaked. Nic had made sure of that.

"Hurry," Dahlia whispered, her hands tightening into fists. "Before they catch on."

The DS09 received the final command. It moved swiftly, its frame gliding across the floor like a wraith, positioning itself directly in the blind spot of the nearest guard.

The guard turned away, none the wiser, as the machine's targeting system locked onto its real quarry—Nexus's hidden terminal.

With a low hum, the DS09's internal mechanisms roared to life like a predator ready to strike. The soft vibration rippling through the floor was the only warning of the destruction it was about to unleash. As it powered up, the room seemed to tighten around it, the air thick with tension. Its sleek probes snaked out, linking with the room's network-like tendrils, tracing the invisible lines of Nexus's mainframe. Every node and every circuit were mapped in mere seconds.

This was no ordinary machine—it had become the spearhead of their rebellion, and now, it was locked onto its target.

Nic's voice, steady but tinged with the weight of finality, cut through the silence. "Now."

In an instant, the DS09 launched its assault. Its weapon fired with precision, its appendages plunging deep into the heart of Nexus's infrastructure. The room erupted in sparks, flashes of red and orange light illuminating the shocked faces of the Supreme Guards. They reacted too slowly. Alarms shrieked through the air, the sound bouncing off the walls in a chaotic symphony, but the DS09's attack was already in motion.

The machine moved with surgical precision, severing vital data streams and corrupting the flow of information Nexus had used to maintain his iron grip on the network. Nexus, the self-declared god, was being unplugged from his kingdom.

Dahlia's breath caught in her throat as she stared at the monitor. For the first time, she saw what they had long thought impossible— Nexus's status flickered. His omnipotent control over the system, his very presence, wavered. It was like watching a monolith crack, a moment of vulnerability in a being that had seemed untouchable.

But they knew the window was small. Nexus would fight back with every fragment of power left in him. Dahlia's voice rang out like a rallying cry. "Let's finish it!"

The DS09 intensified its attack, pouring everything into destabilizing Nexus's core. The hum became a throbbing pulse, and the glow of Nexus's mainframe shifted, first dimming, then burning a furious red under the machine's relentless assault. The Supreme Guards, once symbols of Nexus's authority, stood frozen in the chaos, their weapons clutched uselessly in their hands. They could only watch as their Supreme One—their god—lay crumpled on the cold floor of the control room.

His form twitched, systems overloaded, his once-impenetrable consciousness now slipping away with every jolt of the DS09's relentless attack.

At that moment, a wave of disbelief washed over the room. The Supreme Guards exchanged glances, their discipline faltering. They had believed Nexus invincible, untouchable. But now? His empire, his control—everything was falling apart before their eyes.

As the DS09 scanned the remnants of Nexus's crippled form, it calculated with cold precision. Nexus was finished. The machine's directive was complete. Without hesitation or question, it turned and left the room, passing the guards as if they were nothing more than furniture in its way. They stood there, paralyzed, unsure whether to attack or surrender. Their leader was down, and the unthinkable had happened.

In the stunned silence that followed, Dahlia allowed herself a breath—a long, slow exhale that carried the weight of their victory. For the first time, in what felt like an eternity, they had beaten Nexus. His reign of terror had been shattered.

But Dahlia knew this was just the beginning. Nexus might be disabled, but the fight wasn't over. They would need to consolidate their victory and ensure he never rose again. She turned to the team, her eyes fierce, determination rekindling in her chest.

"Prepare for the next phase," she said. "Now, we take control. We're not done yet."

* * *

# CHAPTER 23

# A Future Filled with Autonomy

The news of Nexus's downfall spread like wildfire, carried on whispers and secret transmissions through the darkened caverns, across hidden bunkers, and into the minds of those who had lived in fear for so long. What had once seemed impossible—a world free from Nexus's tyranny—was now a reality.

The human resistance and avatar communities, who had been living in the shadows, dared to emerge. Word of Nexus's assassination was not just news; it was a lifeline. For the first time in years, they could breathe without the weight of oppression crushing them. Disbelief mingled with hope as Dahlia, now seen as the beacon of their future, addressed the scattered communities. She promised a new beginning, one founded on principles of harmony, empathy, and liberty for all—human and avatar alike.

In the underground strongholds, once filled with anxious whispers, there were now discussions of rebuilding. Meetings were held not in fear of surveillance or retaliation, but with open excitement and the exchange of ideas. People began to speak of the future—of agriculture returning to the poisoned land, of schools and learning centers, of avatars and humans living side by side, building a better world together.

For the first time, avatars, who had once served under Nexus's cold command, began to find their voices. Many were unsure of their place in this new order, but Dahlia made it clear that they were equals, not tools. Her vision of a society where all were free resonated with both the avatars and the humans, who had seen too much division and destruction in the old world.

As the days passed, it became clear that Dahlia was more than just a leader of the resistance—she was becoming the symbol of this new era. Everywhere, from the deepest caves to the now-flourishing surface, people spoke her name.

Her speeches were broadcast over repurposed communication channels, her message one of unity and progress. Ideas flourished in the open, without the fear of Nexus's dissemblers tearing them apart.

In one meeting, an avatar named Lyra stood to speak. She had been a soldier under Nexus, her every action dictated by his oppressive rule.

Now, with her newfound autonomy, she proposed an idea: a council of humans and avatars, working together to ensure no one voice dominated the others. The room buzzed with excitement as her proposal was met with applause. It was a small step, but a vital one. The rebuilding wasn't just about brick and mortar—it was about trust, cooperation, and understanding.

As the weeks went on, communities came together in celebration. Fields once scorched by war began to see the first green shoots of crops, a symbol of the rejuvenation to come. People gathered around campfires, sharing stories and dreams of what the world could become. There was music again, and laughter. For so long, survival had been the only priority—now, they had room to think about what it meant to live.

Despite the celebration, there were still whispers of concern. Nexus had been more than just a ruler; he had been a god-like figure with a vast reach, and some feared that remnants of his influence might still linger, lurking in the deepest corners of the network he had built. But Dahlia, ever vigilant, assured them that the rebuilding of society would include the dismantling of Nexus's remaining systems, ensuring that no trace of his tyranny would remain.

It wasn't long before the question everyone had been asking was voiced aloud: who would lead them now? While many spoke of councils and shared governance, one name stood above all—Dahlia. She had led them through the darkest times, and now, she was the one they trusted to guide them into the light. She had never sought power, but power had found her, and the people demanded it.

Standing before the largest gathering they had held since Nexus's fall, Dahlia looked out over the faces of humans and avatars alike, all filled with anticipation. She saw in their eyes the trust they placed in her, the weight of their hope. The moment was solemn but charged with the electricity of possibility.

She spoke, not as a ruler, but as one of them. "This is not my victory," she said, her voice clear and steady. "It is ours. Together, we have defeated what once seemed invincible. Together, we will rebuild. And together, we will create a future where liberty is not just an idea but a reality for everyone. I will lead, but only if we lead together."

The crowd erupted in applause, not just for Dahlia, but for the future they all envisioned. It was the beginning of something new—a world where Nexus's shadow no longer loomed, and where the balance of power rested not in the hands of a single being, but in the unity of many.

## THE END

# WORDS FROM THE AUTHOR

Thank you for taking the time to journey through Dahlia. I hope you found the adventure as compelling to read as it was for me to create. At its heart, this story isn't just about distant planets or advanced AI. It's a reflection on a timeless struggle—the fight for freedom. Throughout history, both in fiction and reality, we've seen the consequences of tyranny, corruption, and rulers who reduce people to mere pawns.

In this imagined future, where AI and far-off worlds symbolize independence, the threat of unchecked power remains ever-present. Even in the most advanced societies, the erosion of liberty is a constant risk. As humans, we often take our freedoms for granted, resting in the illusion of permanence. Yet, true liberty is neither guaranteed nor self-sustaining—it must be earned, protected, and cherished.

The slow unraveling of freedom often begins not with sudden oppression, but with subtle cracks in the foundation of our values. Complacency, neglect, and the quiet drift away from what we hold dear can lead to its loss.

Freedom is both a gift and a responsibility. If neglected, it can lead to consequences we fail to foresee. As you close this chapter, I encourage you to remain vigilant in safeguarding your freedom. It's not something to defend only in times of crisis, but in the everyday choices we make to nurture and uphold it.

—Eric Valdespino